PRAISE FOR *THE NIGHT GUESTS*

"Darkly beautiful and laced with gorgeous atmosphere, *The Night Guests* will hold you captivated from its opening séance to the pulse-pounding conclusion. Brimming with romance, intrigue, and deception, this thrilling gothic tale is perfect for fans of Sarah Waters and Hester Fox."

— Paulette Kennedy, bestselling author of *Parting the Veil*

"A terrifying twist on traditional gothic tales, Marina Scott's *The Night Guests* is the compelling story of a woman fighting to reclaim her power after the ruinous fall of her family. With nuanced characters and immersive details—both historical and horrifying—Scott's atmospheric writing pulls readers into a macabre world that will haunt them long after the last page is turned."

—Erin Litteken, international bestselling author of *The Memory Keeper of Kyiv* and *The Lost Daughters of Ukraine*

"Nothing is as it seems at The Dawning, or in Marina Scott's eerie and unsettling *The Night Guests*, both of which are swathed in layers of gaslighting and gothic secrets that, like the heroine, force you to question everything, all while being lulled into a delightfully maddening dream of a tale."

—Olesya Salnikova Gilmore, author of *The Haunting of Moscow House*

"Haunting and unnerving, tense and atmospheric. A gothic tale rife with all things curious, enigmatic, and ghostly, Marina Scott's *The Night Guests* will send shivers down readers' spines as it lures them into its pages and envelops them with this entertaining, chilling story."

—Gabriella Saab, author of *The Last Checkmate*

"Ominous, mournful, and deliciously creepy, Scott masterfully unpacks themes of grief and loneliness in this slow-burn historical gothic novel, perfect for fans of Mexican gothic. You will find yourself looking over your shoulder long after you finish this book!"

—Amanda Jayatissa, author of *Island Witch*

the NIGHT GUESTS

ALSO BY MARINA SCOTT

The Hunger Between Us

the NIGHT GUESTS

a Novel

MARINA SCOTT

LAKE UNION
PUBLISHING

Published by Lake Union Publishing, Seattle

www.apub.com

EU product safety contact:
Amazon Media EU S. à r.l.
38, avenue John F. Kennedy, L-1855 Luxembourg
amazonpublishing-gpsr@amazon.com

ISBN-13: 9781662531729 (paperback)
ISBN-13: 9781662531712 (digital)

Cover design by Joanne O'Neill
Cover image: Hærdaceous Pæony, by Kazumasa Ogawa (1860–1929), 1896, colored collotype © Penta Springs Limited / Alamy Stock Photo; © NSA Digital Archive / Getty; Portrait of the singer Matilde Juva Branca, by Francesco Hayez (1849 - 1851), 1851, oil on canvas © Mondadori Portfolio / Hulton Fine Art Collection / Getty Images

Printed in the United States of America

To my CPs, who believe that my words matter.

Chapter 1

Omaha, Nebraska
1903

Mother sits stiffly in the velvet chair, a false smile stretching her lips. It has been ages since we've been to the Hollands' house, and judging by the looks Mrs. Holland gives us—so bloody pious—we should never have come.

Mother rolls her shoulders back to a desperate angle and lifts her chin, as if an imperious stance will erase the shame that hangs over us. I reflexively sit up straighter, but my attempts to replicate Mother's posture fail on all accounts. Twenty-five years old, unmarried, and perpetually tired, all I want is to stretch my throbbing legs, sink into the cushion, and disappear.

I look around the room, taking care not to look anyone in the eye. Whenever I see familiar faces, I also see their scorn. These people—whom we used to call our friends, who used to drink my father's whiskey and listen to my brother's jokes—now try their hardest to ignore our very existence.

It's clear that no one expected us to attend tonight's séance, let alone placed in the first row. When the invitation first arrived, I thought it was a cruel joke. No one had asked us anywhere for ages, and suddenly a light-blue envelope made an appearance, inviting us to experience the new wonder in town, Leroy Marshall, medium extraordinaire. I had wanted to stay home, but according to my mother—who embraces anything that provides her even the slightest reprieve from her grief—we should be open and receptive to the lesser-known avenues of the spiritual world. It might help us heal after my father's death.

I study the lush carpet under my feet. The carpet at our family's estate used to be like this—soft, thick, clean. And now look at us. Mother trussed up in her best mourning dress with two thin rips in the lace. Eyes pinned to the empty armchair in the center of the room. I smooth my cotton dress, listening to the hushed voices, wondering if they're buzzing with ghostly anticipation or talking about us.

My stomach contracts from hunger, and, as if summoned by it, my thoughts wander to our former cook's sumptuous cooking. My mind conjures images of a beef stew, followed by the clear vision of a shank of lamb with the cook's signature plum sauce. This produces a loud grousing in my belly, and I force myself to focus on something else. The food I think about is from *before*. From the days of the lush carpet. These days, neither butcher nor baker will extend our credit at their shop. We're reduced to two-day-old grits with a sliver of butter.

I carefully check the room to see if a certain Mr. Robert Walker—or Bobby, as he asked me to call him after two waltzes and a shared flute of champagne at the Hollands' fall gala last year—is in attendance. He proposed a month after the gala, and my father gave us his blessing. The Walkers own a small bank on the east end of Farnam Street—Walker Savings Bank—making Bobby a true, respectable gentleman and not a tradesman. Marrying a tradesman is not advisable in our circles. Our former circles, anyway.

I don't see Bobby's clean-shaven face with his signature angular chin anywhere in the room, and the disappointment, sharp and bitter, gnaws on my insides. He rescinded his proposal as soon as my father's gambling debts surfaced. For no one wants to be associated with the family that lost all their fortune to gambling and are unable to pay their bills. Such sin is frowned upon. Not gambling, of course, which is considered a regular pastime. Poverty is utterly more sinful. It offends.

Perhaps his absence is a blessing for my hurt ego. A soothing salve for my ruined dreams of becoming a member of the Walker family, one of the richest in Omaha, and my gateway to a stable future. I clench my fingers around the seams of my brown cotton dress and banish the disappointment. I'm meant to be a spinster, like Mrs. Holland's sister sitting all the way in the back by the wall, drool slowly slipping out of the corner of her wrinkly mouth.

I turn to Lizzie Holland. "Are the Walkers not invited?"

A small smile appears on Lizzie's heart-shaped face, and suddenly she reminds me of the Lizzie I used to know—the pretty and mischievous girl who eagerly shared society gossip. "Mrs. Walker's here," she says, nodding to her left. "You look displeased. Were you expecting someone else?"

I return a false smile, but I don't respond. She knows perfectly well whom I was expecting to see. It's foolish to think about Bobby. No good will come of it, only humiliation laced with an acute heartache.

Something glistens by my feet. I lean down and pick up a small wooden carving. I turn it in my fingers, examining it. It's fairly rough, but I can see it is a boy soldier in a military coat. Both arms are carved close to the body, but his head is tilted up, a small mouth agape in a silent scream. Lizzie's brother must've dropped it earlier today. Boys always play war games.

"Is this Phillip's?" I show the wooden figurine to Lizzie. "It was on the floor."

A shadow falls across the room.

"He's here, Nina." Lizzie pulls on my sleeve, drawing my attention to their houseguest. She leans forward in her chair, locking her fingers together in her lap. She pauses before adding with a sigh, "And he's pleasant on the eye. Don't you think?" Her green eyes gleam with adoration.

Following her gaze, I shove the boy soldier into my dress pocket and try to fix my eyes on the man in the center of the room.

He sits in the armchair perfectly still—a sculpture carved out of marble. His long legs are leisurely crossed at the ankles. The flickering candlelight sharpens his high cheekbones and square jaw. He's dressed in black pants, immaculately creased in front, and a silk shirt in the same color. A silk necktie with an odd yellow embroidery is a nice contrast against his pale skin. His thick, raven-black hair and equally dark brows complement a black waistcoat that emphasizes a broad chest and slim waist. There's no jacket. The smell of the burning wicker rises in the room and circles above us, tickling my nose. Lizzie warned me Leroy Marshall insists on candles and burning wicker because the spirits are drawn to the shadows and incense.

"Ladies and gentlemen, welcome to my small gathering. My name is Leroy Marshall, and I've been blessed with the hospitality of your town. As some of you already know, I've also been blessed with certain spiritual gifts. Over the years, I've experienced many changes in my abilities, and each of my powers has altered my life. Today, one of my strongest spiritual talents is piercing the veil between the world of the living and the world of the dead." He pauses, letting us absorb his words. "Our lives are empty without God." Looking crisp and poised, he continues in a deep voice, each word loud and clear. "And we should always be grateful for his presence. But we should also keep our minds open and invite his other servants into our world. Tonight, we will witness intrusions—the presence of otherworldly spirits trying to contact our world." His gaze slowly travels around the room and falls on me, lingering longer than is appropriate. His eyes don't leave my face when he leans forward and says, "May your heart be full of light."

People nod, and hushed, intense murmurs fill the room.

Lizzie snatches my hand and whispers, "Nina, he's looking at you."

It must be my lucky day.

"He's going to call upon you," Lizzie says, and I sense a note of jealousy in her voice.

"He's looking at both of us. He might call on *you*," I reply, swallowing hard.

Lizzie's eyes light up at my words. She might be more infatuated with her houseguest than I initially suspected.

I pull my hand from Lizzie's sweaty grip. "If he calls on me, he might find himself deeply disappointed." I lean close and whisper to make sure no one can hear us. "I'm not making a spectacle out of myself."

Lizzie shakes her head at me disapprovingly. "If the spirits want to talk to you, you should answer their call."

"I don't know, Lizzie. It frightens me to think about the dead." I don't *allow* myself to think about the dead is closer to the truth. My mother attended séances even before my father's passing. In fact, it was the rare point of tension between her and my father, who never believed in spirits, God, or the devil himself. Part of me, the rational part, knows there is nothing after death—just the eternal sleep of tired souls—but when our house creaks and groans at night, I sometimes wonder. Whether something's hiding in the night when the darkness is the deepest.

Just this afternoon I brought it up with Tilda, our only remaining housemaid, and her response took me by surprise. "Death leaves a mark, Miss. Dark energy of sorts," she said. "Evil spirits are attracted to places branded by death. I know folks who had to flee their houses because of that."

Brushing off Tilda's words, I draw my gaze back to the center of the room. Leroy Marshall is not quite what I expected. He's mysterious. Attractive. Handsome even, I admit begrudgingly. He's still looking at me, and some people now turn to look at me as well. Their attentive eyes follow my every move as I fidget in the chair.

I lower my gaze, folding my hands into my lap. I don't need this attention.

"We shall begin," Leroy says.

This is when I see him. A boy eight, maybe nine, years old stands behind Leroy, by the door leading into the hallway. His right hand squeezes a woolen cap, and his left hand is braced against the doorframe.

His eyes are glistening. At first, I think the boy's crying, but then I notice his clothes are wet as well. Water drips on the floor in rivulets and gathers in a pool by his shoes, which are crusted with red dirt. The boy smiles at me, the skin gathering around his lips into a mound of deep wrinkles, and suddenly the boy looks old enough to be my grandfather.

I shiver as a chill, sudden and sharp, burrows under my skin. The air stills. The shadows gather around the boy's small frame as he slowly shakes his head and puts his pale, oddly twisted finger to his lips, as if asking me to keep his secret.

"Who's the boy by the door?" I whisper hoarsely to Lizzie. "He looks like he fell into the fountain in the garden."

"Must be a friend of my brother's," Lizzie whispers back without taking her eyes off Leroy. "I'm sure one of the maids will take care of him. Children are not allowed at the séance."

I glance at the door again, but the boy's already gone. Only a pool of water remains in his wake.

"Please give me the notes," Leroy commands, drawing my attention back to him. He turns to Mrs. Holland, and Lizzie's mother turns slightly pink when he smiles at her. Her blond hair is parted in the middle, her plaits arranged around the top of her head in a crown. She's wearing a modest yellow dress with a high white lace collar. "The spirits are ready."

Lizzie nods, and her blond curls, almost identical to her mother's, bounce around her heart-shaped face. "I can feel them too. Do you, Nina?"

I glance back to the door, to the spot where I saw the boy. "I don't feel anything," I whisper. "What am I supposed to feel?"

"The chill. It always gets cold when they come."

Another shiver, like tiny ice chips against my skin, scatters across my arms. "Maybe you should ask the maids to close the windows."

"The windows are closed so that spirits don't escape the room and come into our world," Lizzie whispers.

"Not all the windows are closed." I nod at the window in the farthest corner of the room, where the curtain moves in the breeze.

"Hush, ladies," someone barks from behind us.

Lizzie turns away from me, her attention back to Leroy.

Mrs. Holland hands Leroy a stack of folded papers. He turns them over and shows the audience they are sealed with wax. Then he starts shuffling the stack of notes as if he's about to play a game of cards. He gazes at us with stark seriousness. The look on his face is almost bashful. "At the beginning of this evening, some of you wrote letters to your departed loved ones. I'm not aware who wrote what or whose note I'm about to pick from the stack. Every note is sealed. I'll choose the note at random, and I won't break the seal. I won't read the note myself. Instead, I'll commune with the spirit of your departed, who in turn will convey to me the content of the note. I'll reveal to you what the spirit shared with me, and only then will I break the seal and read the note."

Something shifts inside me as I look over at Mother's strained face. I saw her writing a note earlier. Another letter to my dead father, most likely. That's all she's been doing lately—writing letters to her dead husband and bringing them to his resting place in the middle of the night to burn over his grave. Tilda and I accompany her on these odd excursions because we can't allow her to travel alone.

What would Amos, my twin brother, do if he were here now? What would he do if he knew how increasingly difficult Mother is becoming? How she is withdrawing more and more, hardly speaking to me. Maybe if Amos were home, Mother would come out of her bedroom more often. After all, Amos is her perfect boy who never does anything uncanny. But my twin is far away from home, and no one can tell me if he'll ever find his way back to me. Not even Amos himself.

Mother turns and catches me studying her, and I force myself to smile. Her eyes are hard rocks, pressing me down. She never looked like this at Father. Or Amos. Not with such coldness. She turns back to Leroy, who finally stops shuffling the envelopes.

He picks a note from the middle of the stack and—eyes half closed—holds it tightly in his left hand. He presses the note to his chest, over his heart, and holds it there for a few long heartbeats. Suddenly, his breath catches, and he exhales sharply. Slowly, as if not quite certain of himself, he puts the rest of the notes on the floor by his feet. Then he leans all the way back into his armchair and shuts his eyes. There is something sad and lonely, even inexplicable, about him.

Everyone seems to be holding their breath as Leroy's undeniable gravity takes control over us. I catch myself leaning forward, a breathless anticipation uncoiling in my chest. My heart pumps steadily in my ears as I wait for Leroy to say something.

"Is anyone here? A spirit? A guardian spirit, perhaps?" His voice is deep and melodious—the voice of a confident man.

Lizzie takes my hand again, and I don't withdraw this time.

An icy breeze sweeps over my face. A candle in the farthest corner of the room blows out. I look over to the half-opened window, but the curtain is not moving anymore. An unsettling pinch in my stomach draws my attention back to Leroy.

"The veil is lifted. The door is open. You may come in," he chants. "You're welcome here. Come in. Come in."

Something raps on the ceiling, and a few of the guests shriek. Another rap, stronger this time. Then another, followed by three more. Lizzie tightens her grip on my hand. More raps, fast, one after another, a strange staccato.

"They're here," Leroy says, opening his eyes. "They're ready to talk."

The air around us is thick with a nervous buzzing, our collective breathing the only sound as we all wait for whatever comes next.

"This note is from a grieving father," Leroy says. "He lost his son a year ago . . . to the water?" Leroy searches the people in front of him. "A drowning, I reckon."

I freeze in my seat, my mouth dry. The boy by the door. Was he the spirit of the drowned boy? Is it even possible? I suddenly have many questions, all of them frantic. They're burrowing into the deepest corners of my mind.

A man in a loose-fitting jacket steps forward from the back of the room. His chin is shaking as if he's suppressing a sob. "My son, Carl. He drowned a year ago."

"Who's this gentleman?" I whisper to Lizzie and gesture at the man, but she shrugs, puts her index finger to her lips just like the boy did a few minutes ago, and doesn't reply.

Leroy nods solemnly. "You wrote the note. You asked this question: 'Are you all right, son?'"

The man stumbles forward and drops to his knees, tears rolling down his face in thick rivulets. "Is he? Is Carl all right?"

Leroy gets to his feet and, with long, firm steps, makes his way to the man. With a sigh, he puts his hand on the man's head. "Your son, your Carl, is well. He's here, talking to you." His voice is distant, as if he's listening to something or someone else. "He says you shouldn't be crying. Not now, and not at night when you slip away from your house to cry outside so that your wife doesn't hear you. Carl's happy." His hands drop loosely by his sides. "And he wants you to find happiness too."

The man lifts his face up and gazes at Leroy in awe, like he's God himself. "Thank you," he whispers and pulls out a silver dollar from the pocket of his jacket. He presses it into Leroy's palm. "Thank you." He pushes himself off the floor and stumbles out the door.

The room erupts with applause.

"This cannot be real." I turn to Lizzie. She has a faraway look that tells me she isn't listening. Her eyes are wide; her lower lip is trembling. My words float, hollow and useless, in the empty space between us.

Return what's mine. A sharp, angry whisper, followed by a small hand sliding down my arm. I frantically turn around, a scream about to burst, but there's no one. Everyone else's attention seems completely fused to Leroy.

It must be my imagination, the medium's voice lulling me into some weird state. The notes, the desperate father, and his drowned son.

It is a lot to take in. Or I'm turning into my mother. I push this thought down. Then I take a deep inhale and settle back into my seat.

Leroy is back in his armchair. He breaks the seal, unfolds the note, reads it silently, nods, and shoves it at the woman closest to him. She reads the note and gets to her feet. "The note reads: 'Are you all right, son?'"

More applause follows.

A fierce flare of anger burns in my chest. What a silly question to ask the medium. The boy, Carl, is already dead. Can he really be all right? Is this all some kind of a twisted theater?

Leroy picks up the stack of notes from the floor and chooses another. He goes through the same process again, leaning into the chair, closing his eyes, listening. It's gloomy outside now, and candlelight and shadows dance across the angular planes of his face. He looks tired, his skin paler than a few minutes ago. His left hand, the one holding the note, trembles violently.

"Another tragedy. Another loss. A raging storm; a carriage drawn by an unruly horse afraid of lightning. A sharp corner. A crash." He opens his eyes. "So much pain and loss in this room. So much grief."

My stomach tightens. It sounds awfully familiar.

He lifts his right hand to his forehead and rubs it fiercely, as if chasing away the shadows. Then he drops his hand into his lap and lifts his chin, his eyes trained on Mother.

"Your ache, your loneliness, comes from your unfulfilled expectations. You expect God to lead you, to heal you. But God won't make you whole." He leans toward my mother, who's sitting upright with her shoulders tense, her eyes wild. She fiddles nervously with the mother-of-pearl button on her lace collar. "Even God needs assistance sometimes. There are those who can help, and they will if you open your heart."

My mother inhales brusquely. She lets go of the button, and her hand wraps around her throat as if she's trying to suffocate herself.

Cold sweat forms between my shoulder blades. Is that her note Leroy has in his hand? This is beyond embarrassing. I cannot allow these people to make a fool of my mother. I want to tell her to leave, not to listen to this strange man. But my throat has gone dry, and the words won't come.

"You wrote this." Leroy extends the note to Mother, as if he's trying to give it back to her. "Because you believe your husband's spirit is still around. You can sense his presence, can't you?"

My mother's eyes well with tears. Her lips shake as she mutters a hardly audible "Yes."

"Oh, Mama," I whisper. Her grief-stricken face is so gaunt, I'm afraid she's about to faint.

Lizzie casts me a sideways glance and whispers, "I told you he's extraordinary."

We shouldn't be here. Guilt crawls out of its cage and rears its head. It's all my fault. I allowed this to happen. I hoped I was helping Mother to deal with her loss. I believed that whatever it was that made her write those letters and go to the cemetery in the middle of the night, exhausted from all the sleepless hours and unable to be comforted, was temporary. I went along with her because I convinced myself that's what I needed to do. Never did it cross my mind that in her deep, endless heartache, Mother would believe that my father's spirit was still lingering in this world.

"He's here, your husband." Leroy pauses. His face grows distant, as if some uncertainty lurks beneath his words. "Your Robert," he continues in such a faint voice, it could have been the rustle of the curtains in the breeze. "He's here." My father's name scrapes against my nerves like a sharp fingernail against glass.

My mother's strangled moan rises to the ceiling, filling the air.

"Mother," I say. "Don't listen. It can't be true." I search her face, looking for the slightest hint of skepticism, of suspicion. I find none.

A few people turn and look at me, scornful and outraged.

Leroy's attention is on me now too. His eyes are black as coal. He says something else, but all I hear is my pounding heart. Mother jumps to her feet. I scramble to mine.

"The note. What's in the note?" a woman's voice asks from the corner of the room.

A heavy silence descends.

Leroy gets to his feet. A flash of curiosity on his face. A puckering of the lips followed by a glimmer in his eyes. "'Do you get my letters, Bert?' That's what the note says." He shows the note in his hand to us. It is still folded and sealed. "And Bert confirms. He reads every single one of your letters."

I press my hands to my chest as if I were just punched. How does he know my father's nickname? How does he know about Mother's letters? I feel like I'm being pulled underwater, and every breath I take sinks me deeper into the abyss.

There's a movement to my left. A loud crash, an ear-piercing screech as a chair scrapes against the wooden floor and falls with a loud thump. I turn and see my mother lying, unmoving, on the floor.

Chapter 2

The day after the séance, Mother starts to play piano again.

She hasn't touched it in months—the polished surface has been collecting dust ever since Father's funeral—and suddenly, the music floats in our drafty hallways.

I stand in the doorway and watch Mother. The sound of music fills every inch of the space. The notes flow and swirl around us with an odd, effervescent energy. And there, in the middle of the room, is Mother with a small smile and white teeth, and her neatly plaited hair that catches the sunlight, and her wedding ring that gleams as her fingers fly over the piano keys.

The gnawing sense of grief mixed with surprise rushes through me. After her fainting episode, I expected she would return to her room, where she spent her days. I didn't expect her to come out so soon after the séance, because Mother always had her moments. Even when Father was alive. But those were rare occasions, sparse throughout the year. She'd retreat into her bedroom and stay in her bed for days. During those times, and under the guidance of Father, I learned not to ask for her attention. I taught myself not to go to her bedroom. I never knew what Mother's moments meant or why she'd choose to leave us for an extended period of time.

Instead, I figured out how to live without Mother. Father's explanation of her occasional absence was brief: Mother was overburdened by her responsibilities and needed to rest. During those times, Amos and I would wait patiently for the day when her bedroom door would be thrown open and she'd come out in her high-collared, flowing silk dress. Her hair all made up and her smile cheerful, her eyes always searching for Father first and then Amos. I was always an afterthought, a nuisance.

It was Mother's idea to lighten up the hallways with custard-yellow wallpaper filled with small red roses, coiled with delicate spikes. "Let's bring sunshine into the house," she said after one of her vanishing acts. Father, who always agreed with anything Mother proposed, eagerly hired workers to install the wallpaper not just in hallways but in every room in the house.

After Father's funeral, I was terrified she might not come out of her room at all. Each morning, I woke with worry tightening my chest. I thought the unfortunate séance would plunge her deeper into the place of despair. But whatever happened that night at the Hollands' offered Mother unexpected relief.

As the days go by, Mother keeps on playing piano. At night, she feverishly writes letters to Father, and we continue to walk to the cemetery. I don't think she sleeps at all, but every morning she smiles at me, and her smile reminds me of the days when this house was full of life. Full of people and music and laughter. The séance must've cured her heart of whatever darkness was consuming it.

In response to Mother's improvement, my own mood elevates until a medical bill from Dr. Fuller arrives and plunges me into despair. The mere thought of money makes my stomach curl in knots. I'll have to pawn something in order to pay the bill, and I'm trying to save whatever we have left—which is almost nothing—for the winter months. The roof needs mending. We don't have any timber. And the unpaid bills that lie in a solemn pile on my father's desk need attention too. I've never been in a situation like this. No banker to ask for a check. No friends to call for help. There was always my father—all-knowing and commanding—his answers clear and reassuring. Now, alone and almost destitute, I'm facing impossible problems.

I ask Mother if she has any thoughts on how we can pay the bill, but she just sits there soundlessly, her gaze—fleeting and weightless—fixed on the yellow wallpaper. I'm not sure she hears me because, without a word, she gets to her feet and turns away, and my question is left unanswered. As she steps around me, I want to grab her hand, pull on her sleeve, make her listen, but I can't bring myself to move. And so I'm left alone with the unpaid bill.

A day later, at breakfast, a thought appears in my buzzing mind and snaps into place like the missing piece of a puzzle.

"Bring me my mother's silver. Have you polished it yet?" I ask Tilda, who's hovering by the door. Tilda is from rural Iowa, and Iowa raised her tall, tough, and strongly built. Her father's farm gave her physical strength and pragmatism, but what it didn't give her was money and good prospects. A few years ago, Tilda, accompanied by her determination to create a new life for herself, arrived in Omaha in search of work. She doesn't talk much about her time in our town, but I suspect that time wasn't easy. Nowadays, she's the most reliable person in our household. The one not haunted by the past. The one who stands firmly on her two feet.

"Yesterday, as you asked," Tilda says. Her blond hair is swept away from her forehead. Her skin is not perfect, but her blue eyes are full of life, and her smile always softens her face, making her look much younger than her twenty-eight years.

"Bring it up to my room." I pause. I should not order Tilda around like this. She's been on her feet since the early morning—preparing our meager meals, washing dishes, sweeping floors, ensuring Mother and I are being taken care of. "Please," I add softly.

As Tilda walks away, I get up, taking my final sip of coffee. Its bitter taste bites on my tongue and fills my mouth with acid. It is unbearable to drink it and remember the real coffee we used to drink just a year ago. With the memory comes the hunger, a painful pang in the stomach. I'm always hungry. Always craving more. I quell my memories, ignore my stomach, and run up our wide marble staircase, my fingers tracing the red oak banister chiseled by age. I go to my bedroom and wait for Tilda to bring me the silver. Perhaps my plan is a mistake, and my heart is bursting with discontent at just the thought of it. But I'm out of solutions. So it must do.

Later, Tilda and I are counting teaspoons when I hear her heavy sigh. She's standing straight, in her usual brown dress with a white apron smeared with egg yolk. Her lips pursed as she appraises the spoons in my hands.

"You don't approve," I say and slowly roll the silver into a thick woolen cloth.

"It's your grandmother's set. Maybe we can find something else of value." She doesn't look at me, but in the bleak light of the room, her eyes change from blue to deep cobalt, a sea during the storm. "Your mother will miss it." She hesitates and adds, "You'll miss it too."

"Mother won't notice it's gone."

"She will."

I scoff. "She doesn't notice anything anymore. Not me. Not you when you set her breakfast every morning in front of her. Or the condition of this bloody house. All the decline. How much repair is needed. I doubt she notices what she eats."

"There must be some other way."

I sit down on the edge of the bed, shoulders slumping. "I don't think there's any other way. We need money. And this." I take the bundle and place it into my lap. "This can pay Dr. Fuller. And maybe I'll have enough left to pay you too."

Tilda sighs, shakes her head, and doesn't say anything else.

"Pray tell me, what would you do in my place?"

She rolls her shoulders and appraises me with a sharp focus. "You could pawn your grandfather's portrait instead of silver. That painting gives me shivers every time I look at it," Tilda says. "I know you don't like looking at him too."

She's right about old Opa's portrait. Every time I study my German grandfather's stern face, I feel as if he's evaluating me, his disapproval crawling beneath my skin. "Mother would definitely notice that Opa's gone. I can't do it."

"Then silver it is, Miss. And, I reckon, it'll pay more than a portrait of an old, angry man."

We leave at high noon. The sunlight outside is warm and bright and blinding after the gloom of the shuttered house. The air is crisp with freshness. I inhale deeply, purging the scent of dampness and mold from my lungs.

"I think this walk will be good for us," I tell Tilda, and she nods in response. And when we're back, I'm going to take a long bath and wash myself of whatever deeds I'm about to commit. At the gates, I turn around and look at the Dawning. My eyes trace the sloping red roof, a few shingles displaced by a high wind, and the lines of the tall gates surrounding the estate. Its poles are already pockmarked in rust. Even from this far away I see the huge iron knocker shaped as the head of a wolf on the front door. The house looks back at me with shuttered windows as if waiting patiently for my return.

"Why would Father build such a big house away from town? No one would know if something awful happened to us. No one would hear our screams," I say. "And when I leave, what's going to happen to it? It requires so much maintenance."

"Where would you go, Miss? All alone? Your mother won't let you."

"My mother doesn't seem to care much. Sometimes I wonder if she wants me to leave." I shrug. "I'd go to Chicago. Find a job as governess. Or work for a charity. I can be whoever I want to be away from this wretched town, Tilda." I turn to her and smile. "You can come with me. When Mother recovers, we could leave together. Go to a big city. Do great things."

"Oh, Miss. It's not that easy out there, in big cities. It's hard to survive on your own. Especially with no money." Tilda's voice carries a sharp edge of anger that takes me by surprise. "I came to Omaha because I thought it would be easier here. It's smaller than Chicago." Her voice breaks, and she turns away from me. "It's smaller, all right. But it ain't kind to women. Especially young and pretty." Her hands roll into fists. "It ain't kind," she repeats. Tilda had a hard life before she came to work for us two years ago. Her father was a drunk and heavy with his hands. Tilda ran away from home when she was fifteen and worked at saloons and gambling dens for a while. I can only imagine what kind of experiences she had.

There is a hard knot in my throat. "Tilda." I softly touch her shoulder. "What happened to you? You can tell me."

She looks into the distance, her eyes darker than usual. "If you leave, you'll be just another woman who came to Chicago looking for a fresh start. So many go there, and so many disappear. I had a friend who left a few months before me. Last I heard she ended up in some low-life holes in Chicago. In the Bed Bug Row."

I don't know what the Bed Bug Row is, but the sound of it chills my spine. I've heard about the girls who vanish into obscurity in big cities. I never thought I could be one of them. But what have I truly seen of the world? I've never left Omaha. I've never traveled on a train. What do I know about what it takes to survive in a big city? I'm not like Tilda, who has worked for her food since she was a child. Perhaps my dreams of leaving are foolish.

"I'm sorry for whatever happened to you and your friend." My voice is hollow. I feel awful for bringing Chicago up. For being naive. The idea of a big city was so appealing, so seductive, talking about it was like falling into a dream, finding an escape. Even if it was for just a little while.

"Maybe you should pick a smaller town. Families in small towns look for governesses. Teachers. Look in newspapers. See if anything catches your eye."

She makes a good point, and I almost agree with her, but the thought of exchanging one small town for another doesn't sound as appealing as getting lost in a big city.

"You had a hard life, and you handled it well. I'm not as strong as you are."

"My life was hard, all right. But it gave me a useful skill, Miss. I know how to spot a lie."

"What do you mean?"

"I don't know how to explain it, but I know when people don't tell the truth. I look at their faces, and I know."

"My God, Tilda, I should be careful with you. Does it mean you can read me like an open book?"

Her face softens. "You don't have to worry about me, Miss." Tilda is older than me by just a few years, but in this moment she looks ageless. "My home's here, in Omaha. I ain't going anywhere. I'll stay in your father's house as long as I can."

The walk to town is long and tiresome. At some point, the air fills with the stench of manure. The fields spread out on both sides, and the path is filled with wet mud that clings to the thinning soles of my shoes. The pallid sun peeks through the clouds and warms our faces. Beads of sweat start to gather on my temples and slide down my neck and under my coat and dress. Tilda walks by my side, her steps wide and firm, seemingly unbothered by our brisk pace. I pause by the Rask farm—the only farm that is situated on our land—and assess the quietness of the place.

"This place is so desolate," I say. *Almost like the Dawning,* I want to add, but for some reason I don't.

"The Rasks are not here anymore," Tilda says.

A gust of wind sweeps through the fields. The smell of manure and dirt is stronger now. "What happened to them?"

"The land turned bad, and they left."

"Did my father know?" I ask. There is a peculiar itch in my mind, something forgotten. Something ignored. A sense that I know the answer to my own question. "About the land? The sickness?"

Pursing her lips, Tilda looks at me from the corner of her eye and nods. "Your daddy knew." The way she says it, measuring her every word, makes me wonder if Father did something awful. Something that pushed the Rasks away from their farm.

We walk in silence the rest of the way. The path is rocky and rutted. The flats and small hills dissolve into the monotony of all the similar walks I've taken since my father's passing. Omaha's outskirts spring on us before we know it with tall, gloomy buildings and depots and a tangled mess of poor houses and wide streets. We enter the town and get on the streetcar. I sit in front and watch the streets with unseeing eyes while the awareness of my decision presses on my shoulders like rocks stacked one upon the other. Perhaps it would've been better to send Tilda alone on this errand. But it seemed wrong to send our maid to sell my family silver. Someone could have taken her for a thief.

The streetcar stops a few blocks down on Twelfth, near the Union Pacific building, to let the passengers off and on. We get off, turn the corner, and head toward the swinging door of a two-story brick building.

"Nervous?" Tilda asks, and I nod. "Don't look anyone in the eye," she instructs me. "Keep your eyes on the floor."

I nod again, my throat dry. The quiet humiliation burns in my veins. Tears gather in the corners of my eyes, but I blink them away. When you lose your status, your dowry, and your future, no one tells you that being poor will ostracize you in a blink of a moment. No one tells you that being poor has a special shameful cadence—like a broken piano string—that follows you wherever you go. Your dresses go out of style. Your shoes wear thin. Your household staff leaves you. A seven-course meal turns into burnt oatmeal. And your only housemaid suddenly becomes your lifesaver with her uncanny advice on where to pawn your family silver.

Following Tilda's instructions, I use the side door designated for women who want to attend the establishment. But there are no women inside. The stench of beer is as thick as a wall. The patrons, men, are clustered around the tables. The dining room is square shaped and stinks of unwashed human bodies. The ceiling hangs low, and as soon as I'm inside, I feel trapped. Everything around us is soiled with grease, spit, and sin. The murky daylight coming through the windows is rendered useless by layers of thick dust on the glass.

As soon as we step inside, a silence descends. I feel the men's eyes on me, but I keep my gaze fixed on the dirty floor littered with gobs of tobacco. There's a loud ringing in my ears. It muffles all noises. A small blessing.

Tilda and I approach the barkeep, a tall and burly man. His bushy, unkempt sideburns are the color of burnt prairie grass. He is missing a few front teeth. When he gives us a broad smirk, his mouth looks like a deep gaping cavern about to swallow us whole.

"Excuse me, sir." My stomach somersaults like a circus gymnast, and I try to smile. But my lips won't stretch. I'm about to burst into tears. "I'm here to see Mr. Sol." My voice breaks on the name. Tilda told me about this place a few days ago when I wondered if I could sell some of my family heirlooms discreetly, avoiding certain pawnbrokers who were in close contact with members of society. Tilda suggested I go see Solomon Brodkey, a pawnbroker on Douglas Street.

The barkeep's unnaturally cheery expression slowly morphs into amusement as he looks me over. His eyes slide over my face, my navy blue wool coat with golden embroidery and gold buttons to match, and focus on Mother's silk satchel I'm clutching to my chest. He shifts his weight from one foot to the other and cranes his neck to the side, as if trying to make a better assessment. His face suggests he doesn't see many women wearing expensive coats in his establishment. As if confirming my thoughts, he slowly shakes his head.

Tilda, her eyebrows drawn into an apprehensive line, leans forward and says something, but he pays no attention. He pats the surface of the bar—his wrist thick, his knuckles hairy—making some kind of point, shaking his head again. Tilda purses her lips, and her shoulders fall.

My cheeks are aflame. This situation is awful. This vile place fills me with so much shame, it sticks to my skin like tar, but I cannot go home without money. I step around Tilda, my stomach folding on its own. "I need to see Mr. Sol. It's important."

"I gathered," the barkeep says with a sly, toothless smile. "He ain't here today."

Tilda leans over the counter, placing her palms firmly on the dirty surface. "Oh, he is here."

"No, he ain't."

Tilda raises her eyebrows. "Tell Mr. Sol he has visitors. Tell him he'd want to see what we've got."

I want to laugh in relief. Or maybe cry. Tilda's special skill to spot a lie is indeed invaluable.

"Sol ain't seeing no one today." The barkeep inspects the glass in his hands, smeared with marks. His thick fingers—skin raw red—press hard, creating a foggy layer of condensation.

I don't realize how desperately I clutch my satchel until the joints in my hands start to spasm. One by one I unclench my fingers. I lift my chin a little higher, even though my knees go suspiciously soft. "And I gathered he doesn't close his business even for Sabbath." I'm tired of feeling frightful all the time, and I want to be done with this place. I open the satchel and pull a silver dollar out of my purse. I softly place it on the counter and push it toward the man. "Please let Mr. Sol know Miss Wilson is here to see him."

"Wilson?" He leans forward and taps his thick fingers on the counter before taking the dollar. "Should've said that sooner."

"Didn't you hear me?" Tilda asks, setting her hands on her hips. "I told you Nina Wilson is here to see Sol."

His eyes slide over to Tilda, and he tosses the dollar in the air, catching it swiftly a second later. "Sometimes you talk funny. Like a proper lady." He chuckles. "Well then, ladies." The words seem to be stuck in his throat. He slides the glass across the counter, glancing sideways at me. "Come with me." With a deep and exasperated sigh, the barkeep nods over his shoulder.

We follow him into a room behind the counter. As soon as we enter, he closes the door behind us with a violent push. An unpleasant chill fills my belly. The intelligent thing for me to do is to leave or at least ask him to keep the door open. But I'm here for a discreet transaction, away from prying eyes, and so I don't say anything. I slowly turn around, looking for Sol, the pawnbroker. But the space is empty and windowless. The air is pungent with dampness, but at least it doesn't stink of stale sweat. A chair made of wicker stands in the corner. An oil lamp is placed on the floor. The walls are unexpectedly clean and white.

"Put it there." The barkeep points at a wide-open dumbwaiter that gapes at us from the farthest wall.

"I don't understand," I say. "I'm here to see Mr. Sol."

"Sol ain't seeing no one, Miss. Put whatever you have inside. On the cart."

It doesn't feel right. Maybe I can find another way to get the money to pay the medical bill. I should go home and pretend this never happened. Pretend I never came to this seedy place to sell my grandmother's silver.

I look at Tilda. She looks at me and nods.

My heart thumping so loud that it's all I can hear, I take out a bundle of silver and hold it in my hands, hesitant to let it out of my grasp.

"Ain't got all day," the barkeep growls and snatches the bundle from me, throws it on the cart. He sticks his head inside the dumbwaiter and roars, "Wilson." Then he proceeds to pull on ropes, sending it down. The pulleys groan and squeak as the elevator slowly drops out of our sight. We hear the dumbwaiter stop, and someone opens its doors and takes the silver from the cart.

My hands are shaking. My core clenches tightly, overwhelmed by turbulent emotions roiling through me—shame, relief, anxiety. I feel like I'm drowning, like I myself am in that dumbwaiter, pulleys creaking with a familiar rhythm, lowering me into the void. Somehow I manage to stand still and hold my breath. Life has changed so much in the span of a few months. Before, I couldn't even think about entering a saloon. Now, I am in an empty back room with a stranger, trying to pawn our family silver to an invisible pawnbroker.

"Sit if you want." The barkeep points at the chair, then scratches his head and leans on the wall. "Never thought you'd show your pretty face here."

I don't have the slightest idea what he means by his odd remark, and I don't feel comfortable sitting in his presence. I shrug half-heartedly because I don't want to irritate him. "I'll stand. Thank you for the offer, though."

He spits on the floor and folds his arms across his chest. "Sol will be happy."

My heart speeds up at the thought of getting good money for the silverware. "The silver is valuable. Indeed, he should be happy with it."

We wait.

Tilda starts to pace the small room like an animal, nervous and alert. I can barely keep my uneasiness at bay. Finally, the cords screech again, and the dumbwaiter is coming back. As soon as it arrives, the barkeep opens the door, but there is no money inside. Just a small square piece of paper. The barkeep hands it to me.

"It says I owe three hundred dollars," I say slowly. "Is this a joke?"

"Ain't no joke. You owe money, Miss. Your daddy used to play here. I reckon Sol assigned his debts to you."

Gloom falls over the room as the realization dawns. My father's gambling debts.

The barkeep holds my gaze for a few seconds and starts to laugh. He's enjoying himself tremendously. "Well." He slaps himself on his hips. "Time for you to go, Miss." He points at the door, but I cannot move. This is not happening.

"You hear me? We're done. Both of you, get out."

Slowly, as if in a dream, Tilda and I shuffle to the door. My limbs heavy, my head dizzy, we walk past the counter. And before I know it, I'm outside, blinking rapidly in the bright sunshine. I take a few steps, trying to fill my lungs with air. But the pressure in my chest never releases its iron grasp on my heart. Just like Tilda, it accompanies me all the way home.

September 5, 1903

Dear Amos,

I hope this letter finds you well. Do you feel fall in the air? It must be pretty cold where you are. I have heard weather turns cold in upstate New York sooner than in Omaha.

I am sad to inform you, but the Dawning has turned into a place of misery and pain. Every day inside this house makes me want to disappear, run away to some welcoming place where no one knows me. You probably know this feeling too well. God, how I wish you would be allowed to communicate with us. The rules in that awful place are too strict. It is truly disheartening.

I dream about our father's funeral often. The memories of it are carved into my brain. Oh, what a dreadful, dreadful day that was. Does it haunt you as well, Amos? I keep trying not to think about it, but the encroaching memories find their way into my mind and at the most unexpected moments. I remember the gray sky. And I remember the loneliness. The service was short. The weather was brutal. We stood under the freezing rain until my feet were numb from cold and my stomach curled on itself from hunger.

It seems even the Dawning does not want to let go. I keep finding Father's hats and gloves and ties scattered throughout the house. Always in a different room. Always in the middle of the floor. As if he just was standing there, getting ready to leave the house, and had dropped his belongings absentmindedly. Something about it makes him feel alive. Every time I see Father's clothes, my heart sinks, and I stand silent for a moment, looking at the belongings of the man who died months ago. When I find these painful reminders of him, the unease lingers like a shroud over my heart for hours.

I suspect it is all Mother's doing.

A while ago, Mother stopped paying wages to our staff, and everyone left except Tilda. I begged Tilda to stay and promised to pay her late wages before long. I offered her a room downstairs by the kitchen—until I scrape the funds—and to my immense surprise and relief, she stayed. Sometimes I think if not for our social standing, I could be good friends with Tilda.

I do wish you were here to help me bear this burden. You are so much better at solving problems than I shall ever be. You always know what to do. But I am sure the doctors would not let you go home. I have not the slightest idea how to bring our financial affairs in order. Our parents did not prepare me for the real world. We have a month to come up with the funds to pay our tax bill. Do you know what will happen if we cannot pay it? I try not to think about it because some thoughts are too frightening.

I think my pen is leaking. Do you see all the smudges? In case you're wondering . . . they're not tears, Amos.

With all my love,

Your sister Nina

Chapter 3

Our dining room feels damp, as if the walls absorbed most of the rain from the night before. I eat dry toast for breakfast. The butter and jam ran out a few days ago. Staring directly ahead at the wall in front of me, I try my best to keep my face blank. If I allow myself to look across the table at Mother, my chin starts to shake. Little quivers of suppressed tears.

Mother looks thinner than days before. Her cheekbones are so sharp, they might cut through the skin. Two red splotches burn on her gaunt cheeks. She's in the same dress she's worn the past few days. The dress gathers around her small waist in waves, falling awkwardly around equally skinny hips, like some used-up rag picked up in the stalls of the Capitol Avenue Market House. Her eyes gleam feverishly.

"Mother, what should we do with the land bill?" I ask. The crunch of her toast stabs at my eardrums. "You're the lady of the house. You need to tell me what to do." I've been holding my anger inside for a long time, and I can probably hold it a little longer, though how much longer I'm not so certain.

She finally looks at me. Her gaze is sharp. Sharp as the bread knife that lies in the center of the table. "Your father will figure it all out." She pauses and waves her hand around the room. "He always knows what to do."

My blood bubbles like boiled water. My thoughts are a tangled mess. To stop myself from venturing deeper into the anger, I shove a piece of scratchy, tasteless bread into my mouth and slowly chew on it. Then I take a sip of a bitter chicory coffee to wash it down. "Father is dead. He won't be advising us anytime soon."

"You have no faith, darling."

"Faith in what? Spirits?" The heat builds and swirls in my chest. "Are they going to pay our bills?"

Her eyes blast me with ice as she pushes herself away from the table. "Your rudeness is unacceptable, Nina. No wonder you're not welcome in town anymore." She glides across the room and disappears into the hallway.

I stay frozen in my chair, clutching its edges and grinding my teeth. The air is so quiet the floorboards scream under Tilda's steps, and when she enters the dining room, the clicking of her shoes seems to echo through the house.

"Miss," she says. "What can I do to help?" Her voice is tired, as if she's in need of rest too.

"Pay the doctor's bill?" I laugh bitterly.

A strain—as if she wants to say something but doesn't know how—crosses her face.

"What is it, Tilda? Tell me."

"I ain't no help with the bill, but there's someone who might help your mother. He's done it before."

I narrow my eyes at her. "You don't mean . . . the medium, do you? Leroy Marshall?" I'm not certain why I thought of him, but as soon as I say his name, my pulse speeds up.

"I know you didn't take to him. I recall you called him a charlatan. But people listen to him."

"I'm not certain *charlatan* is the right word to describe Leroy Marshall. I don't know what he is." I shrug, chest heavy. "It doesn't matter what I think about him or what I call him. But you might be right. Maybe . . . maybe he is the one to get Mother out of the world of the dead and back into the world of the living."

"Your mother responded to him quite well."

"All right. I'm going to invite Mr. Marshall to visit Mother here, at the Dawning, and convince her that my father wants her to move on. That Father himself has moved on. Hopefully, Leroy Marshall will persuade her to let go of this . . . madness . . . this idea that Father's spirit is roaming our hallways." I look at the yellow wallpaper, the red roses and the green leaves scattered throughout, and the crystal chandelier, grimy and covered in spiderwebs, hanging high on the ceiling. How I wish I could leave this house and let it rot. But after my conversation with Tilda about the dangers of big cities, I'm not so certain I'm brave enough to do so. This morning, the idea of leaving feels a bit thin. Like a fading memory. And, of course, there is my promise to Amos to take care of Mother in his absence. I must keep my word, and maybe that choking guilt that constantly assails me will finally dissipate.

"If this man does what you ask him, if he tells Mrs. Wilson that her dead husband isn't with her anymore, it will render him a fraud. I doubt someone like him would agree to it. Because if it gets out, people will get upset," Tilda says. "He gets paid good money for his abilities. He doesn't need to pretend he speaks to the dead. He truly does, and the dead listen."

"Tilda, my goodness." My curiosity about our maid sharpens. We never talked openly about the spirit world until now. "You believe in ghosts? You believe in Leroy Marshall?"

"I do," Tilda whispers and drops her gaze. "He's a true medium, Miss. He brought my departed brother through the veil when he stayed with the Masons. Their cook let me in through the back door to watch his séance. I could feel Frankie's presence. He was thirteen when he died of influenza." She sighs, playing awkwardly with the frayed threads of her apron, and shakes her head. "I don't know how to explain it, but my little brother was there. I swear. He held my hand. There was a special kind of tingling in my bones when he touched me." She looks up at me, and there's obvious admiration in her face. "I can spot a lie, Miss. Not once have I thought Leroy Marshall was a liar. Not once have I doubted him. I don't know how Mr. Marshall does it, but he talks to the dead."

"Well then. Perhaps it's what Mother needs. That special tingling in her bones." One way or the other, with Father's help or not, Leroy Marshall will know how to give Mother closure. "He'll come." I nod too fast, too eagerly, and spill my coffee. The brown liquid drips down my chin. Instead of using a cloth napkin, I wipe it off with the back of my hand. My mother would cringe at my table manners, but there's no one here to judge me. "I know how to persuade him. Money. Money can persuade anyone. Perhaps . . . perhaps I can offer him my silver locket." My hand flies to my collarbone and squeezes my locket. It always gives me comfort, but now the metal feels uneven and scratchy under my touch. I remove the locket, open it, and study my and Amos's portrait. It's unsettling to see our happy faces. The portrait was done three years ago, at the time when we thought nothing and no one could ever break us apart. There's so much hope in that portrait. So much heartbreak. "Silver's valuable. He can sell it for a lot of money."

Tilda shakes her head. "Just ask him for his help instead, and he'll do it. He never refuses those in need of his services."

I smile. "He never refuses because people pay him." I tilt my head, studying my housemaid. "I haven't realized you know so much about the world of the dead."

"There are stories, Miss. Stories and things no one can explain."

I think back to the séance, to the room filled with the scent of burning candles, and how that boy stood by the door, a pool of water by his feet, his face sharp and otherworldly. Is it possible that he's one of those souls Leroy talked about, wandering in our world, looking for a place to stay? My hands start to shake. No one else saw the boy but me. Maybe I imagined him. Or maybe he was there. If I believe the medium, if I believe in the existence of the other world, then I don't have to face the possibility of it being in my head. The possibility of madness. Wouldn't that be freeing?

"Anything to help Mother." Goose bumps dance up and down my arms as I pick up my coffee cup to distract myself from my own thoughts. "I don't really have a choice, do I? If I don't do something, anything, she'll go completely mad." And I'll go mad with her. I try to infuse as much confidence in my voice as I can, but my words falter, betraying my real feelings. Sleepless nights, long walks to the cemetery, constant hunger—all of it stretched my sanity thin. Mother has visions too. She claims Father is in the house. She plays music for him. She writes him letters and spreads his clothes around the house.

I slam my cup on the table with more force than is necessary. Beads of coffee spray on the white tablecloth like dried blood. Leroy Marshall might be a real deal or a charlatan, but for now he's my only hope. If he can get Mother out of her grief and back into the real world of unpaid debts and crumbling walls and leaking pipes, maybe she'll figure out how to pay the bills, and maybe I'll be able to get back into society. And maybe Bobby will reconsider our marriage. I try not to think about what happens if Leroy refuses. Or worse—fails to provide Mother some much-needed closure. What would become of us? Would we be destitute, looking for some distant relatives to take us in? Would we forever rely on someone else's charity, someone else's goodwill?

I swallow hard and push my thoughts away. "I'm bringing Mr. Marshall to the Dawning."

I leave Tilda in the dining room and rush to my room. I start climbing the stairs hastily, adrenaline pumping in my blood and propelling me forward. Suddenly I'm out of breath. I pause in the middle of the staircase, gasping for air, my hands slick on the banister. What's happening to me? My legs burn as if I scaled a few flights of stairs, but I'm standing in the center of the staircase, appraising a few more steps I must conquer. I shake my head. I need to do something about my restless nights. I must be staggering with exhaustion.

Before I leave the house, I remove my pearl earrings and drop them into my mother's silk satchel. I remove my locket. I hope earrings and the locket are enough to convince Leroy Marshall to help Mother. The earrings were a birthday gift from my parents when I turned fifteen. Ten years have passed since then, and yet it feels like it all happened to someone else and in some other life, not mine.

Time as a concept has a funny quality. I vaguely remember certain events—my first ball gown presented to me by my parents, my first horse, my first kiss with Bobby, my first pearl earrings. These moments are foggy and faded. Forgotten. And then there are deep holes of events, buried in time, and yet they're still raw, sharp, and agonizingly fresh.

I splash water on my face, letting it clear my mind. Morning sunlight bursts through the tall window, reflecting off the mirror and brightening the room. I study my reflection for the first time since the séance. I've aged. My face is so pale and gaunt, someone could easily mistake me for an apparition. In contrast with my skin, my locks are as black as raven wings. I smile, and my face twists in a grimace.

I leave before tears start to stream down my face.

The clouds are gathering in the late-morning sky when I ride my bicycle to the Hollands' family house on Izard Street. I pass by the Union Pacific Railroad bridge and enter Omaha on Douglas Street, passing by one of the infamous brothels at Ninth where Amos used to spend his time. A streetcar glides by, and its passengers crane their necks at me and my bicycle. The streets around me are bustling and flowing with people on horseback, in streetcars, and in carriages. Some whistle at me as I ride wearing my loose-fitting silk bloomers. By tonight, Omaha's society will spin gossip about the Wilson girl who rides a bicycle like a man.

Lizzie's father built their sprawling, castle-like house in the esteemed Walnut Hill neighborhood in North Omaha. The three-story building made of wood and brick is tucked away in a back alley, shaded by cottonwood and pecan trees.

When Lizzie sees me enter their parlor, her green eyes light up like two jadestones under the sun. A few candles burn brightly on the fireplace, which is unusual considering the time of day. A tea set is perched on the Chippendale mahogany table by her side. She straightens her spine, readying herself to leap out of her leather armchair. Her simple green dress with a high collar and white lace contrasts oddly with the lively bird-themed wallpaper and whitewashed ceiling. She smiles at me, but then her face turns somber as she looks at Mrs. Holland, who is sitting on the beige settee by the window with a small book in her hands. I shift my feet uncomfortably, the oak floorboards creaking as they announce my arrival. The huge grandfather clock on the wall measures my heartbeats.

"Good afternoon, Mrs. Holland." I smile at Lizzie's mother. "Hello, Lizzie." I stretch my arms to her with a wide smile.

"Nina, you're here," Lizzie says in a tense voice. She runs up to me and holds my hands and smiles; her breath is warm and sweet with tea and sugar. "I'm so happy to see you." The way she says it, the lilt of her words, reveals the strain in her voice, and for a fleeting moment, I see truth. For whatever reason, my friend doesn't want me here. I wonder if it has anything to do with my resistance to Leroy's charm during his séance. Or Mother's collapse in the middle of it.

"How is your dear mother?" Mrs. Holland asks, echoing my thoughts. Her voice is sharp. Her eyes bore into my face unpleasantly. She doesn't get up from her seat.

"My mother is not well." My voice quivers—with despair or impatience, I can't tell exactly. "She's the reason I'm here. I'm wondering if I could see Mr. Marshall."

A moment of silence descends, heavy and awkward. The clock ticks. Lizzie stops breathing, her mouth falls open, and a bright flush of red appears on the bottom of her neck. Mrs. Holland sets the book on her lap, curls her hands into fists. Her lips twist into a scowl.

"Mr. Marshall is not accepting visitors today," Mrs. Holland says. Her voice is so icy and cutting, it could freeze the Missouri River. "At the moment, he's indisposed. You might not realize, but what he does takes a lot of his energy. Talking to the spirits is not an easy task, and it requires a certain exertion. He must restore himself before he's able to see any visitors."

Visitors? Is that what I am now—a random, unwanted visitor?

"How long will it take for Mr. Marshall to restore himself?" I ask. "I hope to see him today. It is a matter of utmost importance."

Mrs. Holland stands up, her brows creasing. "Lizzie will send you a note when . . . when appropriate. In the meantime, send our warmest regards to your mother, please. I do hope her recovery is swift." She turns to Lizzie. "It's time for your piano lesson, darling."

What a pathetic excuse. Lizzie hasn't had a single piano lesson in years. She simply cannot wait to get rid of me. The images of me coming back to the empty home, to my ailing mother, crack my chest open like an eggshell dropped on the floor, severing a part of my hope that everything will be well in the end. That someday Mother will be her normal self, my promise to Amos fulfilled.

"Please, Mrs. Holland, send someone to Mr. Marshall to let him know I'm here to see him. It's a matter of life and death." Something caresses the back of my neck, a gentle whisper, a light touch of the air. As if someone is watching me. I ignore the feeling and say what I meant to say during the séance five days ago. "Otherwise, I wouldn't be here. You've made it abundantly clear you won't have me. I'm not welcome in this house."

Lizzie gasps, her hand flying up to her lips. "Nina, don't say that." The sunrays break through the clouds and catch on her blond curls, highlighting them in gold.

I hear a noise behind me, a creak of the door, a few footsteps, a light sigh. Perhaps it is my imagination again. My wishful mind conjuring the sounds. "You haven't called on me in months, Lizzie." At my words, the hurt pools in Lizzie's eyes. "But it doesn't matter now. I understand I'm not as important as I used to be. Amos is away, and my father's dead, and our financial situation is . . . difficult. I know what people are saying." It's not appropriate to bring up certain subjects so openly, but why should I hide my thoughts any longer? No one says anything as I pause. The air is charged with awkwardness. Lizzie swipes at her locks, entranced by the plush carpet on the floor. I force myself to continue. "Please, if you don't want to help me, help my mother." A teary choke in my voice surprises me. I hadn't realized I'm about to break down in tears.

"Nina—" Mrs. Holland starts to say, but she never finishes her sentence.

"Your situation sounds dire," a familiar low voice drawls from behind me, interrupting Lizzie's mother. In two sweeping steps Leroy Marshall enters the room, his movements precise and confident. He looks just like I remember him, pale and clad in immaculately pressed raven-black clothes. The same necktie is wrapped around his throat, and his black shoes glisten with a flawless shine. His eyes are shaded by exhaustion, but his attention is sharp. He doesn't look as drained of energy as Mrs. Holland made it sound. His gaze is intense as he takes me all in.

"Mr. Marshall," I exhale.

A frosty breeze follows him, swiping over my face, my hair, sinking its claws into my skin and rattling my bones.

"Please call me Leroy, Miss Wilson," he says with a beautiful smile, seemingly unaffected by the strange coldness. "May I call you Nina? Or is that too presumptuous of me?"

Chapter 4

I draw myself tall. "Miss Wilson, please." I feel a pang of annoyance. Who does he think we are to each other? The fact that he helped carry Mother to the sofa when she fainted doesn't make us friends. We're not even acquaintances. "I'd like to talk to you about my mother." I swallow hard, and his eyes, brown flecked with gold, trail my throat. "She's not well. She needs your help."

He rubs the bridge of his nose, puzzled. "I'm sorry to hear it, Miss Wilson, but I fail to understand how I can possibly help you."

An odd emptiness grows inside my chest. "You speak to lost souls, don't you, Mr. Marshall?" My voice turns raspy, as if pieces of gravel scrape against my esophagus. "You conjure spirits. You mend broken hearts." I almost laugh at my own words. I sound ridiculous. But then I remember my mother's slumped-over-the-piano posture, the feverish gleam in her eyes, her pale hollowed-out cheeks, and I school my face. She is my burden. The sensible part of me, the one who listened to Father openly mock spiritual gatherings, believes the man in front of me can give closure my mother needs. But the other part, the one that thinks madness lurks around the corner, the one that questions the unexplainable, wonders if he truly talks to lost spirits. It is disquieting to think that the dead might be listening to us. "I know you can help her. If you just talk to her. One more time." As I speak, Leroy's eyes trace the loose curls that brush the sides of my neck and my dress. There are beads of sweat from my ride I meant to wipe off my forehead before I entered the parlor. I swipe at my forehead, and my cheeks heat under his inspecting gaze. "Would you consider coming with me? To the Dawning?" I inhale his scent of earthy aftershave mixed with burned wicker.

He raises an eyebrow. "The Dawning?"

"Our estate."

"Nina, Mr. Marshall can't go with you." Lizzie reaches out to me as if to pull me away from Leroy but relents under her mother's strict gaze. She used to be my best friend, and now she isn't even an ally. One day I will ask her what happened, what changed between us. I don't recognize her anymore. My friend used to be kind and funny, and now she is as indifferent and distant as my own mother. And why is she giving me these odd sidelong glances as if she thinks I bring trouble?

I roll my shoulders in defiance. "Mr. Marshall, could we speak in private, please?"

Leroy's mouth twists in amusement. Lizzie stares at me in shocked silence.

"In private?" Mrs. Holland barks, keeping her chin high and her back perfectly straight. "This is utterly inappropriate. You're forgetting your manners, Nina." Her eyes are hard. Her words, heavy and painful, burn my skin like a slap.

Anger sinks its claws into my marrow as I turn to Mrs. Holland. "Where were your manners when you turned your back on my family as soon as my father's debts became known? We missed you dearly at his funeral. Why didn't you come? Was it your manners that stopped you?" I'll never forget my mother's white face, a shocking contrast to the black lace of her dress, looking at the cemetery gates, expecting the Hollands, who never came. We stood alone in front of my father's grave. No friends, no support, no one by our side. Just our own family, whatever was left of us, and our shared burden of loneliness and grief.

"Nina," Lizzie exhales, blinking slowly.

"How dare you—" her mother starts but is interrupted yet again by Leroy.

"Rachel," Leroy says softly, addressing Mrs. Holland, who stares at me in stern disbelief. "There is no need for such harsh words." He pauses, as if giving her a chance to acknowledge her rudeness. When she doesn't say anything, he adds, "Miss Wilson's seeking help. That's all it is. And it is my vocation to help her."

Lizzie's mother scoffs. "All she's seeking is trouble." She turns to her daughter. "I'm retiring." I stiffen as she brusquely walks past me to the door, and before anyone else can say a word, she is gone. Lizzie follows her meekly.

The situation is going awry, but I cannot leave without talking to Leroy, and so I stay, unmoving. If they want me gone, they'll have to drag me out of this house. My eyes flit nervously to Leroy, and to my immense relief, he smiles and waves at the door. "Looks like you got what you've asked for. A private audience with the medium." His smile is wide. He seems unperturbed by Mrs. Holland's dramatic exit. "We can stay here, or perhaps you prefer the office?"

"Let's go to Mr. Holland's office," I say. "I don't feel comfortable in this room." Indeed something shifted in the air. The space is stiller. Shadows gather around me, tightening my rib cage, suffocating me.

I follow Leroy up the stairs to Mr. Holland's office and step inside, squinting from the unexpected brightness. The French windows are open, heavy velvet draperies are pulled aside, and the sunlight is streaming freely into the familiar room. The smell of leather and paper is oddly soothing. I slowly close the door behind me and turn to face Leroy, but my gaze is drawn to the big mahogany desk that looms by the window. Books and documents are scattered across its shiny wooden surface in some chaotic manner, as if a breeze flapped the pages around. I look up at Leroy, who's standing a few feet away from me with an expectant expression on his handsome face.

"Mr. Marshall," I begin, my voice flat. "My mother's drowning in grief. She's prone to the most terrible moods after my father's passing. But since the note reading we attended in this house a few days ago, she believes my father's spirit now lives in our house. If before the séance she wrote letters to my father occasionally, now she writes them every day. At night, she spreads Father's clothes throughout the house because she's convinced he's back and needs to dress." I pause to gather the thoughts coiling and whirling in my mind. "And she plays piano for him daily. It's madness." He stands transfixed and watches me so intently I wonder if he thinks I'm losing my mind too. "I hope if you talk to her, if you use your message of healing, she'll get better."

"A message of healing? I'm not sure what you mean." There is a grin in his voice, but his expression is attentive. Yet it seems forced. Is he not taking my words seriously? Does he take me for a tattling child?

My voice grows a notch higher as I push forward. "Talk to her about my father, Mr. Marshall. Just like you did during the séance. Tell Mother you talked to him again, and he wishes for her to go on with her life, to be happy, and that he himself is moving on. Tell her what you said to that man, the one who lost his son to drowning." As soon as the words are out, a breeze snakes up my neck, as if someone puffs air onto my skin. Papers rustle on the desk by the window. A slightly built figure, the shape of a boy, lowers itself into one of the armchairs by the desk. But he doesn't really sit down. Instead, the boy hovers over the seat.

"What's happening?" I whisper, more to myself than to Leroy. I'm under so much duress, I'm hallucinating again. My pulse is beating in my temples, loud as a church bell. If I ever get money to spare, I must talk to Dr. Fuller. Perhaps all I need is some kind of tincture to calm my mind and my nerves. He gave something to Mother the day of Father's accident, and she was able to sleep through the night. Perhaps I need the same tincture. I look over Leroy's shoulder, but the room is empty. There is nothing there.

"I think I know what's happening. Your mother had an encounter with the spirit of her husband. And now, understandably, she desires more. She needs more." His eyes narrow on me as he examines my face, almost clinically. "Does your mother believe in God?"

"I'm not sure what she believes."

When my father was alive, we went to church every Sunday. I remember how the heavy church door creaked. How the hushed murmurs of the parishioners filled the space around me, pressing on my temples. The heavy smell of burning candles, stale sweat, and sharp perfume. Mother would be dressed in her most expensive crimson silk dress, me in my best satin shoes, Father and Amos in their best wool suits. Mother believed it mattered to be seen in church, to show our religious devotion. She believed in God and prayers and whatever the priest was preaching. She believed in salvation, right until the day my father died. Right until the moment he was gone. Sucked into oblivion. She stopped going to church then. Didn't mention it once. I guess she finally realized that no God could stop Father's carriage from crashing. Death was more powerful and definitely more possessive than God. No divine power could return what had been taken from her.

Before father's death, I didn't believe in God the way Mother did. My father's skeptical mind influenced my view of the world. But right now, at this moment, standing alone in the room with billowing shadows, facing the medium, I suddenly long to be in a house of God, where no apparition can reach me.

"Will you come with me to the Dawning? Talk to Mother?"

"Talk about what, Miss Wilson? I'm still at a loss here."

Irritation stirs in my chest. Why this pretense? He knows what I want him to do. He understands me perfectly well. He's the one with the power to help my mother. Perhaps he wants me to beg. "Summon the spirit of my father." My voice is low—low enough that no one from the Hollands' household can overhear me in the hallway. "And if he doesn't come, pretend he's there anyway. Tell Mother he asks her to move on because he's leaving our world with no intent to return."

"Are you asking me to lie?" There is a hint of laughter, a lilt of an unspoken joke in his words, in the gleam of the golden flecks of his eyes.

"Isn't it what you do for a living?" My chin trembles with anger. "Pocketing some coins while telling grieving parents their children are in a good place? That they're doing all right?" The words burst out of me before I can catch myself, and I'm mortified. I bite the inside of my cheek. I should've held my tongue. All I'm doing is alienating him. The coffee I had this morning churns in my stomach. I wince, trying to find the right words to say to remedy the situation.

He laughs, a short and surprisingly warm sound. "Miss Wilson, you're asking for help, yet you're going out of your way to insult me." With a small smile, he steps closer, and I suddenly feel trapped between the closed door behind me and his tall frame. "I don't think I can do what you're asking me to do, Miss Wilson. The spirits don't like skeptics."

"I'm not here to prove you wrong. Or to make you into a charlatan." Chuckling, he runs his hand through his lush hair. Why is he so unfairly handsome? "You don't understand. I'm not here to insult you. I'm asking you to help my mother. You're the only person who can get through to her. She believes you. Please, Mr. Marshall, I beg you." My voice hums with desperation, and I hate the sound of it. "I'll pay you. Your time won't be in vain." I clutch my satchel and pull out my locket. My face flushed from embarrassment, I show it to Leroy. "Please, take this as the payment." I wince. Never in my life have I thought I would stoop so low. "This is all I can afford, but I hope it's enough."

He takes the locket, opens it, and studies the portrait for a long minute. The sun catches on his hair, and the shadows playing on his cheekbones make him look almost otherworldly. "Is that your twin brother? You don't look like twins."

"We don't," I say, my heart tightening with so much longing for Amos, it might fracture.

"Wasn't he sent away? To an institution?"

My hands curl into fists. "I see you collect gossip." God knows how much I hate this bloody town and its incessant chatter. Its desire for a scandal. Nothing is off-limits. Not even human tragedy.

"Miss Wilson, you're offending me yet again. Put your locket away, please. I don't prey on misery. Nor am I a rumormonger." There is something in his tone that tells me he's not really hurt by my words, and I feel ashamed of my outburst. Everyone in Omaha knows our story. What happened to Amos. How our family name was stained by shame. I'm certain Mrs. Holland herself volunteered to supply this information.

I stand awkwardly for a few frantic heartbeats, my hands opening and closing the purse. I'm almost mesmerized by Leroy Marshall staring at me with an expression I don't understand. There is warmth in his eyes. A flash of sorrow. And also some curiosity.

"The portrait was done three years ago," I say. "When Amos was healthy and living at home." A year ago my brother was sent away to upstate New York to heal. And ever since, the visions of him keep popping into my head at most unexpected moments—his sad smile when he said his goodbye, the frost that bit into my skin as I watched him descend the stairs. I see it so clearly, as if it all happened yesterday. "It's all I have left of him." Tears are burning my eyes, but I refuse to cry in front of Leroy. "I have a feeling Mother will do something awful without your help." My voice croaks from all the despair coiling in my throat. "Just talk to her. I'll do anything you want; just please help my mother."

He rubs his jaw thoughtfully. "What are you offering, Miss Wilson?" There's a seductive quirk to his grin that makes my knees go soft. He has a charisma I never encountered before in a man. "I won't take the locket. Or the pearl earrings I noticed in your purse."

"I'll do whatever you want," I whisper, my face burning.

A glint of a shadow. My heart rate spikes as I force myself not to look over at the armchair, but despite my efforts, like a moth drawn to the flame, my gaze slides over Leroy's shoulder to the desk behind him.

Return what's mine. A soft whisper of a child.

The floor shifts and slides underneath my feet, and I lean into the door behind me. Not by the chair this time but in the farthest corner of the room, the boy I saw at the séance is smiling at me, water mixed with mud dripping on the floor.

This is not happening. Not again. I'm indeed going insane. Perhaps Dr. Fuller will take my earrings in exchange for a sleeping potion.

"Miss Wilson?" Leroy's voice floats to me through the choking fog in my head. A gentle touch to my shoulder. "Miss Wilson?" My gaze slides back to the medium.

Return what's mine.

"Anything," I cry out to drown the voice in my head. "I'll give you anything you want. Just come with me to the Dawning." Fighting the urge to run, I look over to the desk. The boy is nowhere in sight. The air is warm again. I inhale and let my tense muscles relax. It was all an illusion. An odd dream produced by my exhausted psyche. The boy cannot harm me, because he doesn't exist. "Mr. Marshall?" I direct my attention back to the man in front of me. "Will you help my mother or not?"

With a deep sigh, Leroy shoves his hands into his pants pockets. With just one word he can grind my hope to dust. What will he want in exchange for his help? Most importantly, what am I willing to give? A tremble in my bones tells me I'm desperate enough to agree to anything. My breath turns heavy. Is there anything I'm not willing to give him? I try not to think about it as I hold my exhale, waiting for his answer.

"I'll go with you, Miss Wilson. I'll talk to your mother."

"When?"

"When do you want me?"

"Right away."

He studies my hands. I haven't realized until now how hard I'm clasping them. My knuckles are white.

"Let's not waste another minute, then." He nods at the door.

The relief is sudden, crashing into me like a wave. My knees buckle. Leroy catches me by my forearms and pulls me up. I find the ground under my feet and finally allow myself to breathe. "What do you want in return?" I ask, my voice raspy.

He drops his hands; his fingertips sweep against my wrists. "Perhaps one day we'll find out." He leans closer, and his lips brush over my ear. "Today is not that day, Miss Wilson." His mouth lingers above my ear for a few more seconds before he withdraws. Our eyes meet, and I think he's about to say something else. My core tenses in anticipation, but he's already opening the door, and the moment is gone.

Chapter 5

After I show him my bicycle, Leroy disappears into the house to ask the Hollands for their carriage. I stand outside, watching the sky stitched with heavy clouds, hopeful, more hopeful than I've felt in months. I'm finally bringing closure for Mother. Maybe there is a God after all, and my thoughts somehow reached out to the heavens, and he listened.

"We're ready to go, Miss Wilson." Leroy's voice interrupts my reverie. There is a carriage in front of the porch. Leroy's brows are raised at me in a silent question. I nod and climb into the front seat by his side. My bicycle is secured in the back. Leroy takes the reins and directs the carriage down Farnam Street.

"I thought I'd seen a lot in my life." He chuckles and slaps his hand on his knee. "But I've not seen a woman on a bicycle." His eyes, shining with amusement, sweep over me, assessing my clothes.

I glance at him from the corner of my eye, for some reason not daring to meet his gaze directly. My face is flushed, and I'm not sure what to say. He has already turned away and is looking straight ahead, but a small smile is still playing on his full lips. I take in his broad shoulders, raven-black hair, and long eyelashes. Not a trace of judgment. He's definitely handsome in a bit of a roguish but mysterious way.

"I'm not the first woman who chose a bicycle as a mode of transportation, Mr. Marshall. And I'm sure I'm outmatched in a big city like Chicago," I say. "Omaha is behind on all the progress." The town is behind on many things: education, women's rights, and housing limitations—resulting in slums growing in the outskirts of Omaha. Yet brothels keep on springing up everywhere like mushrooms after a rainstorm. Women have to use a separate door to enter a saloon. I cannot have a bank account because I'm not married. But I'm not going to talk to Leroy Marshall about deeds and property rights and our financial predicaments with the looming tax bill.

"What does your mother think about it? Your riding alone through the streets of Omaha?" Leroy asks softly. A grin flashes on his face so quickly, I'm not certain if it was a smile or a play of light and shadows. "Does she even know about this dangerous contraption?" He turns to me, his eyes gleaming with laughter.

"Contraption?" I snort and shake my head. "Mother doesn't have an opinion. Not really. But Amos, my brother, calls my bicycle *progressive nonsense*."

I remember the day Father brought the bicycle home and Mother stared at it, incredulous. "You want our daughter to ride this thing?" she'd asked, her voice trembling either from anger or surprise. Neither Amos nor I was sure as we stood together by the doorway.

My father snaked his arms around Mother's waist and pulled her into his arms, tucking her against his chest and dipping his head into her chignon. "Yes, I want her to ride it. Let Nina set new and adventurous expectations for our Omaha ladies. Let them see that a woman can operate a two-wheeled vehicle."

"You sound crazy. Impossible," Mother said, but her smile was wide as she leaned into my father, resting her head on his shoulder. Her hand covered his, her diamond rings catching the afternoon light.

"It's called progress, darling," he said.

Whenever I ride the bicycle, I think of that moment. And I always remember my parents, how they stood together in the hallway, embracing each other. I wish I had lingered a little longer around them that day. Looked at them closer. I didn't know our life was about to turn upside down. I couldn't know how fast my parents' love would morph into anger and wrath. And how that anger and wrath would be directed at me, destroying, burning everything we had to ashes.

"Progressive nonsense?" Leroy's laugh is warm, appreciative of my brother's humor.

"Amos found himself in a state of perpetual disapproval when my father gifted me the bicycle. I even started to suspect he wanted it to himself and maybe that's why he *pretended* he didn't approve." The horse whinnies, interrupting me, and tosses its head, chasing away a fly from its hide. At some point, Leroy whips the traces, directing the horse into a turn.

"Luckily for me, I don't need my brother's approval," I add.

"I reckon you don't," he says softly. "I'm sure your brother sincerely cared about you being safe."

His words burn through my chest. No one cares if I am safe or what I do with my days anymore. Not even Amos. There is no one around me to provide me with guidance or show kindness. There are moments when the absence of care is liberating, but on most days, loneliness blooms inside me.

When I don't reply, Leroy turns to me. "I didn't mean to make you sad, Miss Wilson."

"I'm all right," I say with a deep sigh. "I love my bicycle. It's quite an exercise to ride it." It really is a fight of mind and body to ride against the wind, up the sloping fields to the city, and navigate Omaha's streets with their potholes, busy traffic, and curious gazes. But it's also exhilarating—dangerously so—to be fast and reckless and feel the cool air on my skin. "It makes me feel alive."

The air smells of rain and horse manure. As we pass by Dresher Tailors, I remember my day trips into Omaha with my father and Amos, who used to order their suits there. "Gentlemen, shoulders and collar give style to any coat," one of the tailors used to say. Amos would always chuckle in response while I smoothed the lapels on his jacket, assuring him his shoulders indeed looked extremely stylish. I avert my gaze, trying to forget my stops at the Westlakes' ice cream parlor, where Lizzie and I indulged on their lemon and Neapolitan creams.

A few carriages pass by, but I don't make eye contact with anyone. The collective weight of people's stares pulls on my shoulders. I wish I could sink into the ground to escape the attention. All I want is to be able to catch a breath and not be watched, judged, or gossiped about. I'm sure people will talk about my family whether I greet them or not, so I choose to keep my eyes set on my knees and my hands in my lap. Leroy, however, lifts his derby hat in a soft-black finish a couple of times in acknowledgment. Does he realize he's inserting himself right into Omaha's rumor mill by riding with me? But perhaps he doesn't care. After all, with me or not, he's already a part of that mill.

As we exit Omaha's main streets, mudflats stretch out on both sides of our carriage. The road in front of us is worn away by horses' hooves and carriage wheels. To this day, I wonder why my father decided to leave the city and build the Dawning, our estate, in the sprawling prairies outside Omaha. The parcel of land is on a small hill, overlooking tall prairie grass. Father shamelessly had traded land and built his fortune on the backs of the Nebraska farmers, driving some of them away and forcing others to sell their land cheaply. He built the Dawning to commemorate his new business beginnings in Omaha. My father's pride. His life's work. It took up so much space that just a few years ago I couldn't tell where our family's land started and where it ended. Neighboring farmers hated us. But now the land has been sold to pay the debts. Only the Dawning remained untouched.

In my mind, I see the house with its red sawtooth roof, shaded windows, and weathered peach stucco. The wraparound porch made of black wood looks like a blemish against the peach. Father once said that this particular piece of land was a good investment. Amos told me the land where the house was built belonged to the Omaha Tribe. "It's not really ours," he said, his sour whiskey breath making me dizzy. "And the Rasks' farm is built on the tribe's ground. I bet they don't even know it." He burped and added, "Don't tell Father. It infuriates him when people talk about his real estate schemes." I remember going cold at his words. Even taking a breath at that moment seemed impossible. I didn't think about it much then. But now I think of the draft in the hallways, the dampness that clings to our bones, the spongy walls, and the mold creeping along the lines of the floor. Perhaps my father's schemes broke human laws, and the land where the Dawning stands shouldn't be ours at all because it didn't make us richer like Father promised. Instead, it cut us off from town and trapped us in the mudflats. The Dawning stands alone, desolate and slowly turning into a relic.

The farm fields are behind us as we enter the prairies. Everything is still and eerily quiet around us. Too quiet. Even the air feels different—tense and heavy. As if something is watching us from afar, from the shadows.

Return what's mine.

I spin around, my chin trembling. "Jesus," I shriek and clutch my chest as if I am about to faint.

"Is everything all right?" Leroy asks, shooting me a glance over his shoulder.

"Did you hear it?" As I strain to listen, my voice is hoarse and low.

"Hear what?" His eyebrows are high on his forehead as he turns to me.

"The voice."

Leroy swallows hard, his Adam's apple moving up and down. "No." A hint of confusion in his voice, as if I can't possibly mean what I just said. Of course not. There is no voice calling out to me. It's all in my head. "What do you hear?"

"A voice of a child. A boy. It must be my exhaustion." I stifle a sigh about to burst out of my chest. "I haven't been sleeping well. If at all. I have nightmares often." Strange how simple sleep deprivation can play dangerous tricks on one's mind.

"What does the voice say?"

"He wants me to return something. Something that is his and not mine."

Leroy looks at me, a brow raised. "And do you know what that is that you have and he wants? Do you know the boy?"

"I don't know what I have, nor do I know who the boy is," I whisper and rub my forehead. "It must be your séance. The grieving father of the drowned boy. His story has been haunting me ever since."

"The spirit world is mysterious, Miss Wilson. Maybe during my séance, a lost soul came through the veil and you, indeed, saw him. The boy you keep hearing." A shiver runs through me. What if Leroy indeed opened some kind of portal for the dead to cross? But why am I the only witness to it all? As if echoing my thoughts, Leroy adds, "Have you ever thought that you possess certain abilities? That you, too, can talk to the dead?"

"Heavens, no." Father believed séances to be nonsense. He thought ghosts were idle gossip. But what if he was wrong?

Leroy laughs and doesn't say anything else.

"How do you know the Hollands?" I ask.

"Mrs. Holland attended one of my first séances in Omaha. She was so impressed, she invited me to stay with them for a few days. My visit—it was intended to be just a visit—somehow extended into a few weeks. I didn't really know the Hollands at all before then."

"And yet you accepted their invitation."

"I'm a welcomed guest." He shrugs slightly, his shoulders flexing beneath his jacket. "I accepted your invitation as well, didn't I?" There is a teasing note to his words, but I choose to ignore it.

"It's a short visit. Nothing else."

"I'm not forcing my way into your house, Miss Wilson." He sounds colder, more distant than a few minutes ago.

"I'm sorry, Mr. Marshall. The exhaustion gets the best of me." I hold tight to the edges of the seat, feeling the wood dig into my skin. "I'm not trying to offend you."

"Sometimes I wonder." He chuckles softly, but his posture loosens up.

I rub my hands, trying to chase away the chill that suddenly takes hold of me. "How did you get into this business of mediums and spirits?"

"You want me to reveal all my secrets?"

I look at his sharp profile against the prairies, the strong jaw, his deep-brown, almost black eyes. "Not all of them. Just a few." I smile. "After all, I've invited you to my house. I deserve to know something."

A hint of a smile tugs at the corners of his lips. "All right . . . just a few, then." He pauses, as if deciding where to start. "My father was a shoemaker and a drunkard. I grew up in the streets of the small town of Chesterton, Indiana, fending for myself the best I could." His voice carries an unexpected hardness around its edges. "I didn't have my father's reputation, but I got his unwavering determination to destroy myself. I gambled. I got into fights. I became a thief who procured goods for a criminal who introduced me to a medium. A woman."

I straighten my back at that. This is not the story I expected, but I'm not sure what I expected to hear. His openness is surprising and exhilarating somehow.

"She took me in, showed me the tricks of the trade. The medium and I traveled together for a while, and when she died of influenza, I discovered my own talent. She was the first spirit I summoned."

"How?" I gasp.

One side of his mouth twitches, as if he's suppressing a smile. "I didn't take you for a believer, Miss Wilson."

"Your story is amusing. And intriguing. And I'd like to know more."

A soft laugh. "Well, that's a story for another day, Miss Wilson."

An odd sense of foreboding stirs in my chest. I'm not certain I believe him. An odd itch is nipping at my mind. His tone, the way he talks, feels rehearsed. There is something in his words I cannot connect, cannot untangle, but my muddled-from-exhaustion mind doesn't let me think, and the annoying itch trails me through the prairies.

"Tell me, Miss Wilson." Leroy's voice jolts me back to reality. "Why is the Dawning so distant from everyone else? It seems awfully inconvenient to be so far away from town."

I sit up straight and lace my hands on my lap. "My father bought thousands and thousands of acres when he came to Omaha. Then he expanded some more. He wanted to build farms and houses. He figured he'd build the house on the top of the hill and oversee what was happening at the bottom of the hill."

A low whistle. "That's a lot of land, I reckon."

"He sold most of it when times got hard." I swallow a sharp lump as I struggle to reconcile the man who admired the progress, believed in industrialization, and yet, in a drunken haze, gambled our lives away.

"So it's just you and your mother in the house?" His eyes search my face, as if he's trying to see right through me. "Must be very lonely. To be so desolate."

You have no idea, I want to say but don't. There is no need to reveal all my bitterness and fear and my soul-deep longing for Amos. "Our housemaid, Tilda, stays with us."

We drive on in silence for a few moments until I ask, "Did you leave anyone behind when you came to Omaha?" My face heats up. I shouldn't have asked. Asking questions like this is not something a woman of my class should do.

"What does the town gossip say?"

I'm sure people talk about Leroy Marshall behind closed doors in their parlors, at dinners while chewing on steaks, at the saloons over ale. But I wouldn't know about it. We haven't been invited to any dinners anywhere for so long, it all feels like a long, drawn-out nightmare. I'm certain Leroy has heard rumors about us. "I don't indulge in gossip. It's always so ill intentioned. Harmful. There is no truth in gossip."

He turns to me again. "I'm not married, Miss Wilson." His voice is warm. His gaze is impossible to break. "If that's what you're trying to ask me. No wife. No children. No family."

"So you move from town to town and what? Perform séances as a form of spiritual wisdom?"

A faraway look crosses his face as he tilts his head, thinking. "Something like that. Yes. I help people heal." He pauses. "And what did you plan to do with your life, Miss Wilson? Before all your troubles? A well-to-do husband, a house full of children, I assume?"

His words stir a sharp, heavy awareness in my chest. "Something like that," I say flatly. "I don't think it's a viable option anymore."

He turns to me, a glimmer in his eyes. "I'm sorry about what happened to your family. It's an awful tragedy."

"Thank you." I bite my lip to stop it from trembling.

"I'm sure you will have it all someday," he says softly. If his intent is to reassure me, I'm not certain it's working.

We approach the house. There's a dense patch of trees on the south side of it, a shadowy spot in the otherwise bright and open air. The windows are set high in the walls, but they are wide, inviting the light of day. Old oak shutters are open. A tall birch near the far south corner of the house is leaning toward the windows. Its skinny branches drag against the glass when the wind comes. As we get closer, I notice some of the branches are leafless and broken. The dead bark peeled away. Leroy must've noticed the decline, the desolation. How can you not see the ghastly, dry branches of the birch, stretching out high as if in a prayer to the sky. The urge to ask what he thinks about the house is almost overwhelming. But I bite down on my lower lip and don't ask, and he doesn't say anything either.

When we arrive, I escort Leroy inside. He pauses at the entrance to take in the trappings of wealth that still surround us—a small tapestry on the wall I don't dare to sell, a few paintings, and silver candlesticks. The woodwork inside the house is stained chestnut to contrast the white-and-yellow wallpaper. The crumbling ceiling, the dusty corners, and the bronze chandelier, not polished in ages and covered in spiderwebs. The dining room doors are wide open for some unknown reason, and Leroy walks inside.

"My mother's bedroom is upstairs," I say as I follow him.

"I'm admiring the portrait over the fireplace." He nods at the portrait of my stern German grandfather, whose gaunt face is staring down at us. A look of delighted surprise flashes behind Leroy's eyes. "A relative of yours? You look nothing like him."

"My grandfather," I say, looking up at the portrait. As usual, Opa's eyes seem to burn with disapproval. "I've never met him." I don't remember his German name. Amos and I always referred to him as "our German opa." When Mother moved to Omaha from her small town in Pennsylvania, she brought some of her family paintings with her, along with the wooden crosses that she put up on the walls throughout the house.

I lead Leroy out of the dining room and up the stairs to my mother's bedroom. We stand in front of her door, and I cannot bring myself to knock. Leroy probably sees my fear and hesitation, because he softly moves me to the side.

"Let me," he says and knocks at the door. "Mrs. Wilson. This is Leroy Marshall. I have a message from your husband." He pauses, listening to the deafening silence on the other side of the door. Then he adds, "From your Bert."

There's a thump, a rustle, and my mother's hurried footsteps. The lock finally turns, and there is nothing more beautiful than the sound of the old hinges creaking as she swings the door open. Mother's tall, birdlike frame appears in the doorframe, and I almost gasp at her ghostly appearance. Her hair is frazzled, and her face is white. Her cheekbones are sharp, and her eyes are rimmed with shadows.

She leans heavily on the door, as if her legs barely support her. "Please, come in," she mutters so faintly I might be imagining it.

"Mother," I say and take a step toward the door, but she shakes her head as a shadow passes behind her eyes.

Every muscle in her body tenses, as though she senses Father's presence. With a slow turn of her head, she focuses on Leroy. "Just him," she says, her voice a dry whisper. My spine locked, I stand paralyzed by a hammering and acute ache in my chest. The finality of her words snaps something inside me.

Leroy nods, his movements slow and fluid.

As I watch him walk into my mother's bedroom, a sudden frost shoots through my veins. A premonition of something awful to come. Shouldn't I be relieved instead? Shouldn't the tightness in my throat loosen?

Before the door closes, I see Leroy take my mother's hand and kiss it briefly. His eyes are fixed on her pale face with such an odd intensity, my skin tingles. He whispers a few words, his voice a soft whooshing breeze. My mother nods and shuts the door. The air doesn't supply me with enough oxygen as I lean on the wall, my knees weak.

Chapter 6

The next day my mother comes down for breakfast cloaked in a long green satin dress with a white laced high collar. My father's favorite dress.

She glides through our icy hallway like a ghost. With her pale skin, her eyes rimmed in red, she looks like she has risen from the grave. But her lips are pulled in a taut smile I haven't seen in a long time. She lingers in the doorway, as if she cannot enter the dining room, where the table is laid for breakfast. Where, holding my breath, I'm waiting for her. Her gaze slides around the room, settling on nothing, seeing nothing. Finally, with an odd look of surprise, as if she just realized I'm in the room, she walks inside.

"Mother, how are you feeling?" I ask in a high and shaking voice, sounding like a child.

"Much better, my dear." She opens her arms and lets me hug her, but she doesn't hug me back. Embracing her is like holding a fragile, bony bird. Too much of a squeeze, and she might break. She withdraws quickly, her face set. The wrinkles that run from the corners of her mouth to her chin are deeper and harsher than a few days ago. I press my lips to her cool forehead. By the time I pull away, her face is already turned, so I can see only the hardened lines of her profile.

She sits at her usual place at the table and eats her breakfast silently, her eyes fused to the clump of oatmeal on her plate.

I shove my own food into my suddenly dry mouth.

Before the death and debts and madness descended on us, our breakfasts used to be feasts for our stomachs, taste buds, and eyes. The plates overflowed with eggs, bacon, and juicy slices of ham. Marmalade and jam were placed in various-sized jars and lined up by color—from the lightest to the darkest. Crispy wedges of toast were set on plates by a silver coffeepot. And the coffee itself was always scorching hot and never diluted with chicory. There was so much food, enough to feed half of Omaha, but we barely ate it. Amos would grab a triangle of toast, plant a hurried kiss on Mother's cheek, and rush out of the house. Father nibbled on his eggs and read his morning newspaper. Mother had a cup of coffee and nothing else. There was always so much food. So much indulgence.

Look at us now, eating half-burned oatmeal like it's a delicacy from the restaurants of Paxton Manor.

"Mother." I distract myself from the memories flooding my mind. "There's something I want to discuss with you."

She dips her spoon into the oatmeal and doesn't acknowledge me.

"How did you sleep last night?" I push forward, a little breathless and uncertain, as I swallow a spoonful of oatmeal. It tastes like sawdust and drops into my stomach like a rock. I'm certain Tilda's trying her best, but her cooking standards are not great. In the previous life, our former cook's feasts were famous in Omaha. The Fletchers hired her as soon as our father's debts came due, and the wretched woman took all the recipes with her, leaving Tilda with nothing but her own imagination. "After Mr. Marshall's visit?"

Mother doesn't reply; her jaw moves up and down as she chews.

"Have you slept at all?" I take a deep breath and push down the anger heating up my chest. "What time did Mr. Marshall leave?" Last night, I paced in the hallway, waiting for Leroy to come out from Mother's bedroom. When an hour passed—maybe two—and there was no sign of him, I came down to the kitchen, looking for Tilda, but she was already in her room. I didn't want to bother her, so I spent the rest of the evening in the parlor, retreating to my bedroom at half past ten.

"Mother?" I pause, giving her an opportunity to reply, and when she doesn't, I add, "Has he left at all?"

She looks up at me briefly. "What an odd question, darling. Of course he left. It was around midnight. He was utterly exhausted."

"Did you . . . did you talk to Father?"

She nods curtly. "Bert stayed with me all night. Mr. Marshall said I'd feel Bert's presence for a few more hours into the night."

I expel air from my lungs. "Is that why you walked the hallways? To be with Father?" I heard rushed footsteps in the middle of the night, and I assumed it was Mother. Her walks through the house bother me a great deal, but the relief of Leroy giving her closure is overwhelming. "I couldn't sleep, and I've heard you wandering the hallways. You went to Father's study again. Did you spend the night there?"

Slowly, as if she's submerged in deep waters, Mother puts her spoon down by the plate. She dabs her lips with her napkin and fixes me with an icy gaze. "This conversation is utterly inappropriate."

Unlike with Amos, Mother was never acutely aware of my concerns or me in general. There were moments when she did pay attention: when Bobby proposed, and she noted our union with the Walkers would elevate my status even higher than the Hollands', or when Amos was sent away, and she furiously blamed me for my twin's misdeeds. But since Father's death, her focus has entirely shifted away from me.

A low thump, and I jolt in my chair. Another thump, louder this time. I glance at the window again, expecting to see a bird, wings flapping, black eyes glistening, but there's a face pressed to the glass: nose flattened, eyes jet black, a mouth wide open. The drowned boy. The breath heaves out of my lungs, and I grab the edges of the table to steady myself. Fear, cold and all-consuming, cuts through my skin and bones. The boy's grayish-blue lips move; a swollen black tongue juts through the opening. His head tilts too far back at an unnatural angle when he rises in the air, floating like a dust speck, his arms outstretched to the sides. He starts throwing himself at the window in bristly thuds. The glass splinters; tiny spiderwebs of cracks run across the window.

The stench of wet earth and something pungent and rotten settles heavily in the room.

I press my hand over my mouth to keep a scream from escaping. I scramble to my feet, point at the window with a shaking finger, and back away from the table, distancing myself from the boy.

My mother sits, serene amid the commotion, and eats her oatmeal. How could she not hear the boy's thundering strikes against the glass?

The spirit behind the window giggles, a jarring sound. A wild shriek rises in the back of my throat. I hug my middle tightly, shielding myself from the apparition. He nods and points at my mother. His blackened fingernail scrapes against the glass. A horrible, earsplitting, brain-numbing screeching sound.

"Mother, get away from the table," I scream. "From that window." What if Leroy didn't come alone? What if he brought his ghosts with him? Cold sweat blooms at the nape of my neck, dampening my dress and sliding down my spine. What are we to do if the ghost breaks through the window and enters the house? I try to remember a prayer—any prayer—but my mind is blank.

Mother lays down her spoon, lifts her head, and looks at me, her gaze surprisingly clear. "What's wrong, darling?" She raises her thin brow at me as she used to do whenever I said something trivial.

"There's a ghost of a drowned boy right outside the window, and he's trying to get inside the house." I point to the window, but no one is there. The boy is gone. No cracks, the glass not shattered.

The quietness of the room washes over me like a violent torrent. Someone whimpers, and, with horror, I realize it's me. Panic squeezes my chest like a vise, wrapping around my rib cage, tightening my lungs with every breath I take. Its sharp spikes, little daggers, dig under my skin and set my veins on fire. What is happening to me? Is it just exhaustion, or is my mind getting muddled by madness?

"The weather is extraordinarily nice today," Mother says in a sharp and clear voice that slices the air like a knife. "Don't you think so, Nina?"

The shock of her words is so sudden, I gasp and force myself to look over Mother's shoulder at the window. The morning is murky, and the clouds are gathering into a storm. The wind must've picked up, because the trees look all twisted, their branches tangled.

"What do you think about the weather, Nina?" Her tone is casual, as if we're having our regular breakfast on a regular day and there's nothing out of the ordinary.

"It's cloudy and, most likely, chilly." I push the words out, her ridiculous questions nagging at my nerves. "It looks like another rainstorm is on its way."

"Hmm," she says with a look of smug delight, leaning back into her chair. "You see and hear perfectly well, then." She sits very still and very quiet, her eyes appraising me sharply. "I started to wonder if your sight and hearing are impaired somehow."

My heart drops. I feel dizzy, a heavy unease settling in my chest. "What do you mean, Mother?"

"I don't think discussing such things at breakfast is the right place. Or the right time. Certain things must wait for their moment. But you seem to insist on having this conversation now." There's something unpleasant in her eyes, something cold and final. "It's not easy to say this, Nina. But I don't walk our hallways at night. Though sleep evades me, I don't have a habit of wandering, nor do I sleep in your father's study as you imply. You ask inappropriate questions. You act like a little girl begging for attention." She picks up her spoon and goes on eating her oatmeal, as though she didn't just accuse me of lying, as though the matter of our discussion is of little consequence to her.

Her reaction is so baffling, so unexpected, I stand with my mouth open. Anger, scorching hot and blinding, stirs inside my bloodstream.

Mother finishes her breakfast, folds her napkin, and pushes back her plate. She slowly gets to her feet, turns around, and inspects the window, shaking her head. She unlatches the locks and throws it wide open, leaning out to see if there's anyone outside. The breeze blows through the room, sharp and blustering, stinging my skin.

"There's no one outside, Nina. Come and take a look for yourself."

I step away from the window, moving deeper into the room. "I believe you, Mother."

"Then what in heaven's name was that all about?" Her shoulders are tense. Her back is rigid. She also seems to be on the edge of unraveling, but somehow, unlike me, she holds herself together. She shuts the window.

"I'm sorry, Mother. I must've not slept well myself." I feel weak and small and very much alone.

"Nina." She must've read something in my face, because her voice softens, and there's a subtle change in her, an indefinable emotion that lingers and lightens her stern expression and gives me hope that she'll finally say something comforting and kind. "Pull yourself together, for God's sake."

A shuddering breath is all I can muster in response.

On her way out of the dining room, Mother's hand hovers over my shoulder, never resting, never touching. "You need help, my dear. Help I cannot provide. But I know someone who can." With a dismissive shrug of her shoulders, she exits the room, the clicking of her heels fast and loud, as if she can't wait to leave my side.

I stand stricken by everything that just happened. The need to be consoled is deep and raw, but Mother's words have plunged me into shame. And doubt. I should've known the boy was created by my own tired mind. I should've not behaved like a deranged lunatic. She's going to call Dr. Fuller and send me away.

Until my father died, I didn't know my mother's love had limits. I grew up convinced that whatever I had of her sporadic, seldom attention was enough. After my father's accident, I realized my mother could love only one person with complete abandon, and that person was my father. Since I was a child, I grew accustomed to the endless longing for my mother's love. It lives in my bones, like a weight gained from consuming our former cook's pies over the years. And that's why I accept our current situation, not with ease, but with understanding.

I have no choice. Wanting more of Mother's love, longing for more, is not going to yield anything.

However lonely I feel, I must carry on. What I have must be enough.

The air feels liquid and thick when I slowly approach the window, my feet shuffling on the floor. I look down, almost expecting to see the apparition crouching on the grass beneath the window, laughing at me, pointing at my horror-stricken face. But there's no one outside. Tall half-rotten weeds crowd the lawn. Nothing is out of order except for the trees that stand unmoving, as if they're frozen in some strange dream, their naked branches extending into the sky like arms in prayer.

Chapter 7

The next morning, I position myself in the parlor. It feels cozy and comforting despite the peeling wallpaper peering at me from every angle. The sun is shining through the window, its rays cutting through my unhappy mood. I try not to dwell on the state of my mind.

My chin in my right hand, I open the Saturday edition of *The Excelsior* and let my mind wander to the latest fashion in New York. Russian sables and opera gowns are predicted to be prevalent this season. Something I won't experience, something I probably won't see.

My eyelids get heavy, my chin droops, and I don't hear the knock. I miss the tromp of his shoes. My heart almost stops when Leroy Marshall walks into our parlor, bringing with him the scent of something earthy, like pines and moss. He's in his usual black suit. Slowly walking through the parlor, he holds his black derby hat in one hand and a brown leather trunk in the other. He smiles, setting the trunk by his feet.

I inhale, choke on air, and burst into a cough.

He bows, holding his hat to his chest. "Miss Wilson." He laughs softly, lifting his chin to catch my eyes. He looks younger somehow, happier. "I didn't mean to startle you."

"What are you doing here, Mr. Marshall?" I croak, my eyes watery. The sun suddenly bursts through the clouds, striping the floor in bright, blinding lines. Is he here to ask for that favor I so thoughtlessly promised? Is that why he looks so pleased with himself? "I thought your business here was done. Mother is doing much better thanks to your . . . visit."

"I'm glad to hear that, Miss Wilson. Helping those in need is my vocation." He pulls an envelope from the breast pocket of his jacket. "In fact, I'm here at the invitation of your mother. She asked me to come and stay here, in your estate, for a few days."

"My mother invited you to stay with us?" I've not been feeling well for so long, I must be pulling words out of thin air. Can I even be sure that Leroy Marshall stands in front of me, in flesh and bone? Or is he a figment of my imagination? "She invited you to stay here, in the Dawning?" I repeat slowly, testing every syllable on my tongue. The words sound unfamiliar and distant, as if I'm speaking in a foreign language. The sound of them, the way they fill the space around us, and the odd energy they produce grate against my teeth. "Why would she do that?"

"She believes I can help you, Miss Wilson, deal with your grief. It seems to be taking a toll on you." His eyes roam over my face. No one ever looked at me with such absolute attention. The same powerful pull I felt during our carriage ride courses through me. I banish it and focus on his words. My mother's letter. "Understandably so."

None of what he says makes sense. I try to swallow, but my mouth is dry. "I'm dealing with my grief just fine. Better than Mother, if I must be frank." As the words leave my lips, I feel the overwhelming sense of doubt rush through me. Am I truly dealing with my grief better than Mother? My visions of the boy tell me otherwise. I lower my gaze to hide my discomfort and brush at my skirt, pretending there's a speck of dust or a stray wrinkle that needs tending to.

"Is that so?" He curves his eyebrow.

"Yes, indeed."

"Your mother thinks otherwise, because she asked me to come and help *you*, and I couldn't refuse."

Help *me*? What a foolish thought. I don't understand what's happening, and the confusion steals the words from my mind. I rub my forehead, wishing for him to leave, wishing for him to say it was all a mistake, a misunderstanding. But there he stands, a tall and broad-shouldered shadow. "Why . . . why would she ask you to help me? I don't need help. We're all right." I'm rambling. I sound like a child, my voice self-conscious and weak. I asked him to come. Mother asked him to stay. I was a fool not being able to foresee it.

He steps to the table and leans forward. He's so close to me I feel his body heat as he puts his hat by my coffee cup, his gaze never leaving my face. "I can give you closure, Miss Wilson. You need it as much as your mother." He inspects me solemnly, and his lips move as though he has something to add but cannot decide upon the words. Upon what kind of blow to deliver.

"How? How are you going to help me?"

"Grief is a canvas, the one we can change—or, rather, I'd say *reshape*. We can channel it into something else, something that would bring you peace. But it takes time. Staying in the Dawning seems to be a reasonable solution."

"What a preposterous idea. I don't need to reshape my grief."

"I think it's a curious idea, not preposterous."

"How long are you planning on staying?"

"As long as I'm needed." His drawl is soft and deep like a chant. "Your mother's very interested in my abilities. And if you give me a chance, you'll find them enlightening."

"Mr. Marshall, we don't need lessons in spiritualism. We don't need anything from you." Frustration tightens my throat and threatens to choke me. I scramble to my feet, my chair scraping awkwardly against the wooden planks. I have bills to pay, a declining house to maintain, and an ailing mother to care for. Talking to spirits is not going to solve our financial predicament. I wish Mother would find a different way to solve our problems. The tax bill is due in a few weeks, but instead of talking to lawyers or bankers, she invites a medium. How is Leroy Marshall going to pay our bills? If anything, he is an additional mouth to feed. "Your offer of help is inappropriate and imposing." My voice cracks in fury.

A short, amused-sounding laugh. "Miss Wilson, you should respect your mother's wishes."

My hand presses against my middle. I'm trying to hold myself together, because every word he speaks unspools something inside me, something that threatens to take me apart.

"It's all here. She told me everything." He waves the envelope in the air. As if sensing the impending calamity, the sun disappears behind thick gray clouds, casting an eerie shadow over Leroy's prominent nose and the envelope in his hand. "About your visions. About your raging outbursts. And your sleepless nights."

She wrote him a letter. Rather than talking to me, my mother chose to confide in a stranger. What else did she tell him?

"Let me see it." I reach out for the envelope, but he shoves the letter behind his back. It takes everything in me not to roll my eyes. Whatever game he's playing, I'm not going to participate. "Surely Mother didn't mean to invite you to *stay* here. You must've misunderstood it."

"There's no misunderstanding. I meant it, Nina." A subtle rustle of heavy garments, and my mother enters the room. As soon as her gaze settles on Leroy, her sharp cheekbones turn pink. "Mr. Marshall's welcome to stay as long as he needs."

"Mother—" I start talking, but she puts her hand up, silencing me, and I remain latched to the floor, my back stilted, my spine pained.

"Leroy Marshall brought your father back. I can sense him in the house. We're separated from each other by the ethereal veil, but I know now that it's thin and fragile and can be lifted." She takes a shuddering little sigh. "Isn't that right, Mr. Marshall?"

Has Mother gone completely and inexplicably mad?

Leroy nods solemnly. "Yes, the veil can be lifted. It requires some work, of course. And time. But I know Bert is waiting for you, Elise." Elise? Since when does he call my mother by her first name? "I'm relieved to see how well you're doing," Leroy says and plants his feet wider, taking up more space, as if he already belongs in the Dawning. As if he's a part of this family. He watches my face with bristling attention. "You might not believe me now, Miss Wilson. But give me a chance, and I'll show you the existence of the other world and the spirits that live there. Even though you've already seen some of them."

My mother doesn't look at me; her focus is only on Leroy. "Leroy will help us." She moves smoothly, her dress billowing behind her like a silent shadow. She stands across from me, her violet eyes two deep wells of sadness and grief. "Oh, my dear Nina." Her hand, all blue veins and bony knuckles, reaches out to my face, her fingers brushing over my cheek. "You need Mr. Marshall's help as much as I do. Don't reject him. Try to understand his work instead." She falters, and her face contorts, giving way to sorrow. "You asked for his help before, and here he is, generously agreeing to help you and me. Be kind, and let him in."

"We don't need anyone," I whisper. She searches my face, and I let her see all my pain and grief and fear. "Why can't it just be you and me?" I meet Leroy's eyes over my mother's shoulder. He stands motionless, hands loose at his sides. He reminds me of a prairie coyote I saw once. Same stillness, same elegance, same intense gaze fixed on us, and strained muscles readying to leap. How easily he encroached upon us. Just a few days ago he was living with the Hollands, and now he's spreading his shadow in the Dawning. I was the one who opened the door for him. Who would have guessed how impossible it would be to get rid of Leroy Marshall once invited? Who would have ever guessed?

"Nina, I need this. And maybe you don't realize it yet, but you need this too," my mother says, her voice gentle. Caressing. "Please, let's do this together. You and me." She closes her eyes for a few seconds. "Please, Nina. If not for yourself, do it for me. Please, my dear daughter, do this for us."

Us. She hasn't used that word for so long, I'm not sure I heard her right. "Mother." I wrap my arms around her and breathe in her familiar lavender scent. Tears burn my throat. She's so skinny, so brittle, I'm afraid her bones may splinter beneath my fingers. I drop my hands to not hurt her.

She presses her palm firmer against my face, and I lean my head, melting into her hand. "Nina." A soft whisper. My heart lurches. This is the first time she's touched me since Father died. If she needs me to help her, to guide her through this, I will do it for her. Anything just to feel her love again. If there is any left for me.

"I'll do whatever you ask of me, Mother."

"Good," she says and pulls her hand away, turning to Leroy, already forgetting about me. "Welcome to the Dawning. Tilda has prepared a room for you."

"Which one?" I ask fervently.

"The one down the hall from you." My mother delivers the blow smoothly.

"Amos's room? Why?"

"Let me show you your room, Mr. Marshall." Without a single glance in my direction, my mother glides from the parlor. In her wake, my heart aches with betrayal.

Leroy bows to me again, takes his hat, and picks up his trunk. He follows my mother, his expression already closed off. I stay in the parlor even though I want to flee and hide. I grit my teeth so hard pain shoots through my jaw. There's a roar in my head, a wild prairie wind.

My mind is racing as I pace the room to keep up with my unsettling thoughts. Four steps to the window and five wide strides to the door. The space gets smaller around me with every step I take. First, all I can do is focus on my movements: To the window and to the door. Back and forth. Then I pull on a thread of a thought that keeps coming back to me.

Was it really a worry about my mental state that forced Mother to write Leroy the letter—or was it something else?

September 18, 1903

My dear Amos,

Sometimes I think I'm awfully naive. I thought having closure would help. But I think nothing helps when you are fully submerged into mourning. When your world is bleak and desolate, and you cannot stop your own suffering. You cannot just stop.

I have not been sleeping very well in the past month. If I am fully honest, I have not been sleeping at all. I never had the heart to tell you this . . . but due to the lack of sleep, there is a constant fog in my head now. It makes it difficult to focus. Difficult to organize my thoughts. And I have so many scattered thoughts. Maybe I should start writing them all down.

We have an uninvited guest in the house. And even though I feel repelled by his presence, I am also horribly drawn to the idea of him. The medium, Leroy Marshall, has been staying with us for a few days now. He is a true mystery, Amos. Mother welcomed him warmly to the Dawning and there is no sign of her ever asking him to leave. Every morning, at breakfast, I sense in her excitement for a new day. As if Leroy offers her something no one else can. And the medium himself is always jolly and humorous. If not for what happens at night, I would say he could become a welcome guest.

At night, right after dinner, Mother and Leroy retreat to Father's study. They never invite me to join them. Mother shuts the door, cutting me off. She did say once, "You are not ready yet, darling. You shall wait a little longer." I do not know what that means. What are we waiting for? They close the door and all I hear is their hushed voices and Mother's laughter. Yes, Amos, Mother is not just playing her piano in the mornings, she also laughs now.

And I spend most of my nights pacing in my bedroom, thinking of Mother and Leroy, and praying nothing unholy is taking place behind those closed doors. If such a thing is even possible. Just this morning, I confronted Mother and asked her what was happening in Father's study. If Leroy was doing something to her. Something unimaginable. She just laughed at me. An odd, unpleasant sound tipping into something sinister on the last note. "Lovely," she said. "Lovely how you think, my dear." There was no warmth in her voice.

He is here by her invitation. He is supposed to help *me* to deal with my grief, but somehow everyone forgot about it. I told Mother I want Leroy's help as that was the main reason for his being in the house. At first, there was confusion on her face as if she forgot why she had invited him. The confusion was followed by a flicker of jealousy, and she repeated herself again, telling me I was not ready. "Ready for what?" I wanted to scream, but she was not listening. Every day I try to connect with Mother, to bring back everything that was warm and solid. Every day I am facing her stern face. It grows increasingly harder to love someone who does not love you back.

Leroy is absent during the day. He walks into town to do whatever he does. He comes back for dinner. And he always brings fresh apples with him. This man is obsessed with apples. And Mother is obsessed with Leroy.

I am starting to think I will never sleep again.

I can barely function, but I still manage to move through the better part of the day. I put one foot in front of the other, attend to chores, open and read letters—bills mostly, which I hide in Father's desk—and discuss our meager, laughable menu with Tilda. I feel as if I were a doll: my heavy limbs are being moved by an invisible hand; my foggy thoughts are being strung together by an invisible master.

The days go by and sometimes I do not notice how fast.

Everything is tarnished and broken. The Dawning is crumbling, and I'm crumbling with it. The house is reshaping itself into something I cannot see, nor can I understand. The other day I left my bedroom in the morning, and in the evening, my bedroom door had moved further down the hallway. I counted the steps back and forth to prove to myself I did not go mad. It took me fifty-three steps to reach my room at night. The next morning it took me twenty-five steps to reach the staircase.

I have no words to explain any of it.

With all my love,

Your sister Nina

P.S. I am waiting for you to come home. Are you getting any better?

Chapter 8

Tilda is the first to hear the tapping.

"I didn't hear anything," I say when Tilda tells me she suffered a great headache from all the noise. The knocking started in the late afternoon the day before, when she was washing dishes. It stopped eventually, but when she came back from the market this morning, she heard it again.

"Right over my head, Miss." She points at the ceiling. "Boom." She drops her hand and lifts it again to illustrate. "Boom. Boom." Her cheeks have a special pink glow. As if she took a brisk walk outside. Her blond hair is loose around her shoulders. Her dress is freshly ironed. She doesn't look like someone who's experiencing a headache.

I sit at the table alone, holding a coffee cup, watching Tilda, and trying to take it all in. Neither Mother nor Leroy came down for breakfast this morning, and I'm grateful for their absence because this conversation is nothing but strange.

"It sounded like a child playing with a ball," Tilda says, and this time she pantomimes a child striking a ball. "But it ain't no child. Ain't no ball."

A child. My thoughts drift to the ghost's face pressed against the glass. The gleaming eyes, the gray lips. *It ain't no child*, that much I'm certain of, but is it possible that the specter of the boy somehow was able to get inside the house? If I suspend all my disbelief and assume the boy's truly an apparition and not some odd play of my exhausted mind, ghosts should be able to enter buildings freely, shouldn't they? He was inside the Hollands' manor, but he had difficulty breaking through the window and entering the Dawning. As if the house doesn't want him. Or maybe the boy, for whatever reason, prefers to stay outside.

"There is something I need to tell you. I've been experiencing disturbing visions. Dreamlike visions that feel very real. There are moments when I think I see a ghost of the eight-year-old boy who drowned."

Tilda appraises me with razor-sharp attention. The way she looked at the barkeep in that seedy saloon last week. "You think you can see ghosts," she says and pulls on her blinding-white apron. There is no confusion in her voice. No doubt. She believes me. "If it's a spirit, he must've come with Mr. Marshall. Followed him all the way to the Dawning."

Suddenly, the collar of my dress is too tight, and the material's too coarse to the touch when I pull it away from my throat. "There's something else. When Amos and I were children, about ten years old, our parents had a ball in the Dawning. We were not allowed downstairs, and so we were stuck upstairs with our governess, who was the religious and zealous kind. She believed the only recourse for children to their absolution was the reading of the Bible. That night, she read us verses from the New Testament for about an hour before falling asleep in her chair. Amos and I quickly slipped away from the room and went wandering through the house. We stopped in one of the guest bedrooms on the second floor. You know the four-poster bed by the wall and the big, dusty mirror above the dressing table?" I pause, collecting my thoughts, and when Tilda nods, I push forward with the memory. "Amos was holding a candle. Light flickered and jumped across the ceiling, scaring me. Our shadows were long. Large. I wanted to leave, but Amos pulled on the sleeve of my dress, holding me in place. I looked in the mirror and saw a pale face—black eyes, deep and round like water wells, and a twisted mouth. The specter was floating above the ground, smirking at me. I screamed. My heart was racing so fast, I couldn't catch a breath. But Amos laughed. He thought it was funny that I thought I saw a ghost staring at us from the mirror. It was his reflection. That night, right before I fell asleep, I whispered my wish. I wanted to be able to see ghosts. Real ghosts. I repeated my wish like a prayer until I fell asleep." My mouth is dry and tastes like ash, and I take a sip of my coffee, grounding myself in the here and now.

"What happened then?" Tilda asks softly.

I laugh and set my cup back on the table. "Nothing. I completely forgot about it until now." The memory weighs heavily on my mind. There is no right way to ask the question, so I push forward. "Do you think because I wanted it, and I really meant it when I wished for it, my wish manifested itself?"

"It's an odd wish, Miss. Why did you ask for it?"

"I was ignored by my parents. My brother made me feel miserable that night. I desired to be someone special. Someone who was loved. Someone who mattered. Perhaps I thought everyone would pay attention to me if I had special abilities."

"You got your wish, I reckon. But I don't know why now. Maybe Mr. Marshall's séances have something to do with it."

"You know what else is odd? I think the Dawning is toying with me. One day the hallways are long, and the next day they're much shorter. I count steps from my bedroom to the staircase. And every day I come up with a different number of steps. And the difference isn't just a step or two. Have you experienced anything like that?"

"Not like you, Miss." A couple of creases appear around her mouth. Her wide-set blue eyes darken a shade. "The energy of this house has changed. Your daddy never repented. Your brother never saw the error of his ways. The house must've absorbed their sins." She pauses, looking at me solemnly. "Turned angry."

Can the walls absorb the energy of the people who used to live here? What an odd thing to say. "You're in some mood, Tilda." The goose bumps run up and down my arms. After a moment of silence, I take a deep breath. "Do you believe the ghost-boy is real?" As soon as I say the words, the gloom—thick like a fog—encroaches upon my mind. I should stop thinking like this. I should forget the silly childhood wish. There are no ghosts lurking outside the house, waiting for me to invite them in. This line of thinking won't do me any good. I cannot allow myself this slow but incessant descent into madness. Otherwise, I'd have to admit that Mother was right all along and I do need help. "What do *you* think caused the tapping?"

A flush of red blooms on Tilda's round cheeks when she whispers, "A wraith." Letting out a shaky breath, she wipes her hands at her apron. "A very loud and angry wraith."

I lean back into my chair. "Wouldn't we all have heard this knocking, this tapping, if it was so loud? I didn't hear anything."

"I heard what I heard, Miss," Tilda murmurs. There is coolness in her eyes and a hitch of resentment in her voice.

"Let's check the roof. It might be just a simple leak."

Tilda nods. "I can ask that Polish roofer, Benny. The one who was here last spring. Remember?"

"Yes, I remember him," I lie. I have no idea who she's talking about. Last spring my life was different. The Dawning was different. Bobby was a frequent guest, and I had just started to plan our wedding. There was not a sign, not a single omen of the swift and deadly destruction that followed. When I think of that time, my memories are foggy. Unclear. As though I'm looking into a muddy pond. But everything that came after that—Amos's sickness, Father's death—feels like it happened yesterday.

"It's okay if you don't remember him, Miss." She gives me a small, all-knowing smile. My face starts to burn. I should never forget she can spot a lie easily. "I'll go fetch him, then." Tilda turns away from me.

"Wait. Would he, this Benny, take a couple of our Dresden teacups as payment instead of cash? Could you ask him?" I'm not certain we have any of our opulent Dresden teacups and saucers left. But Tilda would know. She keeps a list of everything we've pawned.

"Let me talk to him. But it ain't water, Miss. It ain't our roof. I know the sound of water dripping. It was something else. This house ain't safe.

Something lives in the walls." She pauses and then whispers, "The dead move inside the walls."

"Tilda, be sensible. There are no ghosts living in the walls," I say, a bit more breathlessly than I'd like. "Maybe it's the pipes. Maybe it's something else. Could be mice or rats, right? Those creatures can be quite noisy. Or some other small animal has gotten inside and is trying to get out. A bird. Or a squirrel. That's why the sound jumps around like a child playing with a ball. Regardless, I didn't hear anything. If the noise was coming from the walls, surely I would have heard it too."

Tilda shifts her weight, and with a long exhale, she says, "Something ain't right with the house. That's all I'm saying." I scramble to my feet and take a step toward her. "It's like a sickness. The silver turned black. I showed you the tray. All silver's black now except for the forks and knives you use." Dread stirs in my chest, its icy grip squeezing my heart. The Rask farm comes to mind. Their contaminated land. Their blight. "I might move back to town. This house frightens me, Miss."

"Back to town? Tilda, no, please, don't do it." My voice is getting higher, tighter, fear coloring the edges. "Give me some time. I'll find a way to fix whatever is happening here."

"Some places are not meant for the living."

I picture the Dawning abandoned. A ghoulish, empty shell of a house, full of sins and ghosts, surrounded by nothing but dry weeds. A pipe groans sorrowfully somewhere inside the house, and instead I see the Dawning in the soft sunlight of a summer morning, full of people and children.

A blast of freezing air whooshes through the dining room. The door to the parlor slams shut.

I jump at the harshness of the sound. "What is this?" I shriek. All this ghostly talk must be getting to me.

"I opened the window in the parlor and forgot to close it," Tilda notes, unperturbed. "I'll go and find Benny, Miss. He owes me some favors. Let me see if I'll be able to collect." Tilda turns on her heel and leaves the room.

I drop back into my seat. I try to pick up my coffee cup, but my hands are too shaky, and I set it back on the saucer. I think back to the moments when the house startles me awake in the middle of the night, when the hallways seem longer and the ceiling seems lower. When there's a rustle by my door, but no one's there. The other night I woke up because I was certain someone was whispering my name.

Some places are not meant for the living.

To save ourselves from the madness of this place, should Mother and I leave the Dawning? Where would we go? What would happen to us?

My stomach roils with bitter chicory coffee. The Dawning, which once was a safe haven—full of my brother's low chuckle and Mother's piano music—is transforming into a living and breathing beast that feeds on our fears, grief, and sins. And yet something deep inside me is tethered to the house, and the thought of us leaving is unbearable.

That same afternoon Benny reports that the roof doesn't show any signs of distress.

"Let me know if you hear it again," I instruct Tilda when Benny leaves.

In the dining room, the windows overlook the trees with dense branches and tall grass underneath them. Bloated-with-rain clouds have littered the sky since the morning, and Tilda fastened the window shutters against the strong breeze an hour before dinner. At seven, we enter the room. The table is not set, and I'm about to inquire what happened to our meal when Tilda arrives, bearing a tray overflowing with food. She places a pot of soup in the middle of the table and sets cheese, broiled salmon, smoked meats, green peas, and fresh bread in front of us.

My mouth falls open. "Where did you get that?"

"At the market, Miss," Tilda says.

"Thank you, Tilda." Mother nods imperiously, dismissing our housemaid.

I feel lightheaded. "Mother, what is this?" I sound like an apparition or a faint whisper of a breeze before a storm.

"Dinner, my dear," my mother says and smiles at Leroy. "Please, Mr. Marshall, go ahead and eat."

Leroy immediately begins heaping slices of meats and fish onto his plate.

"How did we pay for this . . . this feast?" I ask. Somewhere underneath my panic, there is another question. *Why* would we do this?

Mother raises her eyebrows at me, and my heart sinks. Of course, what am I thinking? Mother always prided herself on our family's impeccable manners. We're not allowed to discuss our financial affairs at the dinner table, especially in front of our houseguest. I must keep my mouth shut.

In the quivering light of the candles, my mother eats wordlessly, chewing slowly on her food. To my surprise, Leroy is also silent and doesn't attempt to start a conversation. As we eat, Mother, in her usual manner, doesn't spare me a glance, and when I ask her how she is feeling, she mutters something incoherent.

"Mother, do you know what happened to the Rasks?" I turn to her. "The other day I walked by the farm. It was abandoned." There were days, now long gone, when the Rask children would've been out in the fields all day, enjoying themselves, enjoying their friends and the weather and the soft grass. The hollowness of the place was jarring.

"What an odd question," Mother says. "I had no idea they left."

"They left a while ago. People say something awful happened at the farm."

She shrugs lightly. "It was a horrible tragedy. Mrs. Rask lost her husband and her son on the same night."

"What happened, Elise? Do you know?" Leroy asks softly.

"They drowned." Mother's voice turns sharp. "Both of them drowned in the creek that runs behind their farm. I assume that's why the family left."

Something in the way she sounds—annoyed with the Rasks, almost angry—makes me dizzy with confusion. Why wasn't I aware of this tragedy? Why did no one talk about it in our house?

Leroy nods. "What a horrible death." The sadness cloaks his eyes, softening his gaze.

"Did Father know what happened? Did he go to the funeral?" I ask.

"Why all these questions, Nina? Why does it matter? The Rasks aren't here anymore. Neither is your father." Her eyes mist over with fury as she drops her spoon in the soup, then pushes herself away from the table, her chair scraping noisily against the wood.

"Elise." Leroy scrambles hastily to his feet. "Your Bert's always here. No need to overreact. The veil must've thickened."

Mother swallows, her throat moving up and down, as if she's trying to swallow a hard piece of bread. She turns away from Leroy and leaves the room, her skinny shoulders slumped.

"What happened?" I ask Leroy when he lowers himself back into the seat.

"A temporary setback," he says, with a note of sadness. "Your father was supposed to materialize. But something held him back."

"Materialize?" I croak. "What do you mean?"

"Spirits are invisible most of the time. They can make noises and move furniture. But they also can materialize. I promised your mother that Bert, your father, shall soon appear. But he hasn't. We can sense him. We can hear him. But your mother wants more."

My heart beats so loudly, I'm surprised Leroy hasn't commented on it. "She wants my father to appear in the flesh and blood?" A chill comes in ripples and, like a bad sickness, settles in my belly. This whole thing with my father is getting so much worse, turning into something barbaric and meaningless.

"Not in the flesh and blood. Not the way he was, of course. But in some kind of shape. Not a solid form by any means. That's impossible."

I feel like I'm falling, his words pulling me down, through the floors and walls of the Dawning, into some senseless abyss. "I don't understand," I whisper.

"This type of spirit conjuring requires a lot of work. I must be exhausted because I cannot lift the veil enough for your father to come through. Or maybe your father just doesn't want to appear in a different form. It happens sometimes. The dead can be moody."

"Moody?" I lift an eyebrow. "What makes them so?"

"Don't you want to know?" A chuckle. He loosens his collar. "Are you finally getting curious about the spirit world, Miss Wilson?" His tone is playful, almost flirtatious, but there is an obvious hint of annoyance in his eyes.

I don't get a chance to reply thanks to Tilda, who comes back to collect the plates and clear the table.

Leroy bows good night to me and leaves me sitting in the dining room.

I think about the food, the feast we just had. Anger burns inside me. For months, we were hungry. For months, Tilda and I have been trying to come up with a plan to keep us afloat, to keep us alive. There were days when I was so weak, I thought I might fall and not rise. Months of wanting my mother to do something. Months of letting her grieve in her room and write letters to her dead husband. Months of waiting and waiting for her to take charge. What a desperate fool I am, after all.

Floorboards wail when I get to my feet. I look down, and in the shimmering candlelight, our wooden floor looks black. As I exit the dining room, the door snaps shut behind me with a loud crack. Tilda must've left another window open.

I go up to Mother's bedroom and knock at the door, my hand moving mechanically, as if I'm a windup doll. My mind, though, whirls and swirls and weaves through all the thoughts and questions I want to ask about the food, and the Rasks, and Father. I don't expect her to open the door, but she does. There is a sharp disappointment on her face when she sees me. She doesn't invite me inside. The aloofness in her, the otherness of her, is astounding.

"How did we pay for all that food, Mother?"

"I asked Tilda to pawn my pearl necklace." She looks at me with annoyance, eyes flashing. "We must be welcoming hostesses, Nina."

I reel back as if she pushed me. The unbearable heat courses through my veins and joints. I'm shaking with rage.

"Why is he still here?" I growl. Not really the question I wanted to ask, but seeing her bony face, her eyes gliding over my shoulder as if she's hoping to see Leroy standing behind me, infuriates me beyond my control.

"I'm surprised you have to ask," Mother says and pushes the door halfway, already readying to shut it. "We're preparing for our private séance, and it takes time. Soon we'll be able to talk to your father. All of us. And, Nina . . ." She pauses, and something sharp and angry is suddenly shining from her eyes. "I thought we agreed not to question Leroy's presence in the house. He's important to me." Her voice is emotionless, and her tone's hard. She doesn't look at me as she closes the door.

I stand in front of her room for a few rapid, furious heartbeats. The defeat sits in my chest like a rock. What is it that I'm doing? Why am I staying here, in the house, where no one needs me? Where no one loves me? If I leave now, will anyone notice?

A nauseating feeling of isolation blankets me. I can't leave yet. Not when the tax bill is about to come due. The Dawning, the only real thing that is still here, that needs my help, will be lost forever. I cannot allow it.

As soon as I figure out how to pay this bloody bill, I'll pack my bags. Dangers of the big cities be damned. But then I remember the promise I gave my brother to take care of Mother, and my eyes start to burn. And so I smother my emotions and pace my room, my mind racing through Tilda's words about the tapping and my embarrassing attempt to talk to Mother. No matter how much I walk around my room, my head remains heavy, my thoughts sluggish. At some point, fully dressed, I climb into bed and fall into a dreamless slumber.

Chapter 9

I wake up to a low murmur outside my room.

I sit up in bed and listen. Another murmur, light like a surge of air. Maybe it's wind, seeping through the cracks in the walls. New cracks seem to appear daily now. The floorboards creak as someone moves down the hallway. I slip out of bed, tiptoe to the door, push it open, and peer around the door.

The hallway is full of shadows from the twinkling candlelight, and I see Mother clearly. Wearing nothing but her billowy scallop-white nightgown, she slowly walks the length of the hallway, from one room to another, opening all doors. The shock of her, barefoot and gaunt, takes my breath away.

"Mother?" I call out to her, my voice landing hollowly in the night.

She doesn't respond. She doesn't pause her walking. I follow her down the hallway, down the stairs. The old floorboards screech under her bare feet all the way to Father's study. She closes the door behind her, but she does not lock it. Is Leroy waiting for her inside?

I wait a few moments before slowly turning the handle and pushing the door open. I take a couple of steps and freeze, my chest clenched so tight I cannot inhale.

Mother stands against the far wall, behind Father's desk, in the corner. She's staring at the wood paneling. I expect her to turn, to look at me, but she remains unmoved, facing the corner. Maybe she didn't hear me come inside. Maybe she doesn't care I'm standing in the room with her. I don't know what to think or what to do.

"Mother." My own breath freezes in my throat. I feel like I'm being thrown into a dust storm, time shattering into tiny fragments, and the air swirling and whirling around me, squeezing my chest. I need to go get Leroy. I don't know how to deal with this.

Mother doesn't move. Her breath's coming out fast, her panting loud.

I step forward. Mother seems to be oblivious to my presence. I take a few more steps and place a hand—so very lightly—on her skinny, trembling shoulder. At my touch, she whips around, her eyes wild. She takes one look at me, an uncertain and confused look at first that morphs quickly into fear. And then, her mouth agape, white teeth glinting in the dark, she starts screaming—a cry, starting low and rising in agony. It's coming from deep inside her chest, as if there's something alive and desperate and terrified—her trapped soul—trying to claw its way out.

Someone's arms pull me away, and I shriek.

"It's me. Nina, let go." Leroy's voice comes from somewhere far away. "Let her go."

At the sound of his voice, the fear and confusion release me, and everything slows down. All that is left inside my chest is red-hot fury that burns me from the inside out. "It's your doing," I hiss. "You did this to her."

"Your father did this to her. His refusal to materialize did this to her," he says solemnly. "Elise, please, come with me. Bert isn't here."

"He's supposed to be here," Mother whimpers, tears streaming down her pale face. "You said he'll be here."

"We'll figure out what's holding him back." Leroy wraps his long arms around my mother's shoulders—her body shaking violently in his hands—and leads her out of the study.

I spend the rest of the night pacing in my bedroom, thinking of Mother—scared, confused, staring at the wall—and praying for her to find respite. If such a thing is possible. I don't know if anyone can help, maybe not even Dr. Fuller if I could ever find a way to afford his services. Even if he can help, what would it mean for her? For us? He may take her away, and what would be done to Mother once she was under Dr. Fuller's care? What kind of treatments would she need? No one ever told us what treatment plan was prescribed for Amos. I doubt that doctors asked for Father's consent. Certainly, no one will ask for mine.

So many questions, so many doubts. I must keep the thought of Dr. Fuller deep inside me. Let it simmer. Let it burn me from the inside out.

The next day, to distract myself, I stay in my room and try to read *Jane Eyre*, but the words don't register, and I set the book aside. When the silence of the house becomes too quiet, too oppressive, I lie down on the bed and close my eyes, waiting for the grandfather clock to chime an hour. Finally, after midnight, I open my bedroom door, and, glancing to the right and then the left, I step outside my room.

As soon as I'm in the hallway, my heart kicks an odd and rapid beat, as if it's trying to get out. There's something different about the space, about the hallway. An unfamiliar thickness to the air—the stench of an unwashed body, a foreign presence—is suffocatingly strong. My pulse rises, sharp like an electric current, when my eyes land on the wall to my left. Right above the wall paneling, Mother's black wooden crosses that she hung throughout the house in odd places to chase evil spirits away are all turned upside down. I shut the door softly behind me and walk along the corridor, rightening the crucifixes.

Mother must be out of her room again, wandering in the hallways in search of her dead husband. I pause, hesitant about where to go next. I know I must go to the study and see if she's there, but my body refuses to move. Teeth clenched, I force myself to put one foot in front of the other.

As I edge to the stairs, one hand upon the banister and another clutching a candle, I hear a door open deep inside the house. Father's study. Mother must be there. My mouth turns dry. Under my palm, the railing is cool and spongy, as if it's covered in moss. I hover my candle over it. The handrail seems wider than usual in the candlelight, but the wood looks the same, cracked and rotten. There's no visible growth on it. Yet it feels as if I'm touching a forest floor thick with moss and rotting leaves. I pull my hand away.

The door to Father's study is cracked open, and the air is uncharacteristically cold. I hesitate because I'm not certain I want to see Mother. What will I say to her if she's there, facing the wall again? Will she scream if I touch her? Will she get mad if I interrupt her vigil? If she's there, I'm calling for Dr. Fuller in the morning. Maybe all she needs is a sleeping tincture to settle her restless mind. Amos asked me to take care of Mother, and doing nothing—not asking for help—is breaking my promise to him.

I listen, but there are no sounds coming from inside, just a strange, foreboding feeling oozing through the crack. The study seems to be empty, and so I push the door open wider. All the windows are flung open, and the night breeze moves the velvet curtains in violent bursts. By the wall, the outline of Father's oak desk is sharp and heavy. It's littered with unopened letters and Father's business papers, relics of the past life, and behind the desk is a figure, rocking backward and forward on his heels.

He stops moving for a few seconds. As he faces me, his eyes hollow and set deep inside his skull, I open my mouth, but no sound comes out. I'm out of breath, too frightened to say anything. The man draws against the wall as if trying to disappear inside it, and then, in one big leap, he hurls himself over the ledge of the open window, vanishing into the night.

The scream that finally erupts out of my constricted throat is long and piercing. I know I sound like Mother, but I cannot stop screaming, expelling everything frightened and haunted out of my lungs until I have nothing left.

Someone's warm, strong hands squeeze my shoulders and whirl me around.

"Nina." Leroy's face looms over mine. He is alert and fully dressed in his black clothes. "Are you all right?" I must be silent for a heartbeat too long because he adds softly, "Say something so I know you're all right."

Chapter 10

Later, when I finally collect myself, when I manage to regain a semblance of controlled emotions, Leroy and I close the windows and secure the shutters. We light a few more candles to make sure no one is lurking in the corners of the study. Leroy starts a fire in the hearth, pours me whiskey from a tall decanter he finds shoved in the corner of one of the bookshelves. He presses a rocks glass into my hand and goes to inspect the grounds.

Like a bird, I perch on the edge of one of the armchairs by my father's desk. I cannot stop trembling. My knees pushed tightly together, with the glass pressed against my chest, I strain to listen to the sounds outside, but all I hear is a soft patter of rain. The storm must've swept in during my wanderings through the night. The house is also eerily silent—not a single creak or echo, as if just a few minutes ago the Dawning wasn't breathing, shifting, and coming alive. The shock of what I witnessed—the shadow behind Father's desk, the speed with which it lurched itself over the ledge—keeps me glancing frantically at the window for any signs of a tall stranger.

"We must call the police right away," I tell Leroy as soon as he enters the study, the scent of rain and earth trailing behind him. What was he doing outside? He looks unperturbed by his search, and it provides me a bit of comfort. "We must report an intruder." I take a sip of burning whiskey as I watch Leroy pour himself a glass. The whiskey bites and seeps into my gums, my tongue. I take another mouthful and let it scorch its way down my throat. "What was he doing here?"

Leroy doesn't reply, and his silence unsettles me. It breathes with me—all the way up to my chest and my throat and all the way down to the bottomless pit in my belly. As he lowers himself into the armchair across from me, I take another sip, hoping to settle my lurching stomach. He watches me with some odd, intense energy.

"I didn't see anyone outside. It's raining, so perhaps the footprints were washed away. But the grass underneath the window is not disturbed. There are no signs of anyone breaking into the house. I found the front door locked." Over the rim of his glass, he eyes my lips, the edges of my face, my unruly hair. "If we call the police, what will you tell them?"

"I'll tell them what I saw. A man who broke into the house."

"Is anything missing?"

"I don't think so." I looked over the desk quickly when Leroy was outside, and not a single piece of paper was moved.

"And when the police don't find any signs of said man? What then?" His words hang between us. Would the police take me for a liar? There's no evidence, no facts, that would give solidness to my story about the man. The police would think I had been frightened by a moving curtain or a random flicker of candlelight. I'm sure by now everyone has heard about Mother's collapse during the séance. Any additional gossip won't help our family matters either. As if reading my thoughts, Leroy adds, "I don't think you want to call the police, Miss Wilson." There's something inquisitive and hard in his eyes, something that makes me realize he had no plans to call the authorities from the beginning. "You have nothing to offer to the police, no evidence to show them."

"I saw a stranger jump out of the window," I repeat stubbornly, not ready to admit my defeat. The whiskey stirs in my stomach. The grinding doubt, the absence of anything substantial to support my words, makes me feel ridiculous. "Did you see him when you came in?"

"No." He takes a sip from his glass. "What makes you think it was a person and not a spirit?"

I chuckle darkly, surprised by the abrupt change of subject. "Spirits don't jump out of windows."

"They usually don't," Leroy says softly. "But they disappear into the shadows. Dissipate. And you, Miss Wilson, have been seeing a lot of curious things lately. Tilda told me you count steps to and from your bedroom because you think the hallway shifts during the night. And you see that boy you don't like to talk about. You resist the possibility of the spirit world. Despite that everything around you points to its existence. So how do you know it's not an apparition you saw here tonight?" He stares into my eyes as if daring me to accept a challenge.

A coldness like I've never known before enters my body, slips under my dress and right into my bones. I remember Tilda's words, her conviction there's a wraith living in the walls, and her seething resentment when I doubted her. I know exactly how she must've felt. "I know what I saw, Mr. Marshall." There's a tightness in my chest that hasn't released me since I encountered the man in the study.

One brow raised, he leans forward, and suddenly he's so close to me, I can almost feel his breath on my skin. "How certain are you?" His voice is soft, but his eyes are two burning coals.

I study his face, looking for a flicker of emotion, something that would tell me he believes me, but he looks only serious and inquisitive. As my cheeks heat up under his stare, I whirl the whiskey in my glass. The liquid catches the light, deepening the amber. I take another sip and another, and finally I tip my glass and finish my drink with a couple of swallows. Maybe I do see spirits. Maybe the house is shifting at night. Maybe Mother's madness doesn't live in the deepest corners of my mind. But right now I don't have enough space in my head to think about it.

"It was a man, Mr. Marshall. A breathing, living man. And what makes you so sure there are spirits in the Dawning? My father told you so?" I smile, emboldened by the whiskey.

"To a certain extent, yes, Miss Wilson, your father. But he hasn't been able to visit us for a while now. It's very upsetting. It affects your mother. I've also been trying to lift the veil for a few days now. I believe I peeled it back enough for the spirits to break through. Perhaps what you saw was just that—a random spirit coming through the veil. After all, I didn't see any footprints under the window. I didn't see anyone running away from the house." He looks over to the window, as if making sure there are no signs of the intrusion. Then he tips back his glass, drains it, and gets up for a refill. "It would be impossible to hide on your front yard, Miss Wilson. There are no trees." His soft voice bores under my skull, convincing me it would be difficult to cross the lawn and not be seen. There's nothing I can add that would prove Leroy wrong or articulate the evil I saw in the man's eyes. As he turned away from me, I noticed a thick scar behind his right ear. Do ghosts carry scars from their previous lives? The ghost-boy was drenched in water the first time I saw him, and I was certain he was real.

"What do you suggest we do?" I ask.

Leroy places his unfinished drink on the desk and takes my glass away from me. "We get some sleep." Then he leans over and whispers into my ear. "Let's go, Miss Wilson. Whoever it was, I'm sure they can wait until tomorrow."

Maybe it's the way he says it, the way his breath tickles my skin, but I laugh, and suddenly I feel very young and silly. As if I were a girl who left her bedroom in the middle of the night and got herself in trouble with a houseguest. And he laughs too—a deep and warm sound, warm enough for me to straighten my shoulders and brush my hair away from my face.

"Let's go, Mr. Marshall." I push myself to my feet, too forcefully, too abruptly, and the heavy armchair falls backward, clattering against the parquet floor. I don't bother to straighten it. It can also wait until tomorrow.

At the door, I look over my shoulder at Leroy, who rights the chair and follows me out of the study. As soon as I step outside the room, there is something moving, prickling the edge of my vision—a familiar shape that makes my pulse beat faster. My world goes in and out of focus. The walls are fuzzy, and the floor is tilting. I stumble, but Leroy's strong arm loops around my waist and holds me firmly in place. I allow myself to lean into him, just for a few seconds, just for a few short breaths. He drops his arm, and his fingers slide over my wrist, his thumb brushing across my blue veins.

"Must be the whiskey," he chuckles into my ear, drawing out the words as if he's teasing me. His breath is warm and biting with drink against my skin, and the earth spins faster. I hear my own shallow breathing in the quiet of the hallway. My next inhale gets stuck somewhere in the middle of my rib cage as I lift my head and look up at him. He moves closer and meets me halfway, his lips slightly parting. I don't hesitate; I don't think about it twice as I put my hand on his chest. There is only me and him in the middle of the hallway and a burning candle cutting through the oppressive blackness of the night. Leroy lifts his hand to my face, and something very hot and liquid pools inside my core. Everything in me tenses. I'm starting to arch into him when he drops his hand.

"Miss!" Tilda's voice comes from somewhere down the hall, and the urgency in her voice tightens my skin. The disappointment is a wild animal with sharp teeth, but I step away from Leroy at the sound of Tilda's voice. "I heard the front door open and close." She steps into the light. Her hair is disheveled, spilling from the bun on the top of her head. "Mr. Marshall," she says, turning to Leroy. She juts her chin out at us. "Good evening."

"Tilda," I gasp. She fills up the hallway, taking up all the space. If a minute ago the room was long like a tunnel, it feels small and crowded now. Like a cave.

"Mr. Marshall asked me to stay in your mother's room tonight. To care for Mrs. Wilson."

Leroy looks at me from the corner of his eye. He sees something in my face, because his forehead crinkles in concern. "I took the liberty of asking your housemaid to make sure your mother gets the care she needs." The candle blinks wildly as he holds it higher in front of us. "Tilda graciously agreed."

"You should've talked to me about this." My voice is sharp. Who does Leroy think he is to make decisions like this? "I cannot pay for this."

Tilda hums a sigh and looks at Leroy. "It's been arranged, Miss."

Leroy clears his throat. A small smile dances across his lips. "For whatever reason, your father won't cross the veil, won't show himself, and Elise—your mother—seems to be getting worse. Nothing is working. I'm not really helping the way I thought I would, am I?" He nods at Tilda. "I asked your maid for assistance. You don't have to worry about her wages."

There's something in Tilda's face that makes me think she's delighted with her new circumstances, but I'm not sure. Maybe it's the way she wrinkles her nose and pinches her lips like she's suppressing a smile. Maybe it's the way her blue eyes shine. She's obviously not planning on moving away, and I should be relieved, but I'm not. As if reading my thoughts, Tilda steps into the shadows, away from the candlelight. I look up at Leroy, trying to search for signs of guilt, but all I see is concern. A genuine concern. I should be grateful, but for some reason all I feel is thorns and spikes.

"We must go," he says. "Let's get you to bed." And as I look at him, uncertain how to take his words, he adds, "You need rest." Based on the spin of the walls in front of me and the odd play of the candle's flame, he might be right. My head is heavy, and my step is unsteady.

As we make our way to the second floor, I touch the balustrade, and its wooden surface burns my skin, like a thousand candles violently scorching my fingers. With a jerk, I pull the hand away and stumble over the last step. The walk up the stairs takes longer than it ought to, the stairs spiraling and coiling more than they should. I spin around and face Leroy, who stands five steps below me. I was sure he was right behind me. Space and time seem to move in different directions in the Dawning.

"I count steps to my bedroom because the house is changing, Mr. Marshall. Nothing seems to be the same anymore. The stairs go up and up and up . . . forever. Have you noticed how endless the staircase feels? How steep? And the handrail feels like a living creature under my fingers." I point my chin in the direction of my bedroom. "Mother's crosses were turned upside down. Did you do it? Did you think it was funny?"

He curves an eyebrow, probably considering whether to dismiss my statements on account of the strong drink. "I haven't touched the crosses, Miss Wilson. It hurts to think you blame me for it. Your distrust of me is disappointing. I'm not a trickster. And I'm not entirely sure I understand what you mean about the house. The changes. Everything seems the same as it was on the day I came here."

"No, not the same. How do you not see it? Tilda said she noticed the changes too."

"What has she noticed? A leaking roof? A peeling wallpaper? The foundation that is slanted and cracked? I see it, too, but I don't think I should point it out so bluntly. I'm a guest here, and it's not my place to talk about the condition of your house." There's something desperate in his face when he says, "We can't always trust what we see or what we feel. We need proof. Feelings are not proof."

I choose not to respond because no matter what I say, it will not convince him. There's no proof of the man in the study. No evidence of the handrail feeling like moss. Definitely no proof of the drowned boy. And I'm struggling with my visions myself because I'm not sure anymore what is real and what is imagined.

We reach my bedroom.

"Good night, Nina." The sound of my name on his lips is unusual. "I hope you sleep well." He pauses and rests his hand on the doorframe. "It's been a difficult night," he adds softly. He watches me go inside before turning on his heel and leaving me standing in the middle of my bedroom, alone, in the glimmer of the candlelight.

I sit on the bed for a few moments, uncertain whether to burst into a fitful laugh at how awful this night has been or throw pillows at the wall with rage at the absurdity of my new reality. I do nothing.

I blow out the candle on my bedside, drop onto my bed, and pull the sheets up to my chin. Despite all that happened tonight, the frightful encounter in Father's study and the pungent smells of the Dawning, I contemplate none of it. Instead, I think of Leroy and his strong arms and the angular shape of his face. Of his broad shoulders and how my body responds to his touch—with urgency and hunger, always wanting more. Convinced I won't be able to sleep, I yawn and stretch my legs, but as soon as I close my eyes, exhaustion overtakes me.

The next day I rise with a dry mouth and a pounding headache. The sky is blue; the storm has cleared, and the sun is streaming through the window. A small whisper in a corner of my mind urges me to ignore Leroy's advice and call the police. And I almost follow that whisper, but my mouth sours when I think about the police's curious, studious glances, evaluating the decline, the ruins of what used to be grand. No, I don't need any more gossip. I don't need police in the Dawning.

I bathe myself and get dressed in the same cotton dress I was wearing yesterday. I go downstairs, feeling the cool air of the morning on my skin. The ceiling is high, and the staircase doesn't stretch endlessly. The banister doesn't feel spongy to the touch. Everything looks and feels like it ought to—ordinary and familiar. Normal. Perhaps trapped in the shadows, I've been seeing and imagining things all along.

In the dining room I sit alone and force down our bitter coffee. Neither Leroy nor Mother comes down for breakfast again, and I decide to spend the rest of my day in Father's study, sorting through the bills. I also want to find papers that could shed some light on the history of the Rask farm. Before I leave, I stand in front of our German opa's portrait, his harsh gaze grounding me in reality, making me feel small.

Something has changed in his face. Something is different.

I step closer.

The whites of Opa's eyes are brighter than usual. His skin has an unfamiliar yellow tint to it, as if he's sick with jaundice. The moment is so surreal, I almost believe I'm seeing things again. But then I step even closer, and I see the marble white of Opa's eyes sharply contrasting the yellow tint of his skin.

The air is more stagnant than a minute ago. It feels almost spongy as it caresses my neck a little differently. It slithers under my skin, deeper and deeper, until there is an odd itch. My limbs are heavy, but my head is dizzy. Every cell in my body twitches. I take a shallow breath, and Opa's head turns slowly toward me.

Chapter 11

Madness is like a dream: you can pretend it's not there; you can get away from it if you don't think about it. But what do you do if it stares right at you?

"Tilda," I scream, my eyes glued to Opa, my legs buckling with the ripe terror, but somehow I manage to remain upright. "Tilda, come here, for heaven's sake." I don't hear her footsteps because there is a loud ringing in my ears. Or maybe it is the house wailing for my sanity.

"What happened?" Her voice is urgent. I sense her comforting presence by my side.

"Look at Opa." I point my shaking finger at the portrait. "Tell me what you see."

"I see your grandfather looking down at us."

"That's all you see?" I stand still, but my voice is shrill. "He's turned in a different direction."

Tilda lifts her head higher and studies the portrait with her usual intensity, as if she's trying to determine if Opa's playing a cruel joke on us. "I'm not really sure, Miss. I reckon I've never paid much attention." She takes a step closer to the wall. "There's something different about him. But what it is, I cannot say." Her voice trails off, as if she's caught in her own thoughts.

Instead of going to the study as I planned, I flee to my bedroom. My room feels safe. It keeps the darkness at bay. It keeps me sane. I lie in bed, my eyes closed, and try to think about anything but my visions and my mother's affliction. I listen to the Dawning, focusing on its sounds. It lives its own life: it breathes, whispers, and shifts.

The hours drag on as I stay in my room all day.

I wake up in the middle of the night with a jolt, my short, panicked breaths marking seconds against my chest. At first, I don't know what woke me up. It wasn't a dream, of that I am sure. A sound pierced the silence. Perhaps, deep inside the house, a door slammed. Perhaps, it was a rustle by my bed or someone's frosty touch.

The room smells faintly of wet dirt. A low drum of rain on the glass tells me the storm that's been building in the air all day has finally arrived. I lie still in the deep of the night, listening to my racing heart, hoping it's not another night of nightmares and intruders and crosses turned upside down.

Don't think. Don't think. Don't think. I repeat the words like a prayer, and a few minutes later, I start to drift away when I hear a rustle.

I sit up. "Who's there?"

"Nina." A whisper from the darkest corner of my room.

My hand flies up to my mouth, a scream about to burst. I peer into the space, but I don't see anything. Then, another rustle, and a shadow steps out from behind the dresser. A familiar silhouette. A recognizable slope of the shoulders. A bit taller than me, it moves fluidly and with a great confidence.

I swing my legs over the side of the bed. "Amos? When did you get home? You gave me a great fright." I push my covers aside and leap to my feet. Of course, he had to come to my room because there is a stranger sleeping in his bed. I pull my dressing gown off the chair and shrug it on, not caring to button it. "Thank heavens, you are here." I turn to my bedside table. A scrape of matches as I light a candle and whip around.

My room is empty.

"Amos?" I croak, my voice hoarse. "Amos?" I whisper, even though I know no one will reply. My brother, or whatever . . . whoever was here earlier, is gone.

An odd staccato, almost in cadence with my beating heart—a rapid succession of five knocks, followed by three slow ones—breaks through the night. That must be what woke me up. I force my breathing to slow down, to soften, so I can hear better. The tapping continues, but now it seems to be moving around. One second it is to my right, then my left, and a moment later it's behind me. Is that what Tilda heard?

With a candle in my trembling hand, I walk around the room. The shadows flinch on the wall and across the floor, setting my teeth on edge. An icy draft saturates my bedroom, and I pull my dressing gown tighter. The air grows heavier. It's damp with humidity, and the scent of rot is much stronger now. Like a shallow grave left uncovered in the heat of the day. Lightning strikes, briefly illuminating my room. A peal of thunder follows and makes me jump.

More tapping.

I listen, trying to determine from what side of the room the noise is coming. The knocking is incessant, and it is definitely coming from the ceiling. There's an attic right above my bedroom. Can it be rats? Another rustle by my door, and I whisk around.

The doorknob slowly turns.

"Who's there?" I ask, my voice weak, frightened. "Amos, is that you?" I take a few steps closer to the door.

"It's Leroy."

At the sound of his voice, a sense of relief ripples through my veins. I don't even care to know why he is here. I'm glad he is a person and not a shadow. I wrench the door open and take in his black shirt and black overcoat and black breeches. A few strands of grass cling damply to his boots. The cuffs of his trousers look wet. He came from outside.

"You called your brother's name?" He doesn't look surprised.

My heart skitters as my thoughts about Amos, locked away in the clinic far from home, roil in my mind. Why would I think he finally came home? The healing, especially of something so terrible as my brother's sickness, takes time. Doctors had warned us it might take a year or longer before he'll be able to return. I try to make sense of my reaction, of what's happening, of things that live inside me, of all the visions I see and the mistakes I make. I fail on all counts.

"Why are you in my bedroom at this hour?" I ask, ignoring his question and pinching the bridge of my nose to clear my head.

"Did you hear it, Nina? The tapping?" The dancing light of a candle in his hand creates oddly shaped shadows across his face.

"Do you know what it is?"

He smiles, a flash of white teeth in the candlelight. "It's your father. He was able to cross over. And he's ready to show himself and talk to his family. Are you ready to talk to him?"

Again, I pinch the bridge of my nose with my thumb and forefinger. Press harder. "This is madness. You do realize it, don't you? You're taking it too far."

"Your continuous mistrust hurts deeply, Miss Wilson. Especially considering your own familiarity with ghosts. Why don't you follow me, and you shall witness it yourself." He turns around and disappears into the hall.

The rational part of me is tempted to slam the door in his face, make him flinch, chip at his arrogance. But the less rational part of me wants—needs—to believe I'm seeing ghosts. That I'm not going mad like Mother. And so I follow.

The hallway is dark and cold, but the lack of light doesn't seem to bother Leroy, who moves slowly but confidently in front of me. The floor feels soft, as if I'm walking through the forest, on the ground covered with moss. The wallpaper is browner than usual, unfamiliar black dots like pockmarks scattered across it. The thinning paper bubbles and peels away from the wall. A slight chill, a faint breeze, looms in the air. I look over my shoulder once or twice, but there is nothing but darkness, its crushing presence pressing against my back. I sense a shadowy movement and spin around, but again there is nothing behind me.

"What is it?" Leroy shoves his candle in my face. His eyes are ablaze with an odd excitement. "You're all jittery and jumpy, Miss Wilson."

The rain patters on the roof. The sound is hollow, but it reminds me of the tapping I heard a few minutes ago in my bedroom. "It's the house. It's growing teeth," I whisper. And when he looks at me, his eyes intense with amusement, questioning me, I add, "Look at the walls. At the wallpaper. How can you not see it?"

He shines his candle at the wall to his right. I shouldn't be surprised seeing that everything looks just as it looked this morning—wilted and tired and in need of refreshment—but I am shocked, nevertheless. There is no peeling wallpaper, no exposed flesh of the Dawning gaping at me from behind it. No signs of mold speckling the walls like constellations.

"Sometimes it's difficult to understand you, Miss Wilson." Leroy's voice is low as he inspects the wall. "One moment you deny you're seeing strange, otherworldly things, and the next, you insist I'm blind if I cannot see them." He shines his candle at me. "So what is it going to be? Don't play me for a fool, Miss Wilson."

I swallow and look at him, trying to settle my racing pulse. "I don't know what I believe anymore." When he curves his eyebrow at me again, I continue: "But something is happening to the Dawning, and I'm starting to think it is caused by your ministrations with the spirit world."

"Are you opening yourself up to a possibility that I do indeed talk to the spirits?"

"Perhaps," I whisper. "I don't know. Maybe there's something in these walls that responds to you."

He chuckles and simply turns around and continues his walk to the staircase. We ascend the stairs to the third floor, to Mother's bedroom. Our climb seems unnaturally long. Everything feels foreign, as if I'm walking not in the Dawning but in someone else's house. I know this staircase well. Yet I feel like I don't belong here anymore. I used to run up and down the same stairs as a little girl, chasing after Amos. Just a few months ago, I was standing at the top with a champagne flute in hand, watching men in dinner jackets assemble around Father, who was explaining where the railroad will connect through Nebraska. I stood still, my spine rigid, and Bobby was looking up at me with a wide smile on his full lips.

I wish I could turn time back and return to my life as it was—to the societal status that seemed so impenetrable, so solid, to my marriage prospects and promises of a stable life with a lack of worry.

Down the hallway, my mother's bedroom door is ajar in a silent invitation, gleaming candlelight streaming under it. Leroy glances at me over his shoulder, a reflective, almost contemplative expression on his face. He pauses as if he wants to say something but reconsiders and walks down the hallway. Without a knock, Leroy pushes open the door and enters Mother's bedroom, but I fall behind and linger in the doorway because I cannot believe what my eyes are seeing.

Mother sits on the edge of the bed, dressed in her moth-eaten wedding gown made of silk and lace. It hugs her scrawny figure in all the wrong places. Her long hair, streaked with gray, is loose and flowing down her shoulders in tangled wisps. Her face is pale, sharp cheekbones protruding dangerously. I haven't realized how thin she's become in the span of a couple of days. I can nearly see the bones under her skin.

Otherwise unmoving, she turns her face toward Leroy and smiles, her lips tinged with red spots. Is it wine or blood? The glint of her teeth in the dim light morphs her smile into a hungry scowl. The candlelight, the unnatural whiteness of her dress, her pale skin, and her slow movements give her an appearance of an ethereal creature.

Leroy lowers himself to his knees in front of Mother, and she seizes his hand with her clawlike fingers and presses it to her heart. He whispers something, and she nods briskly in reply. Leroy continues his incoherent whispering, his soft chant. Even in the weak light and from a distance, I see how tense Mother is and how fervently she's taking in every single word he says. He keeps on chanting, and his low hum floats through the air in pulsing waves. He continues like this for a few minutes and then stops abruptly. I wait for Leroy to turn to me and invite me to the room, but instead he lowers his head onto my mother's knees, his shoulders drop, and he stays still.

"What on earth is happening?" I ask, but neither pays attention. A bitter taste invades my mouth as I watch Leroy's head on my mother's lap, his hands cupping her thighs. There's a burning sensation in my belly. What would it be like to feel the weight of him against my body? Startled, I realize I wish his hands were pressed against my hips and not hers. I take a deep yet shuddering breath, inhaling through my nose forcefully. No one is paying attention to me, and it's only when I take a few steps inside Mother's bedroom and say "Why are you wearing your wedding dress, Mother? What madness is this?" that both of them look at me.

"She isn't ready. She isn't welcome here," my mother says, and Leroy nods, pushing himself to his feet.

He comes up to me and stands still, his shoulders broad and his legs positioned wide, as if he wants to take up as much space in Mother's bedroom as he physically can. He gently takes me by my shoulders and turns me around. "You shouldn't be frightened, Nina." His whisper brushes over my skin and springs goose bumps on my neck.

"I'm not frightened. I'm appalled." I try to turn and pull away from his strong hold, but he doesn't let me.

"May your heart be full of light," he whispers into my ear, and before I'm able to take a full breath, I'm pushed outside the bedroom. The door closes behind me with a loud thump. The lock clicks.

I stand in front of the door, my hand lifted to knock. Should I demand to open it? Should I ask him to leave? I press my knuckles to the door, but then I remember the sound of Mother's voice, her wedding dress, and her face full of longing and agony, and I go back to my room. I don't understand the strange pang of jealousy I felt when Leroy touched her. Why did I feel that? I swallow a shard in my throat. That sort of emotion is inappropriate. And useless.

One hour painfully morphs into another as I lie on my bed, hugging my knees to my middle, waiting for the morning to come.

If I close my eyes, I can see my mother, perched on the edge of the bed in her wedding dress. The vision is imprinted in my mind. I think about the way Leroy looks in the flickering light. His burning-with-enthusiasm eyes. Whatever he's doing, it's not helping Mother, not making her better. If anything, Mother is fading away, and I don't know how to deal with this slow yet inevitable vanishing.

But there is one question that hangs, thick and heavy, in the air: What benefit does Leroy derive from all this? There must be something he wants, but what it is, I fail to grasp. Is it money? At that, incredulous laughter tickles the back of my throat, and the sound that erupts out of me is rough and raspy, not even laughter. Who knows why Leroy does what he does. Why does he travel around the country as a self-proclaimed medium? And why doesn't he have a wife? A man in his thirties, with a profitable business, who's not seeking a family of his own, despite being quite handsome and appealing in his own way—a man like him must have a reason for everything he does.

He must leave, and maybe with his departure the Dawning will return to the home I used to love.

When the grandfather clock finally chimes six o'clock, I get out of bed. I stretch, but my back and shoulders remain stiff and achy from tension. A few splashes of water on my face, a brush to my tangled hair, and I'm almost ready. I shrug on a simple house frock, and a few minutes later, I knock on Leroy's bedroom door, but his room is quiet. Is he still with my mother? My mouth feels thick and dry at the thought. What can they possibly be doing at this hour? I push nauseating, burning thoughts away. I must bury the visions of Mother in Leroy's arms, as for what I'm about to do, I need all the fury and determination I can summon.

In the hallway, the smell of burned wicker lingers in the air. I run down the stairs, halting midstep when a shadow, tall and lean, steps into the corner. It moves so quickly out of my eyesight, I'm not certain I really saw it.

"Mr. Marshall? Is that you?" I call out, my voice loud and desperate.

He steps into the hazy light of the morning. His face is still half hidden in the shadows, but the familiar white flash of his teeth tells me he's smiling, and I know he must have waited for me to come down.

"Miss Wilson! You're up quite early." I can feel his eyes on me, appraising, missing nothing—my pale face, my old-fashioned dress, and my dry lips. "Trouble sleeping?"

Anger edges to the corners of my mind, and I welcome it. And before I know what I'm doing, my hand connects with his face. The slap cracks in the air like a gunshot.

Leroy steps closer, catching my hand, which hovers suspended in the air. A bright-red spot underscores his cheekbone. "Nina." His voice is rough. He's breathing hard. "If I offended you . . . I didn't mean . . ." He trails off, and I sense that there is something more, something else he wants to say but for whatever reason doesn't say it.

My throat is too tight to respond. I didn't expect him to look so wounded. I expected an outburst of anger. I waited for harsh words. Anything but this heart-wrenching acceptance. My hand twitches because I want to reach out and touch the red spot on his cheek. I want my cool fingers to soothe the heat of his skin. His face is inches away from mine, inhaling and exhaling the same air. The scent of burned wicker mixes with the smell of his shaving cream.

There's an odd stillness in the air between us that makes it harder to breathe.

A small smile tugs at the corner of his mouth when he gently lifts my hand and presses my knuckles to his lips.

Chapter 12

I jerk my hand away, turn around, and walk briskly down the hallway, his footsteps following me closely. I enter the parlor, my breath ragged. I should've been able to hold myself together, but his question about my trouble sleeping struck me like a shovel to my chest.

Inside the parlor, I turn toward him, and I'm surprised by how unperturbed, how relaxed, he looks despite everything that took place just a minute ago. As if I never slapped him. As if he never kissed me. After being engulfed by rage, seeing him like this—calm and indifferent—I'm almost relieved we can pretend nothing happened. A part of me still wants to make him wince, and I grapple for words to throw at him like blades. But the other part of me brings back a memory of how lost and hurt he looked when my hand connected with his face, and I decide to move on and address the main reason we're here.

"Please explain what I witnessed last night," I say with as much disdain as I can muster. "Why in God's name was my mother wearing her wedding dress?"

"Last night was extraordinary. You witnessed your father's presence. Your parents' reunion." Leroy purrs like a cat and drops into one of the chairs by the window. I'm not sure what I expect of him, but his ungentlemanly behavior doesn't surprise me a bit. In fact, it gives me freedom to be myself and not worry about my own manners.

"I witnessed a sick woman dressed in her old wedding gown, listening to peculiar chants by a stranger."

A peal of laughter bursts from him, and it unspools a burning rage inside me. A need for another violent outburst stirs in my chest, and I step closer to the door, distancing myself from him.

"You are a harsh judge, Miss Wilson." He stops laughing and waves at the chair across from him. "Please take a seat. Don't make me feel uncomfortable for sitting down while you're hovering by the door."

"I don't think you care about manners, Mr. Marshall. And this is going to be brief."

"Suit yourself." He remains seated, shoulders relaxed, a smile expanding by several degrees.

My hands on my hips, I step in front of him, my eyes narrowed and hard. "Preying on the sick . . . deceiving a grieving widow . . . it's dishonest and . . . cruel. Don't you have any conscience left?"

He shrugs, a slight and somehow elegant movement of his wide shoulders. "I know we've been excluding you. But your mother doesn't think you're ready to be a part of our sessions. Not yet. You've been extremely skeptical, hard on her."

"Hard on her?" My voice inches higher. "Doesn't she remember her walks through the house? Her hysteria in the study the other night?" Mother is a very sick woman who needs medical help—help I cannot afford nor am brave enough to seek. "And you . . . you said you don't prey on misery. And yet here you are. In our house. Doing exactly that. I should report you to the authorities."

"Are you sure you want to involve the authorities, Miss Wilson? I thought we agreed the other night that their presence here is not ideal."

I press my hand to my forehead. "This nonsense needs to stop. You need to stop."

He smiles, bemused. "I help people. And I understand your plight, Miss Wilson. I'm eating your food and burning your candles and your wood. I know you cannot afford any of it." There is no disdain in his voice, just wariness. "I know your situation. I'm not blind. I see what's taking place in the Dawning." He looks at me for a long moment, considering his next words. "I feel for you, but have you considered other options? Other than accusing me of fraud or yelling or slapping me. You could leave the Dawning. Have you thought about it? What keeps you in these ruins of the house? Your life here has brought you nothing but grief and fright and ghosts."

How dare he suggest I should abandon the only true thing that is left of my family? When I went downstairs to confront Leroy, in my mind, I was carrying a shield, maybe a sword, ready for a battle. But his words about the Dawning dismantle my determination to fight, leaving me vulnerable. "Get out." I spit the words out. Rage is my only weapon. "Get out of my house. That's the only option I'm considering."

His jaw tenses as he says, "Do you want me to pay for the food your mother so generously offers me in exchange for my help?"

"I don't want your money. I want you out of the house."

"I don't think it's a viable option."

"It's the only option."

He sighs, as if he finds my words silly, and gazes off into the distance. He takes his time to think, and I let him, because I need time to collect myself.

"Miss Wilson," he finally says, "you probably forgot, but you owe me a favor." Each word is a bite. Each word plunges me deeper into desperation. "And I think I'm going to hold you to your word."

There it is—the thing I dreaded to hear for a long while. The favor I so imprudently promised. My fingers wrap around the frayed trimming of my dress, nails digging deep into my palms, leaving half moons carved into my skin.

"What do you want?" I'm struggling to keep the panic out of my voice. He doesn't reply, so I push forward. "What is it you are hoping to get out of our arrangement? For God's sake, what is it that you want?"

Something ripples in his eyes. Something curious and borderline deranged. "It's not *what* I want. It's who."

"I don't understand."

"It's you I desire, Miss Wilson."

His words strike me with the force of a hurricane, and suddenly I'm acutely aware of every joint, every muscle, and every pore in my body. "I don't understand." I fumble for a reason to make sense of what he said. "But it's no matter. There is nothing I can give you. Nothing."

"It's not for you to decide," he says slowly, as if speaking to a disobedient child.

"I'll pay you . . . I'll pay you to leave." I finally say the words I prepared this morning. I will give him my pearl earrings, and if it's not enough, I'll add the silver locket. I'll give him anything he wants—furniture, paintings, Mother's crosses.

His heard jerks backward as he laughs boisterously, clearly enjoying the situation. "One thing I appreciate about you, Miss Wilson, is how utterly and beautifully honest you are with me. It's such a rare luxury."

"Luxury?"

"Everyone lies."

"Name your price."

"You shouldn't be offering money you don't have, Miss Wilson." He pauses, studies his nails for a long minute, as if considering his next words. When he looks up at me, his eyes are serious, almost mournful. "Your father left you nothing but his gambling debts. And I hear you have a tax bill to pay. You're about to lose the Dawning, Miss Wilson."

"How . . ." I stumble over my own words as my tongue refuses to move. The fresh scent of his shaving soap invades my mouth and slides down my throat, turning my stomach. "How . . . who told you about the tax bill?"

Something resembling pity crosses his face. "People talk in this town," he says softly. It's frightening that Leroy Marshall knows everything about me and I know nothing of him. "I understand what you're going through. I told you about my youth. My father was a shoemaker, definitely not a moneyed man." There is a faraway look on his face, as if he's being whisked away to some distant place. "I know what poverty does. How it changes you." His voice doesn't carry a single note of disapproval. If anything, he sounds kind.

It's too hot in the parlor. Drops of sweat slide down my neck. I lower myself onto the chaise. There are moments in life that change everything, but you don't realize it until it's too late to catch yourself before the fall. This moment, right here and now, feels exactly like that: as if on some subconscious level, I know my life is about to turn, and it will never be the same because no matter how hard I try to act as if my life is still normal, everything has already changed.

"Become my apprentice, Miss Wilson, and I'll teach you my trade. I'll teach you how to commune with the dead, and I'll teach you what to do when the dead refuse to talk. Ghosts are moody. Sometimes they don't appear when called."

His words rattle aimlessly in my head. "I beg your pardon?" I must've misheard him.

"I'm proposing a business deal. A partnership. Together, in this house, we'll host séances. People pay handsomely to talk to the spirit world." He grins ruefully. "You and I can make a lot of money."

I slowly raise my head and meet his eyes. "Why would I agree to this preposterous offer?" His voice, his eyes that twinkle with an odd excitement, tells me this isn't the kind of offer I can refuse. But I'll be damned if I don't try. "No, thanks."

"You don't want to lose the house. Or am I mistaken? It would taint your family name forever. You cannot afford that. You want to restore your house and your name to its previous glory. And there was a lot of glory, wasn't there? Your father's vast lands, stables with the most beautiful horses in Omaha, your future dazzling prospects. Everything is gone, and you're about to lose the only thing that is still yours. The Dawning. I know you well by now, Miss Wilson, and I can say you would do anything to prove to everyone that the Wilson name still matters." He assesses me, as if looking for the confirmation. When he finds none, he pushes himself from the chair and stands in front of me, arms folded across his chest. "So what do you say?"

My pulse quickens, pounding at the bottom of my throat. I want to say he isn't wrong. But he already sees my response in the turn of my head and the ravenous hunger in my eyes, because a grin appears on his face, and I don't answer his question.

"I'm giving you a chance to come out from the shadow of your father," he says.

"What makes you think I can do it? Talk to the spirit world? I have no psychic abilities."

"I think you do. The drowned boy only you can see? The changes in the house. Tilda told me about your grandfather's portrait. You think you're going mad, don't you? But you are not. I assure you. I, myself, sense the change, but I can't see it the way you do. I think the house is feeding on all the grief and sadness. There is so much of it here. It's your mother's grief, her inability to move on, her desire for her husband that is destroying the Dawning."

I don't know if I can fully trust him. But the thought of not being like my mother is . . . reassuring. Soothing, even. After so many sleepless nights, the idea of madness became so dense, so solid, it started to feel like a breathing and living thing. Another twin. If I'm not going insane, if my visions are indeed real, then maybe Leroy can show me how to commune properly with the spirits. If his lessons could give me answers I seek, I actually might be ready to become his apprentice. "Can we reverse the changes? Whatever is happening to the house?"

"I can teach you how to expand your abilities, Miss Wilson. How to strengthen them. But first you need to accept the idea that the spirit world exists and you can commune with it. And who knows, perhaps it will be you who will return the Dawning to its previous state. And maybe you'll help your mother find happiness again."

"If I agree, and I'm not saying I'm inclined, how would we do it? People will take me for a fraud, and if I'm caught in lies, I might be arrested."

He laughs softly. "There's no crime when people part with their money willingly." He leans closer, and I can see golden flecks in the brown of his eyes. He's just inches away from me, and in the morning light, he looks much younger than his age. "Miss Wilson." Leroy puts his hand on mine, and I don't pull away this time. "If we do this, you'll make a lot of money. You'd be able to hire your staff back. You'll pay your tax bill. But most importantly, you would reaffirm your social status. Society will take you back with no questions asked. Because they'll need you to talk to their departed ones, to relieve them from their grief, their guilt, and whatever else plagues them." His gaze sweeps across the walls and the peeling wallpaper. "It must be exhausting to always try to come up with ways to fix things cheaply around the estate. Who will be chopping wood when winter comes? You or Tilda? All your problems can be solved in a matter of weeks."

The tight knot lodged in my chest twists tighter. I look out the window. The day is clear and warm. A faint rush of a breeze is followed by a bird cry somewhere in the trees behind the house. My fingers smooth the threadbare cuff on my dress. The old cotton is rough and scratchy. I sold most of my silk dresses to pay for the food. I'm down to one pair of shoes with thinning leather soles. Not even the shadiest pawnbroker in Omaha can help me. "What would I have to do?"

"You'd be a charming hostess, and you'd help me with the setup. I'm going to teach you everything I know. You'll master the basics in no time. In fact, I think we could have our first gathering by the end of the next week."

"So soon?"

Leaning into his chair, he crosses his hands behind his head. "Yes," he says, his gaze fixed on the ceiling, contemplative. "I thought we could do it here, in the parlor. But the room is too small. We'll do it in your dining room."

"How long are you planning to run the séances out of the Dawning? And how long are you planning on staying here?"

"I never stay in one town for too long." He says it so easily that at first, I think he's lying to make me feel better. But there's some heaviness in his voice, deep beneath the surface of his words, and I know he's telling the truth.

"Why not?"

"It's not smart to get attached," he says with a sigh. "We should have a small gathering first. Maybe invite a few of your former friends. The Hollands."

"They despise me. Why would they come?"

Leroy chuckles. "Curiosity is stronger than logic. Stronger than loathing. They won't be able to stay away."

"It feels too rushed. I've only been to one séance," I say and point my chin at him. "Yours. And that didn't go well, if you remember."

"We'll practice. And the more you practice, the easier it will get."

Outside the window, the sun shines brightly, streaming through the glass and illuminating the dust motes floating in the air.

"I need to think," I say, keeping my voice steady. His offer is strange and outrageous. Yet it's also compelling. If séances bring as much money as he says they do, I can indeed restore the Dawning. Taking care of Mother won't be as daunting anymore, as I would have money to pay for her care. The money generated by séances would allow me the freedom I crave so much.

"Of course, Miss Wilson."

I go to my room and fall on my bed. I don't undress, and I don't move for a long time. I stare at the ceiling, letting tears flow freely. Every nerve in my body is humming with a strong current. Every muscle is as tight as a piano string.

If what he has said about the money is true, I can assist him for a short while, and as soon as I have enough, I'll ask him to move out. After all, he doesn't get attached to one place.

For now, all I need to do is adapt to my new circumstances, and adapting is a skill I have plenty of practice with. I learned how to be alone, how to face the financial default, and how to deal with Mother. Being Leroy's apprentice is just one more thing to learn, to deal with.

The light has dimmed behind my window by the time I rise, adjust my hair, and wash my face. I walk down the hallway to his room and lift my hand to knock when the door opens, and Leroy looks down at me.

I tilt my chin upward. "I've made my choice."

He doesn't reply at first. We just stand and look at each other, all my thoughts passing between us in a silent conversation. I suspect he knew my answer before I knew it myself, and now, there's no need for me to verbalize it. He steps to the side, holding my gaze, inviting me in. There is feverish determination on his face.

"Welcome to the fold," he says.

October 10, 1903

My dear Amos,

Do you believe in ghosts?

When we were children—seems like ages ago—there was that incident when I thought I saw an apparition in the mirror. Do you remember it? You laughed so hard that night, I felt like a fool. Even then, we had never discussed anything supernatural as there was no need. But now that I have witnessed something, I would like to know what you think.

I keep having visions of a boy who drowned last summer. At first, I thought it was the grieving father of the drowned boy from the Hollands' séance who brought the ghost of his dead son to our world. But why would the spirit of a stranger want to talk to me? We have no connection, emotional or material, to form any kind of contact. There is nothing that would bind us together.

I thought about it for a long time. And finally, I realized there was one more boy who drowned. Oliver Rask. The Rask farm is on our property. The family abandoned it because the land turned bad.

The boy and his father drowned in the creek behind their house. There must be a link—unspeakable and tragic—that tethered him to me. A mystery I am yet to untangle.

I am certain now it is Oliver Rask I am seeing.

Everyone used to call him Ollie.

Do you remember him, a boy of eight years old, always laughing, always playing with his toy soldiers? I think his spirit wants me to do something, to help him somehow, but I do not know how. Maybe he wants me to soothe him. He must be aching from loneliness like so many of us.

Yesterday, trying to find answers to my questions about the Rask family, I searched Father's desk and, deep in his drawers with brass swan neck handles you hate so much, found letters addressed to Father and written by Mr. Rask himself. Did you know our father was called a "railroad baron"? He was buying land cheaply west of the Missouri River because that was where Father had estimated the new railroad would be built. He was not wrong! Most of his fortune came from trading land, especially the parcels where Omaha's iron wonder, the Missouri River Bridge, was built. One of the parcels belonged to Mr. Rask, who worked tirelessly in the mines of Colorado, saved up some money, and moved his family to Nebraska. When Mr. Rask ran into financial problems due to crops drying up, Father bought his farm. Also, quite cheap. Then he turned around and leased it back to Mr. Rask. I found a promissory note from Mr. Rask in which he pledged his crops to Father for the next ten years. What kind of deal was it, Amos? Working on the land that is not his anymore while our father builds a nice big house on the top of the hill.

I took a long walk yesterday to their farm to find Ollie's resting place, the ground dry and crunching under my feet. I needed a confirmation, something to tell me the drowned boy who visits me is indeed Ollie Rask.

The Rasks left wind chimes hanging on the front porch, and they blew back and forth in a slight breeze that spread the smell of earth and fall. There was a faint sweetness to the air as if something was in bloom, but it is October, and nothing is flowering. I did not see any flowers, only weeds.

I came up to their porch and tried looking into the windows, but the glass was so dirty I could not see inside. And then, suddenly, the air quieted. There was no breeze rippling through the tall grass. The wind chimes stopped moving. I could not hear any birds or insects. All I heard was my ragged, harsh breathing.

It was a lonely and sad place, Amos, and something deeply sorrowful inhabited it. I could feel it in my marrow, in my chest, even in my eyes because they got watery. There was a slow chill that got colder and sharper with every step I took down the porch. Tears burned my eyes, and I did not know why I felt like I was the only living person on earth.

Sadness whimpered in my head, and I wanted to lie down in the mud, curl up on my side, arms over my head, and weep. But I was terrified no one would ever find me, and I would remain lying in the fields and die and rot and become the earth. It was such a desperate and somehow weirdly intrusive thought,

I picked up my pace and started my walk back to the Dawning.

I did not look for Ollie's resting place.

I stopped to catch my breath and saw a shadow in the field to my left. It moved with me, and in response, the hairs on my arms stood on end and I ran all the way home. I do not know how long I ran, but at some point pain stabbed through my sides and I could not inhale fully. I did not look over my shoulder because I was scared. Of who or what I cannot say.

I always imagined the Rasks, just like us, were bound to one place, and that place was their farm.

But Father took it away from them.

And our family destroyed theirs.

With all my love,

Your sister Nina

Chapter 13

Talking to the dead is not at all what I imagined.

Leroy's lessons do not include candles, summoning spirits, or chanting. We don't spend time in rooms where the light comes straggling through the pulled curtains or closed shutters. His lessons have nothing to do with the spirit world.

Nothing at all.

Every day after breakfast, the training commences and takes up all day. I rarely have time for tea or a crust of bread before Leroy is pulling me back to the parlor to show me a new trick, to make me practice it over and over until I can do it blindfolded.

"I don't understand," I say one afternoon after I learn how to tap with a heel on a hollowed-out chair leg. I'm sitting in the middle of the room at our round mahogany parlor table we dragged from the window. Leroy is standing in front of me, arms folded across his chest. He's dressed in starched clothes. His jet-black hair is combed back. I'm wearing my old house frock and scratched leather shoes. I don't remember if I took a brush to my hair this morning. "Why are you teaching me parlor tricks, really? I'm learning nothing about spirits." I remove my shoe and point the heel at his face. "Why am I learning this? I have blisters on my foot from all the thumping. And look at this heel. It's about to fall apart, and I don't have another pair of shoes to spare."

He lets out half a laugh, as if trying to make fun of my question. With a loud thud, I drop my shoe on the floor and don't bother to put it on.

"Spirits, just like people, can be moody, Miss Wilson. Sometimes they don't come. And what are you supposed to do then? Ask your guests to leave? No, you're supposed to put on a performance and wait for the dead to appear."

I almost laugh at how ridiculous he sounds. "How do the spirits decide if they want to grace a medium with their presence or not?"

"This remains a mystery. The dead can be temperamental. Even grumpy. Sometimes they come when called but choose not to reveal themselves. They like to watch."

"The tricks, then." I point at my scuffed shoe that lies on the floor between us. "To put a show on while waiting for the dead to oblige us with their presence." I chuckle. "I have to admit this is more complicated than I thought it would be." I'm not sure what to think of it—the tapping, the trickery, the pretense. Perhaps, over the course of our lessons, it will all make sense, and I'll discover a deeper reason for the tricks. But right now, it feels like we're preparing for a show rather than a séance.

His smile eases when his gaze slides to my feet. He drops to his knees, picks up the shoe, and cradles it in his hands. His fingers skim my foot, lifting my skirt, exposing my stitched-up stockings. The room is suddenly airless. My face is on fire, and my first instinct is to pull away, but his touch is mindful and slow, almost hesitant, and I let him gently slide the shoe onto my foot. His long fingers pause and then slowly trace the outline of my ankle. As if he's learning the feel and the shape of me. The heat of his touch seeps through my stockings, constricting my lungs, making it impossible to take a breath. He looks up briefly, eyes impossibly black and piercing. He holds my gaze expectantly, and when I don't say anything, his thumb presses lightly against my ankle, moving slowly in circular motions. My skin vibrates, my core liquifies, and I inhale sharply.

"Soon you'll be able to purchase proper shoes." His voice is low when he gently sets my foot on the floor and withdraws from me. "There's no right or wrong way to call the dead. Eventually they come. They always do, even the most stubborn ones. You call out to them however feels right to you as a medium, and then you listen."

"For what?" My voice croaks. I swallow hard, trying to keep my composure. His touch is nothing like Bobby's. He strokes me with the confidence of a man who knows the woman's body. Bobby's hands were always wandering, never lingering for long over my curves, always in a rush to get his fill of me. Leroy's touch is slow and deliberate, and it sparks sensations inside me I never knew were possible.

"For a creak. A whisper. A scrape of a foot. Anything that would tell you they have arrived. Sometimes they're so close you can feel their presence on your skin. The chill. The goose bumps." Leroy's words stir unsettling memories of the boy and the absolute coldness that comes with him. How the air stills in his presence. And how the day dims and the night crawls from the corners. The boy's pale face lingers in my mind, longer than I want it to, like an unwanted houseguest. "But you also need to be prepared for silence. In case they decide not to answer your call. And that's why you need to know how to entertain your guests while you're waiting."

"It might be a long wait, I suspect." If anything, this confirms that Leroy's séances are entirely based on trickery and nothing else. If I'm right, if I'm mostly learning how to cheat people out of their money, what does it mean for me in the end? Does Mother's madness cloud my mind so heavily that my subconscious bleeds the ghost-boy into my reality? As I absorb this possibility, I can hear Dr. Fuller's voice in my mind telling me to accept the possibility of madness. The rhythm of his words, the slight rasp in his voice, his soothing tone is so real, I wince.

Leroy frowns and shoves his hands into his pants pockets. "Are you all right?"

After a long inhale, I manage a hoarse "Yes." I should stop thinking about madness and focus on Leroy and his lessons. But for the first time since we started learning the tricks, I wonder if there's some part of me that believes in ghosts. Didn't I wish for the ability to see ghosts a long time ago? What if Tilda is right and my wish was granted? By what power, I don't know, but the thought of the spirit world being real is much more comforting than the thought of going insane. The dead provide an easy answer to every question I've ever asked about myself. About Mother. About Leroy.

"Okay, so . . ." He pauses as he assesses my face. I nod, prompting him to continue. "Even if the dead come and talk to you, your connection might last only a fraction of time, and you need to transition seamlessly—for your audience's sake—between your lost connection and the next trick."

"Teach me how to restore a lost connection."

"I'm not a highly educated medium, Miss Wilson," Leroy says after a long pause. "I can teach only what I know. I have not been able to restore a single lost connection. I don't know how to do it. Once they're gone . . . they're gone."

"Teach me how to lift the veil."

"Everything in due time, Miss Wilson. Lifting the veil is hard. Impossible at times. First, let's learn how to entertain our audience."

I clench my jaw tightly for a moment, but I don't want to argue, and so we go on with our lessons.

Strings are tied to apples, and I bounce them off the walls like balls. I slowly move from one wall to another, counting to five and rhythmically bobbing the apples into the wallpaper. Sometimes I stand on a chair and reach out to the highest corner, where the walls merge with the ceiling. And while throwing apples at the walls, I finally solve a puzzle that's been haunting me ever since Tilda told me about the knocking.

"All that tapping. Was it you?" I ask Leroy between throws.

"I tried to help your mother."

I turn around and take a few steps toward him. "By throwing apples at the walls?"

The lines of his face soften in the dim sunlight. His eyelashes flutter closed for a few seconds as he takes a deep breath. "To make your mother and you think your father's ghost was present. I've lost my connection with him. I didn't know what to do, and I needed you to believe." He runs his hand through his thick hair. "I'm sorry I did it that way. It was reckless. But I wanted your mother to get better. Instead, she got worse. And I suspect it was all my fault. The way I handled it."

"It was foolish."

He rubs his chin. "I know." A crease of concern is etched into his forehead.

My head snaps back, and I squint at him, at his pale skin, his chin shadowed by the rough stubble, as if he forgot to shave this morning, and I remind myself that I'm doing it for the money. That the tricks he pulled on us are not my problem. Not anymore.

We stand opposite each other. Both of us are waiting for what the other will do. If I refuse to go on, I'm certain he'll leave the Dawning. I'm also certain our tax bill won't get paid. Tilda will leave, too, and Mother needs her now more than ever. My mother hasn't left her bedroom in three days. She refuses to eat. She refuses to talk. There are moments when I sense death like a thick mist seeping from underneath Mother's door, cloaking the hallway. And somehow, the house is morphing into something entirely different.

If I let my anger take over, if I let myself feel used and humiliated, then my freedom, my future the way I imagine it, will never materialize. So I shut my eyes forcefully, deliberately, and swallow my rage, my bitterness, because this is the only way to bury it all deep inside me. The ravenous hunger for what is lost and what I don't have is stronger than my desire to throw Leroy out of the house.

I inhale.

I open my eyes.

I go on.

After my lessons, I go to Mother's bedroom to check on her. The hallway is long and narrow, and it takes me a while to walk the length of it. Muscles tighten around my mouth into a scowl as I make my way to Mother. An odd hum inside the house, the sound of things expanding and sprouting within the Dawning's walls, accompanies my every step. The yellow wallpaper above the wood trim is coming off in uneven strips of yellow mixed with brown. The ugly stucco peeking through is a constant reminder that this space is molded and shaped by people who used to live here and now are long gone. Suddenly, I feel bound to the house in some way I don't understand.

There is a tray by the door. Tilda must've left it a while ago, because the pea soup looks cold. I pick up the tray, push the door open with my shoulder, and walk into the room. The air is stale and heavy. It smells like mildew and dead things festering.

And there she is, in bed, a fragile, unmoving shape in the gloom of her bedroom. Mother lies silently, head resting on the pillow, her eyes closed.

"Mother?" I inquire, and when she opens her eyes and nods at me, I help her to sit up.

I feed her, and she doesn't object. I wipe her dribble off, brush her hair, and tuck thick blankets around her. When she is done eating, she breaks into a smile, her eyes fixed on something distant.

"Mother," I whisper, the brush in my hands shaking.

"Nina." Her voice is weak, a murmur, like the breath of a child, difficult to decipher. Her eyes are so wide and so violet, I wonder if she sees something beyond this world. "Bert isn't coming, is he?" There is no trace of her usual sadness or anguish. Instead her face is serene, as if she has finally found peace. "It's your fault, you know. You won't let him come through."

My hand, half suspended in the air with the brush, freezes midmotion. Why would she say something so cruel? The ghost of Father, his ghoulish shadow, stands between us. Mother and I never were close, but his death somehow divided us further. The breach between us is vast, and I don't think we'll ever repair it. I don't think Mother wants us to heal.

"Why are you so unkind to me?" I push the words out between my teeth.

"You know why. First, you ruined Amos. Now, you took Bert away from me."

"Amos ruined himself, Mother. He contracted a horrible disease because he chose lust over morality." I drop the brush onto the floor with a loud clank. She doesn't even flinch. I wonder if her heart beats faster. If her soul is starting to bleed. My own heart beats evenly as I continue. "And your Bert is dead. Gone. He rots in the ground." The words are hard, and she tenses as they fly out of my mouth and stab her between her ribs. One blade at a time. Later, I might wish I held my tongue. Maybe I'll wish I was the kind of daughter who chose not to hurt her own mother—but I'm too tired and too drained by her cruelty to pretend to be someone I'm apparently not.

She doesn't look at me, her gaze sliding away, as if trying to find something else to look at. How long has it been since she looked at my face, into my eyes? Probably since Father's funeral when I held her trembling hand.

I pick up the tray and leave. As I walk down the hallway, my fingers trail along the wallpaper, feeling its warmth against my skin. As if the house is trying to comfort me.

Chapter 14

The next day, after dinner, Leroy hands me the so-called Blue Book—a detailed compilation of information and stories about Omaha and the people who live here. For a fee, the book, bound in cracked brown leather with black bands on the spine, is passed from one traveling member of medium society to another. An intricate design of a snake embossed on the cover of the tome invokes an oddly menacing feeling. The ouroboros, a self-consuming serpent with hollow eyes and a jaw clenched around its own tail, symbolizes creation out of death.

"Even in death, there's life," Leroy explains when he pushes the book into my hands. "This book isn't something I share lightly." His eyes search my face, and, for a moment, I'm mesmerized by the contrast of his black lashes against his pale skin. "In truth, I haven't shared it with anyone. This tome is heavy with secrets. Including your family secrets."

My heart thuds somewhere in my throat as an intrusive thought throbs through me. How heavy are the secrets? I cast a wary glance at the book in my hands. "My family?"

"Nina," Leroy says softly. "You must understand the importance of this notebook. It costs a fortune because of what's on its pages. You're an integral and valuable part of our partnership. Trust is everything in our business." He steps closer. "I want to prepare you. It'll be shocking to read about the people you know. But it'll be agonizing to read about your own family." He takes my hand, the one holding the book, and his fingers gently stroke my knuckles. I look down, remembering how he touched my foot. The moment of heat. "Nina." Leroy's voice breaks through my thoughts, a note of impatience in his tone. "I don't want you to be hurt, but you will be." His fingers travel to my wrist. "And for that I'm deeply sorry."

I meet his eyes, now more intrigued than fearful of what I'm about to discover in the Blue Book. "I'll be all right. I know all our sins."

I go to my room and settle by a candle to study its handwritten pages. As soon as I start reading, a surge of curiosity mixed with excitement vibrates through me like a snapped piano chord. The first few chapters are dedicated to the Hollands and go as far back as Lizzie's grandparents. I discover that her grandfather died of a heart attack not in Omaha, but in Chicago, where he had a second family. The Hollands maintained he passed away surrounded by his Omaha family, but it was a lie. He died in Chicago, in bed with his second wife. She was twenty years younger than Lizzie's grandfather, and somehow the old man managed to sire three offspring. I almost laugh at this outrageous revelation. Instead of being sympathetic of Lizzie's shameful secret, all I feel is deep and hot resentment stirring inside my chest. Lizzie, oblivious to her family history, is living her life without any regrets or any concerns. Look at us now, Lizzie. My life has descended into a nightmare, while yours has not changed at all.

I keep turning the pages. The next chapters are about my family. The first one is about my brother, who didn't leave to New England to study—as everyone was told and no one believed—but to a facility in upstate New York to be treated for a venereal disease he caught in the shacks of the Burnt District. Leroy was right. It's an agony to read about Amos. The weight of the words is too much for me to bear. My family's life lies bare on the white pages. Leroy knows our sordid history, and not once has he mentioned it. Not a hint. Not a slip of the tongue. Was he sparing my feelings? Perhaps he didn't want to add more shame to my already rotten existence.

I sink deeper into the bed, drawing my knees to my chest. I turn the page with a twitching hand. Seeing Amos's name reopens the wounds, still raw and fresh and deep. Hot tears spring to my eyes. My heart is so tight with pain and longing, I cannot catch a breath.

When Amos was sent away, I asked Tilda to take me to the Burnt District. I wanted to see the place that seduced my brother, that he missed so much he couldn't stop going there over and over again. Tilda, deeply appalled by my asking, refused, telling me, "Your daddy will kill me if I do that." I insisted and even promised her a dollar. "I don't need your money, Miss. Ain't a place for you to see." But when I broke down in tears, she begrudgingly agreed. We went in the deep of the night, when the shadows were the blackest. I borrowed Tilda's church dress and her only hat.

She tried to warn me. She tried to stop me, but I didn't listen.

Tilda took me to the Cribs, set in the expansive alleys of Capitol Avenue between Ninth and Tenth Streets. We walked between shacks, brightly lit and the shades not drawn. Through the glass of large windows we looked inside, and I could see everything that took place in the rooms. The girls were so young, so scrawny, so frail, I couldn't stop shivering from horror. My heart turned into a rock inside my chest. Most of the girls appeared drunk. Some were missing teeth. A few had purple bruises and visible teeth marks on their skin.

It was the underworld of Omaha. It was hell. And my brother, my twin, was a part of it. I'll never forget how heavy my body felt with shame and disappointment in Amos. How I wished he was there, by my side, instead of Tilda, so I could shout and slap him senselessly. Clasping my mouth, I ran away from the Cribs, my breath trapped in my chest. I felt tainted and unclean for days. I couldn't comprehend how a place like the Cribs could exist. Who created it? To this day, I cannot understand why my brother chose lust and self-destruction over his bright and promising future. Why did he go there? Why did he participate in the atrocities I witnessed through the windows? Those girls were children handled like toys in the hands of grown men.

This book needs to burn. It must be destroyed. No one should ever touch it again. But the cursive of the written words mocks me, taunts me, and I turn the page.

The next chapter is about Mother. Reading her mental assessment is difficult. She is described as "of an unstable mind and susceptible to mediums." She frequented séances long before my father's accident. Something fiery and nasty stirs within me when I read a recommendation to approach Mother slowly but persistently and through someone she already knows well—the Hollands.

I grab the candle and storm into Leroy's bedroom, willing myself to sound calm. I drop the book on his bed. "The information goes back years ago. Who wrote it?"

Leroy is standing by the window, dressed in shirtsleeves and his usual black trousers. His lips twitching in a suppressed smile, he watches me pace between the door and his bed. "Miss Wilson, it's late. I was undressing." He slowly drapes his jacket over the back of a chair, a bemused smile on his face. "I've warned you it'll be upsetting. Even infuriating. Every city, every town, has a book. A record."

"Who writes in this?" My hand is shaking when I point at the book.

"When a spiritualist leaves the town, he adds his own stories to the book, which is sold to the next arriving medium."

"There is the story of my brother," I say, shame burrowing like a worm deep underneath my skin, making me blush. "My mother. And Lizzie's grandfather."

"Most of the town is in the book."

"But how is this information obtained? It's family matters. I don't understand how such personal things could get out."

A muscle twitches in his jaw, as if he's suppressing a smile. "Household staff is always willing to talk if you pay them well." I think about how Tilda blushes bright crimson when she looks at Leroy. How eager she always is to serve him. No, she wouldn't talk. She's loyal to us. To me. "Let's not worry too much about the book." He smiles as he moves closer, forcing me backward until I'm pressed against the wall. "You're in possession of the dirtiest society secrets. How does it make you feel, Miss Wilson? You have all the power to bring your enemies to their knees." He's inches away, and I smell the familiar scent of his earthy aftershave. He braces his arms against the wall, one hand above each of my shoulders. "So enough with the indignation already." He delicately tucks a curl behind my ear. "Focus on our profitable arrangement instead and what you can do with all that knowledge you acquired."

"Indignation?" I lift my chin and meet his gaze. His warm breath brushes over my skin. Something awakens inside me at his proximity. I cannot think what it is, but to look at him, to feel his heat, is driving me to experience a hunger for his touch so deep, my face is aflame with embarrassment. I'm also terrified. A proper lady isn't supposed to long for a man to touch her in the most inappropriate ways. "I'm rightfully upset. My family secrets are documented by a stranger. It's humiliating and painful."

His eyes linger on my lips, yet he doesn't attempt to kiss me. Instead, he pushes himself away from me, goes to the bed, and picks up the book. "This is your textbook." He pushes it into my limp hands. "Study it. Don't worry about *your* secrets. Not all of them are in this book."

"What do you mean?" I whisper.

"I mean you well," he says with a chuckle and waves his hand around. "Look around you. The Dawning might be knocked down next time the wind blows stronger. You need money for the repairs. And I'm giving you the way to make money to pay for the repairs."

My head is spinning. I feel naked under his inspecting gaze, all my wounds bleeding and gaping. The floor shifts beneath me as I tuck the book under my arm and turn on my heel. I leave the room without another word, stalk down the hallway, back to my bedroom.

Leroy might be a swindler and a liar, but he's right about one thing. The world of the ugliest, most shameful Omaha secrets lies open in front of me. It's all been documented and passed from hand to hand for

God knows how long. I read more pages, study more Omaha secrets, but I always go back to the lines about my family. Straining to read the words in the candlelight, sentences melting into streaks of ink, I scan the book, looking for more information about my parents. About Amos. Instead I find a page dedicated to the Rask family. I reread it twice, and then I stare, dead eyed, into the darkness.

In the following days leading up to our first séance, I start having a recurring dream in which I stand in front of the Dawning and watch it burn. The walls that withstood the financial crisis of the 1880s crumble with a deafening crash. The gravity of everything that happened to my family pulls on my shoulders like a rucksack full of rocks I will never be able to shake off. The vast ocean of grief pulls me down, and I fall to my knees, ashes swirling in the hot air.

Someone places a hand on my trembling shoulder, and I shriek.

"It's me." Tilda's voice whispers into my ear over the snapping of the fire as it rages before us. "The house is letting you go."

We look at the smoldering ruins. As if the house senses our stares, a low sound, like a moan, vibrates through the air, and the roof tumbles down. The shadows around the ruins deepen despite the bright flames. I sense him before I see his short, childish frame stepping away from the burning house.

How is it possible that he is alive and untouched by the fire?

"My God," Tilda mutters.

The boy's pale face is turned toward me. There are deep holes where his eyes should be, glowing yellow like the flames around him, and they look right through me, right into my soul, and I sense it again—his wrath, his sorrow, his desire for revenge. He knows who killed him. As if confirming my thoughts, he smiles, thin lips stretching taught. He strides steadily in my direction, as determined as ever, his shadow melting into the night.

Awareness of my impending death slithers under my skin like a cold snake in search of a home. I whimper and try to pull myself up, but the weight of his gaze is an iron wall that pushes me down.

Tilda slides her hands under my armpits and hauls me to my feet. "Take her." She offers me to the boy, her voice hollow. She's frightened out of her wits.

I try to push her away, to get away from the boy. "Let me go. I didn't know. I didn't know," my voice shouts through the night. The boy is twenty feet away. I glance upward, to the black sky illuminated by the flames, convinced I'm seeing it for the last time. "I'm sorry. I'm so sorry." Loud sobs erupt from my chest.

Return what's mine. A growl. He stops in front of me, his clawlike hands reaching out to my neck as if he intends to wrap himself around me. Suddenly, I'm not sure if he's seeking comfort or revenge. *Return what's mine.*

His name springs to my lips, unbidden. "Ollie."

The boy roars.

I jolt awake with a scream frozen in my throat, wild panic blooming inside me. The remnants of the dream linger like a heavy fog—the flames and Oliver Rask, his voice demanding that I return what's his.

Wrapping my arms around my torso, I frantically glance around. Velvet curtains are drawn over tall windows. Copper-colored furniture. A small round table by the window with a tea set in the middle. Crumbles of dry cake spread on the plate. The cool sheets are twisted around my feet, my fingers clenching the blanket to my chest.

The Dawning doesn't lie in ashes. I am in my bedroom, alone. The hazy morning sunlight breaks through the curtains in random strips of light. But I don't feel safe. The boy's words burn through my veins like a plague. *Return what's mine.* I have no idea what that means. Does he want his land back? His family is gone, and I don't know how to find them.

On the night of his death, John Rask came to see my father. He begged Father to annul their land lease agreement, begged him to return his farm he broke his back working in the mines to afford. Father's debts were mounting, and he was going to use the deed on the farm to pay off some of his bills. Knowing Father, I'm certain not a single kind thought crossed his mind when John Rask asked for the deed. Father always viewed farmers as some wildlings who lived off the land, a feral and uneducated bunch who were useful only when it came to crop collection and market days. The darkness released inside the Dawning when my father threw Mr. Rask out. And when Mr. Rask stumbled drunkenly into the creek that night, the Dawning must've reshaped itself, taking in his sorrow and desperation and shame. When Ollie ran into the same creek to save his drowning father, the gloom settled comfortably in our hallways.

The house rattles weakly, as if confirming my thoughts.

Chapter 15

Five days before the séance, Tilda posts the invitations.

It is supposed to be a small gathering, only friends of the family. *Former* friends. People who abandoned us a long time ago. Memories pass through my mind like a kaleidoscope of pictures—grainy and worn—Father handing a check to Judge Thomas, patting him on the shoulder with a smile. Amos and Bobby walking into the night, my brother looking over his shoulder and pressing two fingers to his forehead, saluting me a goodbye. Mrs. Holland and Mother taking a ride in the Hollands' carriage down Farnam Street, laughing. The pipes rattle in the walls and snap me out of my reverie. I'm not sure anyone will come, considering our nonexistent social status. But Leroy has no doubt everyone invited will be in attendance.

At midnight, Leroy knocks on my door and asks me to get dressed for a walk to the cemetery. Tilda insists on accompanying me. "Not proper to be alone with a man under the cover of the night. Especially a man like Mr. Marshall," she says when I try to convince Tilda her presence isn't necessary. I spend most of my time with Leroy. What does it matter now? "Whatever he wants to show you at the cemetery ain't right. I must be there so he doesn't get any inappropriate ideas." I almost laugh at that. What can he possibly do to me in the cemetery that he cannot do in the Dawning? I agree reluctantly.

"Tilda will accompany us to the graveyard," I tell Leroy, who's waiting for us by the front door.

Leroy nods, winks at Tilda, and holds the door for us as we walk out into the frigid October night. "Not afraid of cemeteries?" he asks her, his voice hushed, and something in the way he says it makes the hairs stand up on the back of my neck.

"Not in the slightest," Tilda answers with a laugh. Her footsteps are light, like she cannot wait for this walk through the town to the Prospect Hill Cemetery. Her eagerness is surprising. What happened to the superstitious woman who whispered tales about the ghosts? She's full of contradictions, it seems.

Outside, a trace of upcoming winter bites my cheeks and makes my eyes water. As we exit the gate, Leroy pulling it back, the rusty hinges screeching, the road turns into a familiar narrow path. It slopes slightly downhill between prairies and farm fields for maybe a mile. Then the path broadens, the fields draw away, and we are in the open space, not far away from the Rask farm.

Leroy's walk is brisk, and his stride is long. It's hard to keep up, and Tilda and I fall slightly behind.

As we approach the Rask estate, the air grows heavier, the night grows deeper, the moonlight not as bright as a few minutes ago. An odd mist swirls violently around their house's roof, as if something alive is trying to get inside. Or swallow it up. My heart sinks to the ground, and I come to a halt in the middle of the path.

The fields and prairies shift, alive and sinister. Pitiless. They crawl closer and closer, a wall of weeds reaching out to us, growing taller and thicker. Their suffocating mass is about to spill into the road. My heart seizes. The mossy, rotten smell is clinging to my skin, my clothes, burning my eyes. The air is filled with malice, the kind that no natural being can feel. It is as black as the night, and it is conjured by deepest wrongs and darkest sins.

For a moment it is all too much—the gloom closing down upon us and the air whispering its incessant tidings of doom. I stand still, tethered above my own body, and all I want to do is throw myself onto the ground and let the earth become me.

"Miss." Tilda's voice pierces the air. "What's wrong?"

"Do you feel it, Tilda?" I whisper hoarsely. My tongue barely moving in my mouth, fumbling against my teeth.

"The air stinks something rotten," she says slowly. "An animal must've died in the field. Dead things in this field. Dead." Her words have a strange rhythm, more of a slow chant than a normal sentence. But she's right. The odor is unpleasant—sweet and sickly. Pungent and not human. "We must go." She points at Leroy, who keeps on walking, never slowing, never pausing, his tall frame masked in shadows and moonlight.

I don't move. Instead, I stare at the Rask house, scowling at the night. "There's something in there. And it's watching us." Suddenly a rush of small birds startles into the cloudless sky, just above the roof. "Look, Tilda, birds. In the middle of the night. How odd."

"Something must've scared them off." She shrugs. "Whatever it is, we must walk. Ain't safe here."

"So you feel it, then?"

She looks at me firmly. "The Rasks buried their father and their son in the farmland. There's a lot of sorrow here. A lot of death." She pauses, and I can hear my own breath, my pulse beating in my temples. "Everything stopped growing after that. Their animals died. No matter what they did, their crops kept on dying too. Then the locusts came. That was disastrous." She shrugs again. "They had to leave. Some places are not meant for the living." I've heard those words before. For a moment, we catch each other's eyes, and I see an expectation in hers. The anticipation of my acknowledgment that the Rask farm is like the Dawning. A place not meant for the living.

As if in response, the air gets colder, its embrace tighter.

When I don't say anything, she pulls on my sleeve, and I force myself to put one foot in front of the other, my limbs stiff and heavy, as if invisible chains are affixed to the soles of my shoes. As the distance between us and the Rask farm grows, the air clears, the fields recede, and we finally enter the edges of Omaha and the narrow unpaved path that snakes between houses and back alleys. We turn onto a hard-packed dirt road, only the moon in the starless sky lighting our way. Omaha's new construction has prospered in the past decade, bringing more brick and stone buildings into the city, but the air, sharp with chill, still smells of manure.

To occupy my mind with anything but the Rask farm, I turn to Leroy. "Mr. Marshall, did you use any of your tricks at your séance at the Hollands'? You knew what my mother had written in her note."

Leroy, who has been strangely quiet for most of the walk, now sighs softly at my question. "I didn't use any tricks, Miss Wilson." He rubs his fingers contemplatively on his chin. "Your father spoke to me that night."

I glance at Tilda, who gives Leroy a sharp assessment through her long eyelashes. A moment later, she looks at me and nods. I take a short breath of relief. "Why do you think Father answered your call at the séance? He was a very rational man. He didn't believe in anything otherworldly. Not even in God." I shake my head, shoving my cold hands into the pockets of my coat. "He barely tolerated Mother's obsession with mediums."

"Perhaps he didn't mind because he had his own vices. Far more expensive."

Gambling. My father frequented poker games while my mother spent her time at spiritual gatherings, talking to the dead.

Leroy whirls and steps in front of me, taking me firmly by the shoulders and examining my face, his brows pulled together. "Let's focus on our lessons, Miss Wilson. We'll talk about that night in due time."

In due time. That's all I seem to get when I try to push for more explanation.

At the cemetery we walk among the dead and take notes of names, dates, and the condition of the tombstones. Some died at a natural age, well into their sixties. But some graves contain children, their time on this earth cut short. The saddest are the graves with mothers and their newborn children.

A breeze, light like a child's breath, tangles in my hair and trails the back of my neck. My skin crawls as I slowly trudge through the death. The air teems with hushed whispers, and I wonder if the dead are trying to talk to me. My hands curl tightly into fists in my coat pockets. Nails biting into skin. My gaze dances restlessly from one grave to another, from one chipped tombstone to another, from marble angels to engravings. I follow Leroy and Tilda, a few paces behind, my shoes sinking into the dirt still wet from the rain the day before. Leroy crouches to check a name on a grave, and he says something over his shoulder, but I cannot distinguish his words. Tilda makes a sign of the cross. Leroy chuckles and says something else; his voice is muffled, the sentences garbled, as if he's talking underwater. A thin white mist swirls around my ankles. The air grows cuttingly cold, and the breeze stills. I look over my shoulder, and there is a child, a little girl in a simple white dress with white flowers in her hair, standing by one of the graves, staring at me.

"Oh my God," I cry out, forgetting all my manners. Mind-numbing dread rolls in my chest, tightening my lungs. Tilda and Leroy whirl to look at me. "There's a girl by the Sinclair grave. It must be their daughter, Helene." I remember the names clearly, as we just spent five minutes studying their resting place.

They both look back at the grave. Tilda's hand presses against her open mouth. Leroy curses under his breath.

"Helene?" I ask the girl, who keeps staring at us silently. Then she lifts her tiny foot and stamps it on the ground. "Leroy." My pulse is a hammer in my temples as I seize his arm and pull him toward me like a shield. "She's angry." A tremor in my voice underscores the fear in my words. "Oh my God."

For an instant—a short heartbeat—confusion clouds Leroy's face before amazement quickly replaces it. "I wonder what Helene wants to tell you."

"You want me to talk to her?" My voice pitches high, piercing the night. The idea is preposterous. And insane. "Why don't *you* talk to her?" A sharp, penetrating chill slides down my spine as the girl lifts her hand and points a finger, gnarled and pockmarked with rot. Her lips stretch; she opens her mouth, and a snakelike hiss, long and screeching, ripples through the night. "You do it. She's pointing at you, I think. And you have more practice than I."

His shoulders slope slightly when he says, "Perhaps not tonight."

There is something sorrowful in his words, and I almost want to follow his suggestion and indulge my own curiosity and ask the girl if she has anything to convey to the world of the living, but when I open my mouth, what comes out is, "I won't do it."

"Are you afraid, Miss Wilson?"

A torrent of thoughts, mostly about the Rask farm, courses through me, washing away my curiosity about the girl. The idea that one's spirit floats around the earth, watching our affairs, listening to our conversations, is too much to stomach at the moment. "I think there are forces in this world we are not supposed to address." It's a struggle to keep my voice from trembling. "Especially in the middle of the night in a cemetery."

His chuckle is low. His eyes gleam mischievously under the moonlight. "You might be right about that. But the girl is here now, and she wants to talk."

"Do we have to talk to her?" Tilda asks, looking at the Sinclair grave, pulling her thick shawl around her shoulders. "I'd rather go home. I don't like it here."

"Soon," Leroy says. "Miss Wilson, ask the girl a question. See if she replies."

I shake my head so violently, I'm surprised my neck doesn't break. The girl and I look at each other wordlessly. Her mouth is moving, but no words come out, only a barely audible, incessant hiss. "I can't," I whisper.

Leroy eyes me briefly, and something resembling raw amusement passes across his face. "As you wish, Miss Wilson." He turns to the girl and asks, "What do you want, Helene?" His voice travels loudly, almost offensively so in the quiet of the cemetery, down the alley to the Sinclair tombstone where the girl stands. And something inside me gives way at his words. He sees the girl too. The frightening thoughts of me going mad, following in my mother's footsteps, lose their sharp edges.

The moon emerges from the clouds. Its light catches the pale curve of the girl's cheek, and I see how her eyes dim and her face fades. She's gone before I take a full inhale.

"She's gone," I whisper. "Why do you think she didn't answer you?"

"We'll never know," he says softly. "They never really tell us everything we want to know."

Chapter 16

The city hall clock chimes at two o'clock, and Leroy points at the cemetery gates. "I want you to meet someone, Miss Wilson. An associate of mine."

"Right now? Here?" I ask, surprised.

"Indeed." He looks up and down the alley, his gaze skipping over Tilda. "Tilda, dear, will you wait in the alley by the gates? My associate likes privacy."

Tilda shoots me a questioning look, and I nod obligingly.

"I'll be right here." Tilda points at the tall birch tree. "I'll wait until you call for me." Her lips are pinched. Her brow furrows in concern.

Leroy and I make our way toward the main entrance. A tall figure leans on the high iron cemetery gates. A man dressed in a gray topcoat, fitted with metal buttons too big and too tasteless for my liking. His eyes glint under a gray cap that is pulled tightly onto his forehead, a smoldering cigarette stuck in the corner of his mouth. His shoes are caked with mud, as if he also has trudged through the back alleys.

He sees us approaching and rolls his shoulders, reminding me of someone, but I can't recall where I saw him. He's shorter than Leroy and stockier. The way he moves, the way he angles himself—hunching forward slightly as if trying to make himself smaller—is familiar. I wish I could see his face, but his cap is pulled too low, and the night is too black.

The man nods at Leroy, turns to face me, uneasiness crossing his face. There is a recognition in his eyes. He knows who I am. His jaw tenses as he studies me for a long minute. "What is she doing here?" As he speaks, I catch a whiff of stale tobacco and two-day-old ale. I keep my eyes on him, but I'm suddenly painfully aware of my thinning coat and scuffed shoes and the stray hair brushing across my face.

"Miss Wilson is my new understudy," Leroy says. He puts his hand against my lower back, pressing slightly, urging me to step forward, closer to the man. "I live with the Wilsons now. But you already know that."

Weaving his brows together, the man looks down at me in silence, chewing on his lower lip. "I thought they're moving away. Was I mistaken—"

"You were mistaken." Leroy cuts him off. "This is James." Leroy looks at me briefly.

I nod at James, who doesn't acknowledge my greeting.

"Understudy, huh?" The man's heavy gaze is fixed on me, as if he's trying to read my mind. "I thought you didn't take students. Or it was just me you never wanted, I reckon." Fixing me with his suspicious gaze, James takes off his cap and runs his hand through his short hair. There is a thick silver ring on his index finger, carved with what looks like Latin letters. He shifts his weight awkwardly from one foot to the other. "If you have her, what do you need from me?"

"We're hosting a séance next Friday," Leroy says.

"You know the tricks?" James turns to me. The cold hostility in his bloodshot eyes is surprising. The man doesn't know me, yet he already resents me.

"Miss Wilson talks to the dead," Leroy interjects, not giving me a chance to respond. "She's a new medium. However, I need you there, James," Leroy says. "To make sure everything goes well. Same appearance as usual. A grieving father who lost his son."

The man spits on the ground and shakes his head. "If she talks to the dead, why do you need me?"

"The dead can be unpredictable." I repeat the lesson Leroy was so clear to deliver. "They might not want to consort with us."

James looks at me as if I sprouted multiple heads. "Unpredictable? What's that now?" He looks at Leroy. "Is she fucking with me?"

"Watch your language, James." Leroy wrinkles his nose, as if he just smelled something foul. "Come to the house next Friday. Same price as before. Three dollars. Same act. A father in the deep throes of grief."

I remember James then. At the Hollands', he was the man who wanted to know how his son was doing after death. I thought he was the father of one of the boys who drowned last summer. It was all an act—and, I have to admit, an excellent and convincing one.

"I remember you. You were very believable. You have children of your own?" I ask sharply. I feel a part of some scheme that has been revealed to me only in bits and pieces, and I'm not sure I like it. But there's no way out of it because I'd do anything to save my family name. To save the Dawning. But James looks like a criminal, and I don't appreciate Leroy's association with him.

James leans one shoulder against the gates, his cigarette still smoldering in his mouth. "Never had no children." His lips peel away from his teeth in a scowl.

"You're a fake," I say.

A strange expression crosses Leroy's face, surprised and rigid, as if he's fearful of what I might say or do next. I've seen him do his parlor tricks, and I've seen him chant and soothe Mother with his odd prayers, but I've never seen him afraid.

"Ain't that the point?" James growls.

"Enough," Leroy cuts in. "Can we rely on you, James?"

"If James doesn't want to come, we will manage without him." I put as much resentment and bitterness into my voice as I can muster. "We don't need him, and we don't need to waste our money."

"What about your unpredictable dead?" James raises a brow at me. "What are you going to do if there's no one to talk to? What will your guests think of you, Missy?"

I jut my chin out. "That's what the Blue Book is for." My mind floods with images of me reading notes and telling lies to my guests about their dead family members, and I feel guilty and ashamed. For a heartbeat. Then I remember how these people treated us like we were a crusted piece of horse manure on their boots, and it occurs to me that maybe the book might be a part of something I haven't considered until now—a possibility of having power over their pathetic lives.

Maybe I should run away from this, but I don't want to. Maybe there are other solutions to our financial problems, but I can't see any at the moment. And it all boils down to one truth—I need money to pay the tax bill.

"She has the book?" James turns to Leroy, his hands curled into fists at his side. "You never let me touch it. Always so careful. And you gave it to *her*?"

"James," Leroy says softly, but there is steel in his voice. "The book is mine. Don't forget that." He draws himself taller, as if preparing for a fight. "I do with it as I please. Do you need money or not?"

James regards us for a long minute as he pulls on his cigarette and blows the smoke into our faces. "I'm going to ask my dead son about my sick wife. See if she's going to join him soon. Maybe you can spin some tales about me. About my homelife."

"Good." Leroy nods. "It should work just as well. We'll come up with a script. Any new deaths in town?"

James scratches his chin, thinking. "There was a late-night stabbing at the White Horse saloon. Over a wench, a moll on the turf. One of the sons of the local judge, the youngest one, got shanked. Heard he was using happy dust."

I don't understand a word he's saying. It must be some kind of street dialect. My heart drops at the mention of the youngest son of the local judge. He was only a couple of years older than me. "Andrew Thomas?" I danced with Andrew once or twice at a Christmas gala hosted by the Hollands. I always felt weak in my knees at the sight of tall, handsome

Andrew. But then Bobby entered my life, and I forgot about the gray-eyed boy who loved to dance. "Is he dead?"

James nods, eyes gleaming. He doesn't even try to hide his excitement at the prospect of a fresh death.

"You knew the boy?" Leroy asks me.

"I . . . do . . . did. We cannot use Andrew's death. It's despicable. It's not right."

James stares at me, his face stone dead.

Leroy steps closer, leaning toward my ear as if he's about to share a secret. "Think about your tax bill, Miss Wilson. Taxes don't wait. They don't have a conscience. They only have a due date." His warm breath brushes over my cheek. "Think about where you'll take your invalid mother when the bank repossesses the house. Will you live on the streets? Perhaps work in the brothels your brother loved so much?"

My eyes start to burn, and I turn away from both men. I hate Leroy for his directness, for his unnecessary cruelty. I bite down on my lower lip because in my heart, I know he is right. My pulse pounds thunderously in my temples at the thought of us losing the Dawning. Leroy might be insensitive, but he's correct about one thing. I'm going to do whatever it takes to pay that tax bill.

"We start at midnight this Friday," Leroy says to James. "It's a small gathering. And, Miss Wilson, let's make sure to send an invitation to the Thomas family. Address it to the mistress of the house."

We turn away, and I wave at Tilda to let her know we are ready to leave. Both men turn in her direction, and as I glance at James, who's looking ahead, eyes narrowed, a tense expression on his face, I know why he resents me so much and why I feel frightened of him. His profile is partially hidden in the shadows, and as my eyes trace over the familiarity of his features, the slope of his shoulders, I see a thick scar behind his right ear. My heart skips a beat or two as I realize I'm looking at one person I hoped to never see again.

The intruder.

My throat constricts. My head pounds. Something bad is about to happen.

I grab Leroy by the sleeve of his jacket and pull him away from James. "Leave now," I hiss.

"What's going on? Is there another ghost?" he asks me in a strangely clipped voice but follows me into the streets.

"Tilda! We're leaving!" I scream over my shoulder and yank Leroy deeper into the night. "Get away from James." I half run and tug and pull, and Leroy, brows raised high, follows my lead. Tilda sees us fleeing down the street and runs to catch up with us.

"What's happening?" Leroy asks between his steps. "Slow down for a minute. Tell me. Are you seeing the girl again? Is she following us?"

"Don't stop." I look over my shoulder to see if James is still by the gates, watching our sudden retreat. But he's nowhere in sight. "James is not who you think he is."

As soon as we round the corner of the street, Leroy stops abruptly, and I run into his wide chest.

"What do you mean?"

Tilda finally catches up with us. "What happened?" she asks, gasping for air.

"James is the intruder. I recognized him. He's the one who was in Father's study that night."

"I see." Leroy pauses, as if trying to find words. He meets Tilda's eyes briefly, and I see something like an understanding pass between them. "You're right. It was him that night. I suspected it for a while now. Maybe he was looking for me. Maybe he was looking for the Blue Book. He's been trying to talk me into selling it, but he doesn't have enough money," Leroy says with a heavy sigh. "I apologize for what happened that night. It was an unfortunate set of circumstances. I hoped, like the fool that I am, you'd never find out."

A heat, scorching and overwhelming, breaks out all over my body. A flash of fury at Leroy in his crisp jacket and combed hair; his cool, dry demeanor; and the suggestion in his words that I am smarter, more observant, and definitely more logical than he expected. "You're taking me for a fool," I say, my voice low. "You think I'm some naive society girl who's so wrapped up in her grief she cannot see further than her nose."

"I never took you for a fool, Miss Wilson. I'm sorry it came to this. This is all on me. I should've told you about James sooner."

"You tried to convince me he was a spirit. Why?" It's getting tiresome to uncover more and more of Leroy's lies. Will there be a time when he's completely honest with me? Will I ever be able to fully trust him? I laid everything bare in front of him—almost everything—but he remains a closed door.

Tilda clears her throat. "I saw James in town a few times, Miss. Before I came to live in the Dawning." Her tone is glib, but I catch a glint of hardness in her eyes as she looks up at me. "He's rough and stupid but ain't dangerous. All he wants is money."

"Are you sure?" I ask her.

She watches me closely when she says, "I am, Miss."

"What do you want me to do to make it right?" Leroy asks softly.

"Don't lie to me. Ever again."

"Miss Wilson," Leroy says, his eyes boring deep into mine. "Every night since that night, I walk the grounds to make sure the house is safe. James won't be getting in. I make sure of it."

"You walk the grounds?" As he nods in response, my anger releases its hold, and something else thaws in my chest, something that was there since the night James jumped out the window. I don't know if Leroy means to protect me and Mother or if he's helping himself by keeping James away from the Dawning and his precious book, but my chest aches with a mix of anger and gratitude regardless.

Chapter 17

The sins documented in the Blue Book creep inside my mind, casting a shameful but compelling allure. I carve out time, a stolen moment here and there, and sneak into my bedroom to take a peek at the book. And once I begin, I cannot stop. Every time I close the Blue Book, I promise myself not to think about the shameful things—and these things are always ugly and shameful—that fill the pages. But the book is like a vast pool of water beckoning me in the desert. I dare not drink it all. Yet I cannot help myself, and I go back for more and more, and it's never enough to satisfy my thirst.

Three days before the séance, I open the Blue Book and read about Bobby Walker and his visits to the Cribs. As it turns out, it wasn't just Amos who frequented the brothels. The man I agreed to marry, the man who broke my heart, has a mistress. Her name is Peach. I repeat her name a few times, my voice full of hurt and outrage. The society men who smiled and nodded approvingly at my father and who congratulated me on my engagement are the same men, steeped in sin, who'd rather spend their time in Omaha's underbelly than with their own families.

How little I knew about the men in my life.

Needing a distraction from my grim thoughts, I stretch my legs, throw my blanket to the side, and slide out of bed. I pad over to the window, pull the heavy velvet curtains aside—the next item on my list of things to sell if our séance fails—and look out into the trees. My heart flutters. Dark, wide-set eyes gape at me through the glass. A starkly pale face. Sharp cheekbones. It takes me a few seconds to realize I'm staring at my own reflection. I avert my gaze to the gray October sky, where dense clouds hang low to the ground. Not even a hint of hazy sunshine.

An odd sense that something or someone is watching me from the line of trees below my window settles in my chest. I scan the landscape, looking for the stocky figure of James, but there is nothing in the density of trees. Just the sky and the breeze and a distant chirping of birds.

How enraging and sickening it is that I must open our house to people who openly loathe my family and who flood Omaha with their poisonous sins. People who'll be attending our séance built their lives from my father's favors and his land speculation. When he died and his debts became our inheritance, they did their damnedest to make sure our pleas for help were never heard while they continued committing their crimes in the name of profit and lust.

I lean forward to examine myself, and the person looking back at me from the window glass doesn't look weak and wavering. She looks like a woman on a mission—eyes wide open, brows drawn together, and jaw set firmly. Then why do I feel so feeble? Why do my knees shake every time I imagine myself talking to the guests?

As if in response to my thoughts, my bedroom door opens wide, its rusty hinges creaking. I whip around, fear pulling hard on my insides. No one is at the door. It's just me and the house, breathing together.

Make them pay. A whisper in my head. The ceiling shudders. *Make them pay.*

My stomach clenches with fury as I picture women and men who are soon to step across our threshold and exude their fake sincerity and spew their greetings with forced smiles.

"I will," I murmur back to the house. "I definitely will." I know their most disgraceful secrets.

The door slams shut. A flock of birds springs from the trees and takes off to the sky, screeching noisily. I watch the birds disappear into the darkening clouds.

"Bert!" A piercing wail breaks the silence of the house. "Bert!"

I run to the door, wrenching it wide open in time to see Mother turn the corner. She's in her wedding dress again, barefoot below the ripped hem of her dress. As she rounds the corner, I catch a glimpse of her pale face and long, tangled hair, and my heart shrinks from fear.

"Mother?" I follow her, but she is so fast, unnaturally fast, her feet making no sound on the floorboards. "Mother." I can barely breathe as I run down the hallway that seems to have no end.

She doesn't look at me, but she pauses at the staircase and looks down over the railing, shakes her head, and starts climbing the stairs to the third floor.

"Bert," she moans. "I'm coming, darling. I'm almost there."

My God, what is she doing? I leap after her, taking two steps at a time, but before I can reach her, she suddenly halts in the middle of the staircase and looks right at me. "Don't you dare." She leans against the banister and looks down.

"What are you doing?" I rasp, my hand on the railing slick with cold sweat. It slips, and I lose my balance and go down to my knees, slamming hard on the stone. Pain is sharp and overwhelming, and everything goes out of focus for a few seconds. "Mother." I breathe through the agony. "Please stop. I beg you."

"You were always such a disappointment, Nina," she says calmly, her eyes fused to the abyss below.

She leans farther, and for a single breath—a horribly slow slice of time—I believe this is the last time I'll see her alive. I don't know if I scream or try to crawl to her up the stairs because everything is a blur and the darkness is closing in, and all I hear is a thunderous pounding in my head. But then Leroy appears—summoned by all the screams, no doubt—and pulls Mother away from the edge. She cries, an awful howling, as if he's truly tearing her away from Father. I never heard her scream like this before, not even in Father's study when I thought she had gone completely mad. I scramble to my shivering feet and somehow manage to move, to run up to Leroy and Mother, and together we guide her to her bedroom.

"You can't stop me. He's waiting." Mother's voice is thick with anger and misery.

"Elise, Bert's not waiting for you. He's moved on," Leroy says in a soft voice usually reserved for his chants. His black hair is brushed away from his forehead. There are beads of sweat on his furrowed brow.

"I don't believe you. Not anymore," Mother says, her lips pressed resolutely. Her face contorts into a painful mask of grief and longing and raw pain.

We put her to bed, and for some unexplainable reason, she doesn't resist. I find a tincture Dr. Fuller gave her on the day of Father's funeral and mix it with water. Leroy and I stay with Mother until she falls asleep.

"What are you going to do?" Leroy asks me as soon as we're alone in the hallway.

"I need time to think."

"You don't have much time." Something inscrutable passes in his eyes, vanishing before I can read it. "Nina." He takes my hand, and I don't pull away. The warmth of his touch is soothing. "You're not equipped to deal with this. No one is. Unless your mother gets treatment, medical treatment, it will end badly." I flinch at his words and wrench my hand away from him.

Sorrow swells in my heart as I realize I have no choice anymore. I swallow hard because I need to get rid of the rotten aftertaste of my broken promise to Amos. I look at Leroy, and he understands the unspoken ask, all things unsaid—or maybe things that could not be said out loud—running under the surface of my thoughts.

"Call Dr. Fuller as soon as possible. Don't think about the cost. I'll take care of it. I couldn't help Elise as much as I hoped to. Your father . . . his spirit is unpredictable. Even difficult. So consider it a payback for your hospitality and my failure."

I don't offer him anything in response. I know doing nothing, pretending Mother's going to get better, is irresponsible. Suddenly, I'm gripped with an exhaustion so deep it almost brings me to my knees. "I need to think," I whisper hoarsely. Then I walk around him as if he were just a fixture standing in the middle of the hallway. The walls murmur softly as I put one foot in front of the other. I keep my body moving toward my room like a windup doll, my heels sinking into the thin carpet. The urgency of my decision nips at my feet like a wild dog, reminding me of my promise to Amos.

Chapter 18

The day before the séance, with an acute awareness of my betrayal, I let my mother go.

In the morning, I send Tilda for Dr. Fuller and ask him to take Mother away to a clinic where she can heal properly. I warn him that it won't be an easy task to convince her to leave the Dawning, but he assures me he knows how to handle women in her condition. His statement frightens me, as I don't know what he means by that. But I do not change my mind, for what other choice do I have? We set a time for his visit.

My words are thick with unshed tears when I ask Tilda to prepare Mother. That afternoon, I sign the papers, and Dr. Fuller examines Mother. It doesn't take long before her screams pierce the air. Her wails, punctuated by the doctor's low voice consoling her, are the sounds of our life collapsing around us. It is weird and lonely, and it all feels surreal, as if I'm watching a theatrical show unfold in front of me: the doctor's soothing words and soft gestures, the loud clacking of tincture bottles, the heavy movements of orderlies in Mother's bedroom.

Unmoving, I stand silently at the door, only the threshold separating us, a wide divide. At some point, disturbed by the noise, Leroy and Tilda come to the hallway, but I ask them to go. Leroy nods solemnly and doesn't say a word. He simply turns around and strolls back to his room. But Tilda lingers. I can feel the itch of her stare between my shoulder blades.

"It's the right thing to do," she says into my back. Her words are careful. Her voice is gentle, as if she's afraid to break me. "It's hard, but it's also right."

I don't say anything, just turn around, and she pulls me into an embrace. Her blond hair is tied into a bun on the top of her head. She's wearing a simple frock, and her apron is ironed and clean. She smells of something earthy—like witch hazel—and soap. I put my head on her shoulder and close my eyes. We stand, unmoving, for a while. There's a catch in her breath as if she's suppressing a shudder. She must be as devastated as I am. The thought grips at my heart, squeezing it.

"Miss Wilson," Dr. Fuller says from the door. "It won't be long now."

Tilda withdraws from me, and I force myself to let her go. When she leaves, I'm left alone, and the house feels frigid and small. Dr. Fuller gives Mother some tincture, and she lies motionless in bed. Her sweaty locks cling to her pale neck. The wild look she gives me when I enter her bedchamber cripples me, and I lean on the wall to support my suddenly leaden body. She stares at me, her lips moving soundlessly, her birdlike hands lost among the sheets. Her eyelids hang heavy. She blinks once, twice. Her last words before closing her eyes are about Father.

The orderlies take her away.

I'm on the front porch when the breeze caresses my face. My skin feels wet; I must be crying. My fingers fumble with the collar of my dress as I think about the things I've done and the things I am about to do. The doctor's carriage disappears out of my view, but I remain on the porch. Will Mother ever find forgiveness in her heart? She never forgave my past transgressions. Why would she forgive me for this?

The world blurs at the edges as I continue to gaze into the twilight, though what or who I'm hoping to see there I do not know. I dig my nails deep inside my palms so hard that pain flashes through me like a blinding white mass. Mother shut me out a long time ago, but I hoped—a morbid, dreadful thing to hope for—that Father's death would bind us together. I thought she'd need me to hold on to. How wrong I was. She never truly loved me—I knew that for most of my life. Her tolerance of me was brittle, and it came apart as soon as she lost everything. She had built a wall around herself, and I was not the one who could tear it down. I became a constant reminder of everyone she had lost, and she in turn became a constant reminder of love I've never had.

The wind strengthens its grip on me, lashing through the trees, whipping my dress around my knees. With a deep sigh, I turn around and go inside the Dawning. I've done everything I could to salvage our family, but only now do I realize nothing was salvageable. There is no regret, no sadness, not even sorrow. Just immense relief.

Inside, Leroy is setting out a row of candles. "We need to say a proper farewell to your mother," he says. The flames flicker as he continues to light the candles.

"I said my goodbyes already." Everything looks out of focus. I might still be crying. "She'll be back." My voice wavers. I'm not sure I believe my own words. "It's all temporary."

He looks up at me, apprehension sliding across his face, and sets a candle on the mantelpiece. "It's a different kind of goodbye. You need closure. Your mother needed it, too, but unfortunately I failed to provide it. Let me give it to you. Living in this house alone, with all your family gone—it must be difficult. I know how you feel. Let me help."

Anger spikes in my chest. The audacity of him, to think he knows anything about what it's like to be my mother's daughter. To live in this house. "Mother isn't dead, and I don't need any closure."

I turn away and take the endless stairs to my bedroom, where the door swings open before I can touch it. My fingers strike the doorframe gently as I step inside, and the wood creaks, welcoming me into the safety of my room.

On the day of the séance, I receive an unexpected gift.

"What is it?" I ask and point my chin at the package in Tilda's hands.

Leroy puts a lit candle on the bedside table. "It's time to get dressed. The guests will be arriving shortly."

The guests are scheduled to arrive at eleven, with the séance to begin at midnight. Dr. Fuller sent a note to inform me that Mother settled well, and according to him, she spends most of her time sleeping. I haven't left my room since her departure, ignoring Leroy's reminders about lessons and his insistent requests to come down for meals.

"Are you all right?" He talked to me through the door last night. "Should we postpone our gathering?"

"I've been better," I said, pressing my forehead on the wooden door. "I'll be ready."

I'm indeed ready, with the help of some whiskey.

"Your dress, Miss." Tilda reaches out to me, holding the package on her palms.

"My dress?" I look at Leroy, who nods, confirming. "But I didn't order any dress."

"I did." Leroy puts a hand on my lower back, urging me to move forward, toward Tilda and the dress. The room grows uncomfortably silent; even the floorboards don't groan when I take the packet from Tilda, put it on the bed, and slowly unwrap it. The dress is made from the most exquisite silk and the softest lace my fingers ever touched. The material billows in my hands like a weightless cloud of luxury. A stitched pattern of black roses on spiky vines covers the dress. The sleeves are long but sheer; my pale skin will glow in the dancing candlelight. I brush my hand over the bodice. The black roses grow denser from the chest down until they blur into a massive wave of spikes and vines that resemble a nest of serpents crawling down the dress.

"It must be worth a fortune," I mutter, stunned. "I cannot afford this."

"The cost is not an issue," Leroy says. His eyes move from the dress sprawled on the bed to my face, trailing every inch of my neck, my mouth, and my cheeks, and finally meeting my gaze. A day or two ago, under his scrutiny, a heat would have built in my belly. But today, all I feel is emptiness. "Do you like the dress?" His voice is low and intimate. "I thought it would be perfect for tonight."

"It *is* perfect, even though it's quite extravagant. And not necessary. If I must wear a black dress, I can wear the dress I wore to my father's funeral."

"We sold that dress last month," Tilda pitches in from the door. "To pay the butcher."

Her words chip away at my dignity.

"If it's the cost you're worried about, don't. People respect money and good looks."

A proper young lady would not accept Leroy's gift. But I'm not a lady anymore. I'm his student, and I have to look my part. "I'll be downstairs shortly," I say, picking up the dress.

Leroy's full lips curve into a handsome smile as he leans forward and takes my hand. He turns it over and presses his lips into the center of my palm. "Wonderful," he says, not lifting his head. My heart's pounding in my ears so loud, I can barely hear him. "I'll see you downstairs," he exhales, and then he's gone from the room, and I'm alone with Tilda.

"You need me for anything?" she croaks. Her face has an odd look. "Help dressing?" Her hands are clenched into fists.

"Are you all right?" My fingers clutch the expensive silk defensively. "You seem upset."

She gives me a half shrug and purses her lips. Is that nerves? But when she finally looks at me, I take a step back. What happened to my friend, my ally who was consoling me in the hallway just yesterday? The woman who stands in front of me is hostile. Her cold eyes can cut glass. Whatever she feels isn't nerves. Loathing, I realize. She loathes me. She looks at me as if she wishes to throw me hard against the wall.

"If you don't have anything to say to me, you can leave." I put as much frost into my voice as I can muster, even though my rib cage tightens under her stare.

She leaves, and I rush to the door to lock it, my palms slick with sweat. But then I feel pathetic and alone. I should've asked her to stay. I should've asked her to explain what's happening to her. Is it possible that it's just her nerves? We're about to host the séance, and if not for the whiskey I took from Father's study, I'd be a tangled ball of nerves myself.

There is a flash of movement in the trees outside, and as I turn to the window, I catch someone shifting, moving in the branches. A small child steps out of the shadows, a breeze swirling through his short-cropped hair. He lifts his face slowly, searching me out, and smiles.

A soft ripple of laughter. *Return what's mine.* A child's voice, almost begging, almost kind, almost human. *Return what's mine.*

"What *is* yours? The farm?" The words inside my head form into a question. "The land? Help me understand." I have so many unanswered questions. So many thoughts.

A giggle that cools me to my belly.

Somewhere in the night, an animal screeches, calling out to me with otherworldly tidings that I cannot untangle.

Through the night, the boy and I peer at each other.

When the clock strikes half past eleven, I enter the dining room, the long dress brushing lightly around my ankles and my heels clicking on the parquet floor. I had some more whiskey right before I went downstairs, sipping it slowly, holding the burning liquid on my tongue as it quieted my racing mind and settled my roiling stomach. Finally, my cheeks pink from the heat of the drink, I was ready to face the cream of the crop of Omaha society and the myriad ways this séance could go wrong.

Pausing by the door, I look over the guests, and the familiar fear surges through me, urgent and electrifying. But this time—fueled by alcohol, no doubt—instead of weakening my resolve, it morphs into a force. Instead of freezing me in my steps, it propels me forward.

I haven't realized how spacious our dining area is until now. How many steps it takes me to walk from the door to the first group of guests. Leroy and Tilda rearranged the dining room furniture this afternoon, pushing the dining table into the center of the room. All the large windows are closed, curtains tightly pulled. The shadows, oddly shaped phantoms, dance on the walls in the fluttering candlelight. Leroy lit thirty candles right before our guests started to arrive. The candles, casting a low amber glow, are placed on the floor in all four corners of the room, away from the curtains. The space is airy and mysterious.

I raise my chin and make my way slowly across the room, my steps echoing in the fallen silence. I meet everyone's eye. I give them a small smile. I say, "Welcome," and I nod, mimicking my mother's imperious nod from our past life.

Most women stare at my dress, their eyes wide with surprise, sliding up and down my figure. They're probably wondering how I was able to afford such a dress, considering our dire financial position. Considering my father's shameful debts. Most men smile and nod back. My shoulders relax, and the air flows into my lungs freely. No one turns away. Everyone acknowledges me as a hostess. Leroy was right. People respect money and good looks.

"Good evening, Mrs. Holland." I stop in front of the Hollands. Mrs. Holland smells strongly of anise perfume. At my approach, Lizzie's gloomy face clears, like she saw the sun coming up. Her smile is so wide, I almost get a glimpse of her pink tongue. "Thank you for coming. Lizzie, would you like some champagne?" I ask my friend.

"I'm fine. No champagne. Thank you, Nina."

"As you wish," I respond with a wide smile.

Her heart-shaped face falls as she shakes her head and mutters something under her breath, brushing her fingers nervously at some invisible speck of lint or dust on her dress. Her gaze glides over my shoulder, and her jaw tenses.

"Miss Wilson," a man's voice says to my right. "It's been far too long." He steps closer, and for a fraction of a second, I'm sure he's about to embrace me. My heart keeps its steady beat when Bobby leans forward, takes my hand, and presses it to his lips. I used to miss him every day. His absence was as acute and painful as a physical loss. My every heartbeat reminded me of his touch. There were moments when I thought I wouldn't be able to go on because so much was happening all at once, my loneliness compounded by the fact of his betrayal. Now, I see him as if for the first time. I don't recognize the man with whom I used to laugh and dance myself breathless and who stands a mere foot away from me invoking nothing in my heart but regret. And dark excitement. Because now, he's just another guest whose money I'm going to take.

"I don't remember sending an invitation your way, Mr. Walker," I say coldly and pull my hand away from his unpleasantly sweaty grip.

"Oh, Nina," Lizzie says, her voice weak, childish. She pushes away a stray curl that has fallen across her pink cheek. "Bobby and I got engaged last week. I was going to write you a note, but I thought perhaps we could all talk tonight instead."

How shameless she is in her betrayal. I pause, assessing my state of mind. But nothing stirs in my chest. Nothing boils my blood. I'm supposed to feel anger or at least resentment, but all I feel is emptiness. "There's nothing to talk about, Lizzie. My warm congratulations to both of you," I say with a smile. "You're a beautiful couple. I'm very happy for you." I turn to Bobby. "I assume Peach knows about the engagement?"

Bobby goes completely still. He blinks slowly. Once, twice. Not a word comes out.

"Who is Peach?" Lizzie asks, her voice shaking, and I wonder if she knows about the girl Bobby frequents in the Burnt District.

"I don't understand what you mean," Bobby stammers. His voice is raw; the words come out thick and heavy.

I brush away the strand of hair from Lizzie's face. "Oh, I must be mistaken. Don't mind me." I laugh lightly. "So much has happened lately."

"Will your mother be joining us?" Mrs. Holland asks, looking a little sallow, but I've already moved on to the next group of people.

"Mrs. Thomas." I give the grieving mother of Andrew Thomas a sad half smile. "Judge Thomas." I turn to her husband, who fixes his pale-gray eyes on me. "My deepest condolences." Andrew had wandering hands and an insistent tongue. Once he pulled me into a corner after a single waltz, put his hands on my breasts, squeezed them painfully, and asked me to go with him into a coat closet at his parents' spring gala. "I was devastated to hear about Andrew's passing."

Mrs. Thomas's face shrinks like a dried apple. Her chin trembles, and I feel awful. I should be more sympathetic. I should feel more, but all I can think about is the séance ahead of me. The judge's eyes tighten, as if he's trying his hardest not to cry too. He nods solemnly and looks at his wife. They don't say anything, and I don't push for a response. Neither of them came to my father's funeral. Neither of them sent their condolences to Mother. And when she wrote a letter asking for help, we never received a reply.

I turn away from the judge and his wife and look for Tilda, who is supposed to be serving champagne. I spot her by the far window, and I start making my way toward her when a thud on the front door, loud and violent, startles me.

Tilda sets her tray on the table and walks out into the foyer. The chatter stops as we all strain to listen. Tilda's voice says something incoherent, and a man's agitated voice replies. Then there are heavy, rushed footsteps, and James stumbles into the room. He's wearing the same coat he wore at the cemetery—the gray wool topcoat with obnoxiously big brass buttons. His brown hair is disheveled and falling into his eyes. Unsteady on his feet, he looks around the room, his gaze landing on me. I notice the hard steel in his eyes that fades away so quickly, I'm not sure it really was there. Perhaps it was a play of the candlelight.

He takes a few shaky steps toward me and sinks to his knees. His hands stretch forward, trying to grip the hem of my dress and forcing me to take a step back. "Miss Wilson, I apologize for the intrusion. But please . . . I beg you . . . let me join your gathering. I must talk to my son. Please." He lifts his head, and there are real tears streaming down his face. He's very pale, and in the shimmering light, he looks fragile. As a devastated father should. "He was only eleven when he was taken from me." A suppressed sob. A deep inhale. "It was so hard on us. Now, my wife's sick, confined to bed. She doesn't get up anymore. I must talk to my son." His voice cracks, and desperate, howl-like weeps escape his throat.

Everyone is watching us in stony silence.

I tentatively step toward James. "I'm so sorry for your loss . . . Mr. . . . How should I address you, sir? And please, get up."

James looks up at me, his eyes wide, pleading. "My name is Peter Moore." His voice breaks. If I didn't know it was all an act, I'd be heartbroken for him.

"All are welcome in my house, Mr. Moore. I cannot refuse a father in grief. I know what you are going through far too well." My words, sad but clear, carry easily through the dining room. "We'll find you a seat at our table. I'm sure Mr. Marshall won't mind. Please get up, Mr. Moore." I put my hands on James's shoulders, and he awkwardly scrambles to his feet. "Tilda." I look over to the door where Tilda hovers in the shadows like a ghost. "We'll need one more chair."

Tilda nods, and a few seconds later she brings in another chair. The approving murmurs of the guests fill the room. Human hearts are simple: fear, love, and envy rule our emotions. People in grief, shattered family bonds, shameful secrets, money lost and money to be made—a lavish kingdom of the medium world.

"I remember seeing you at our house a few weeks ago," Lizzie says, her voice full of sorrow.

Mrs. Holland doesn't say anything, but her thin lips are pinched. Her eyes are sharp. A thorn of suspicion lodges itself in my chest. I don't know if the Hollands know about the Blue Book or Leroy's tricks, but

I'm suddenly wondering if Mrs. Holland knows about James. My heart starts to pound itself out of my rib cage. No, Leroy wouldn't invite to the séance someone who is privy to his secrets.

James nods grimly and wipes his eyes. "Yes, I was in attendance, Miss Holland. Mr. Marshall reassured me my son was happy. It was a great relief."

Lizzie nods approvingly. "I remember now. He read your note, the first one that evening, and he talked to your son. I'm so sorry for your loss . . . Mr. . . . Moore," she says awkwardly and turns to her mother. "Do you remember him, Mother?"

Before Mrs. Holland gets a chance to reply, a collective hush descends on the room.

Leroy stands at the threshold, the flickering light illuminating his tall figure. He's decked out in his usual black pants, an impeccable lace-lined black shirt, and his best fitted velvet topcoat. The pearl buttons of his shirt are all done up. He carries an aura of the otherworld well, and my core heats up as I watch him glide into the room.

"Good evening," he says in a low, intimate voice, but his words reverberate through the space between us. He gives a bow, folding lightly at the waist. "Ladies and gentlemen, may your hearts be full of light. What a wonderful gathering." His gaze slides across the room, and his smile widens when he sees me. Then he turns to James. "Mr. Moore, what an unexpected surprise. I don't remember seeing your name on the invitation list."

I step forward, angling between Leroy and James. "Mr. Moore asked to join tonight's séance. There's so much pain and sorrow around him. Can you sense it? I would like to help him." I pause, letting Leroy reply, and when he doesn't, I continue, "Consult the spirits, Mr. Marshall. See what they say." The words come out sounding natural, the result of much practice, and it gives me confidence to continue with our performance.

Leroy lifts his hand, silencing us. He closes his eyes. He doesn't speak for a long time, unsettling and beautiful. When the silence becomes too awkward, he mutters, "The spirits agree with you, Miss Wilson. Mr. Moore may join us." He opens his eyes. "Let's begin. Please take your seats. Miss Wilson, please sit at the head of the table. The spirits want to talk to you tonight."

A bone-snapping, unnatural cold, like none I have ever experienced, sweeps through the space. The guests fall silent. Not a whisper, not even a breath in the room.

Outside, a peal of thunder rolls through the air.

Chapter 19

Someone gasps, a jarring sound, and everyone turns to look at Mrs. Holland, who's scowling at me. "Nina at the head of the table? Is this a joke, Mr. Marshall?" Her loathing is so thick, it clings to me like mud. "Does she have the required skills? If anything, she'll upset the spirits with her silliness."

"It's not a joke," Leroy says.

"It must be a mistake, Mr. Marshall. We came to see you. Not her." She gives me a look that could curdle milk. I cannot take a full breath. Everything we planned for, everything we counted on in our preparations, is about to be destroyed.

"The spirits decide, Mrs. Holland, not I. And tonight they want to talk to Miss Wilson." Leroy smiles at the woman, trying to soften the sharp edges of her skepticism. "I can attest to what Miss Wilson can do. I've witnessed her gift myself. She is a spirit conjurer." Leroy waves everyone to the table. "Please. No need to quarrel. See for yourself. Allow Miss Wilson to talk to the spirits."

With every word he says, there is a shift in the room's energy. Some of the guests give me curious looks. Some nod, agreeing with Leroy's words. Lizzie stares at me in awe, her eyes wide and her mouth slightly agape. She expected me to be a hostess, not a medium. Bobby's face is serious, almost contemplative. He raises an eyebrow at me, and frostiness settles between my ribs under his scrutiny. He must be thinking the séance an intricately choreographed theater. And suddenly, my knees start to shake. I'm not convinced the spirits will come.

"Let's sit." Leroy waves invitingly to the center of the room, and the guests, as obedient lambs following their shepherd, edge toward the table. "Set your hands firmly on the table, please. Miss Wilson will need your energy to lift the veil."

We take our assigned seats. My palms are sweating, and I rub them gently on my dress under the table, the fabric soft like rose petals, but it provides no comfort. The collar is too high and fastened too tight. The silk suddenly feels like rough parchment against my skin. My stomach is churning with remnants of the whiskey I wish I hadn't drunk before we opened the door to our guests. I might be sick. *Don't let them sense your fear.* The memory of Leroy's lesson breaks through my racing mind. He meant the spirits, but I'm sure the lesson can be easily applied to the people around the table.

"May your hearts be full of light, ladies and gentlemen." Leroy appraises each of the guests at the table, acknowledging each one of them with a slight tilt of his head. "Tonight is extraordinary. The veil between the world of the living and the world of the dead is already thinning. Our loved ones are pressing against it, eager to come in. If you don't feel their presence yet, you will in a short while. Miss Wilson." Leroy looks at me and nods. "Please. Lift the veil. Open the passageway. Invite them in."

I close my eyes and listen, but all I hear is the sound of collective breathing. There is no breeze, no brain-numbing, inhuman chill. The walls don't shift, the floors don't creak, and my German opa isn't stirring in his frame. Everything seems normal. I must be tense, because the sharp ache in my muscles forces me to shift uncomfortably in my chair.

Someone clears their throat, and I open my eyes, look around the room, trying to sense a presence. I cannot put a name to what I feel, but this gathering—and my own emotional turmoil—is not the right time for self-doubt. Even if there are no spirits yet, I must proceed as if they're crowding the room. "Show yourself, whoever you are," I say in a low voice. "I sense your presence. You're welcome here. Come in and show yourself." Lizzie reaches over to me and puts her warm hand over mine. "They're here," I lie.

Mrs. Holland snorts. "What is this silliness, Mr. Marshall? Nothing is happening."

My heart plummets to the ground. The only reasonable course of action at this moment is to proceed with the tricks I've been learning over the past two weeks. If spirits are not cooperating, I must continue with a show. And so I school my expression as I curl my toes and tap on the wooden table leg, hollowed out by Tilda a week ago, with the heel of my shoe the way Leroy taught me. Three quick taps. From the other side of the table, Leroy responds with the same three taps, and the sound carries through the room like an echo.

Lizzie inhales sharply by my side, pulls her hand away, and withdraws deeper into her seat.

"Reveal yourself, spirits. We seek guidance upon our questions. Come in. Come in. Come in," I chant. A few more taps, and I assume it is either Leroy or James going along with the performance. "Ladies and gentlemen, the spirits are here and ready for your questions. Please think about the loved ones you want to talk to tonight. Call them by their names." My voice is distant, disconnected from my body. I sound thoughtful, almost contemplative. "Inhale deeply, hold your breath for a few seconds, and try to remember their faces, the sound of their voices." I pause, letting everyone focus on their thoughts.

A rapping sound from above breaks the silence, and everyone jerks at the abrupt sound. Lizzie's eyes are round and dazed when she leans into Bobby for protection. His attention is on me, candlelight burning in the deep blue of his eyes. Upstairs, Tilda throws apples at the wall with such force, I wonder if the apples are splattering.

"At last," Mrs. Holland exhales, finally convinced.

Whatever doubts I had a few minutes ago are gone now. An excitement is building inside me as I think about this unknown, unmapped territory I'm about to navigate. "The spirits are getting impatient. They want us to ask a question," I say as the rapping intensifies. It now moves above our heads, closer to the windows. A sudden breeze brushes past us, and the candles closest to the table go out. Tilda and I practiced this for days, creating a cross breeze between the dining room and the parlor by opening windows on opposite sides. But Tilda is upstairs now, busy with the apples, and the gust is coming from the kitchen downstairs. Perhaps there is a trick Leroy forgot to show me.

I inspect the room, every corner, every shadow, to make sure there are no spirits. Leroy told me many times there is no guarantee they will come when called, but this is not what I expected. I believed I was capable of conjuring spirits. Have I not seen the ghost-boy? The girl at the cemetery? Have I not witnessed the sudden change in the Dawning? Leroy convinced me I was not losing my mind and my visions were real. So why can't I summon the dead? Why won't they come?

Leroy catches my eyes and holds my gaze. His lashes are long and cast shadows on his cheeks. I bite down on my lower lip—a sign that we're putting up a show while waiting for the spirits to oblige us with their presence. I run my fingers carefully around the corner of the table closest to me, scratching my nails along the edges, and turn to James. "Mr. Moore, your son is here. What do you want to ask?" I say softly.

A sob. James buries his head in his hands and doesn't say anything.

"Mr. Moore, please talk to your son, now. While he's still here. He can't stay for long." I talk to James as if he were a disobedient child. "The pull of the otherworld is too strong."

The rapping stops.

"He's about to leave," Leroy says. "The veil is closing. No one will be able to come through."

Mrs. Holland grabs James's hand. "We share your pain, sir," she whispers hoarsely, "but don't let the veil close."

"Son?" James whispers, hunching over. "Carl?" Tears spring out of his eyes and onto the table.

"He's here," I say. "Your boy wants to know why you want to sell his pony, Mabel."

"My God." James gasps in disbelief. His eyes bulge so much, I'm afraid they're about to fall out of their sockets. "How does he know about Mabel?" He looks widely around the room as if in deep shock. "Son, we . . . I must sell it. You're gone, and Mabel needs to eat and drink. It's an unnecessary expense."

As if angered by the spirit of the boy, I bring my hands down on the table. Hard. The loud sound, like the crack of a gunshot, makes everyone jump. "He asks you not to sell Mabel at Hershey's auction this Saturday. Frank Hershey is cruel to animals." Frank's name was in the Blue Book. Last year, a few people witnessed Frank beating a horse on the streets. He was eventually charged with cruelty against a horse and fined fifteen dollars. Judge Thomas presided over the case. The story never made it into newspapers, but it was meticulously recorded in the Blue Book. "He says if you wait until next month, you can get thirty-eight dollars for the pony, and it will be treated well."

"My Lord, I remember Frank Hershey's case. He beat his horse something awful," Judge Thomas whispers loudly to his wife. He bought the whole charade. There's no way for someone like me—a young girl who doesn't follow court cases—to know about the horse beating. A tight spring that was coiled inside me all this time finally uncoils. People are truly simple and are willing to grasp any straw. All I have to do is give them a piece of truth, sprinkle a few vivid details, and they're eating from my hands. Leroy was right when he called the Blue Book a treasure trove of the small things that matter the most. The personal things no one can know. I steal a quick glance at Leroy. His eyes are closed. His face is relaxed, but the corners of his lips are twitching.

James nods his head vehemently. "Okay, okay, I'll wait to sell."

"He's ready for your question." I close my eyes, pretending to listen to a boy who never existed.

"Son? Your mother's ill. Is she going . . . is she going to be well?"

My whole body convulses. I slam my hands into the table again. I drop my head to my chest and then raise it sharply, almost violently, as if someone has pulled on my hair. "No, Father." My throat exposed, I deepen my voice. "She's soon to join me." An invisible hand releases me, and I collapse forward, onto the table. A woman's voice gasps. James chokes on another sob. I count to five, and, opening my eyes, I pull myself back into a sitting position.

"I suspected it all along." James opens his mouth, and a moan of horrible sadness rips free. "I'm done." He shakes his head. "Please move on to someone else. I can't bear it anymore." His voice is so full of heartache, it sounds almost real to me, and I feel almost sympathetic.

Again, I close my eyes and listen. "Andrew Thomas is here." I pause. "He wants to talk to his mother." I can't force myself to meet Mrs. Thomas's eyes. I know what it feels like to lose family. My own mother's pale, gaunt face floats to the surface of my thoughts. My eyes start to burn. I shouldn't be doing this. Not to Mrs. Thomas. I catch Leroy's gaze. He can see through me clearly, and he knows I'm wavering. James can see it, too, because he stirs in his seat, gives Leroy a pointed look, and starts sobbing again, trying to keep his performance up. And somehow it helps. I snap out of the unexpected guilt and straighten my back. I roll my shoulders and settle my gaze on Mrs. Thomas. "Andrew says he's sorry for not listening to you and leaving that night. He should've stayed home. With you and his niece, Mary. But he was mad because you refused to give him money. He wanted to punish you." James bribed Thomas's maid to find out about the argument and the money. Leroy recorded it in the Blue Book a few days ago.

Mrs. Thomas makes an odd sound, something between a whimper and a cry.

"What would you like to ask him?" I half close my eyes again, as if listening to Andrew's voice.

"Is that true, my love? About the money?" Judge Thomas asks.

Mrs. Thomas looks at her husband; then she dabs at her eyes with a handkerchief, her gaze distant and contemplative, as if she's having a conversation with herself or maybe her dead son. "It's true," she whispers finally, and a lonely tear rolls down her pale cheek. "He spent his money on drinks. On horse races. I wanted him to stop. I wanted him to move away from Omaha, its awful gambling nest. And the Cribs. I think he frequented the Cribs too. He always denied it, but I suspected the worst. We had an argument that night. He left." I see the agonizing guilt eating at Mrs. Thomas. I know the feeling intimately—falling into the void, the acute sharpness of vices that get hold of you, refusal to accept the awful truth, and, later, desperate attempts to claw yourself back to light. I squeeze her hand, trying to console her. I wish I knew how to reach out to Andrew's spirit so he could provide comfort to his own mother. Maybe if I try harder, say the right words, take deeper breaths, the spirits will come.

"Ask him if he can forgive me." Mrs. Thomas clutches her hands to her blue velvet dress with the ridiculously puffed-out sleeves that are currently in vogue.

I pull my hand away from her and go through the same performance as I did with James, even though my neck is getting tense from all the violent jerks and my heart weighs heavy from the compounding sorrow. "I love you, Mother. I could never be mad at you for long."

I pause, waiting for someone to say something about how horrible of an actress I am. It was hope and curiosity that brought them to the Dawning tonight. But now, the curious glint is gone from their faces. Instead, it is replaced with fright.

No one says a word, and I push forward. "Mother, I miss you so much." I force the words out. Mrs. Thomas breaks down in uncontrollable sobs. I don't want to continue, but I need to close the door I just opened. I need to give her solace since it's what she's come here for. "I'm at peace now," I add hastily and collapse on the table.

When I finally straighten myself, I look around the room, taking in Lizzie's expression of marvel and wonder. Her mother's somber expression as she tries to console Mrs. Thomas. James's self-satisfied smirk, and Leroy's approving gaze. I look at the others: the couple who lost their child to fever last month; a banker who is about to lose his fortune in a bad real estate deal. Their stories are recorded in the Blue Book. I know the most intimate details of their lives, and when I speak to them tonight, they won't have a choice but to believe me. Even now, they're already looking at me expectantly, straining forward, brows raised, lips parted, hanging on to every breath I take, to every word I say. Suddenly, the thrill of the ruse thrums through my center. I've been chasing the idea of madness and ghosts for so long, I forgot what it means to actually feel excitement to the fullest, and right now I can't remember the last time I felt so exhilarated. So deliriously alive.

"Shall I go on?" I ask my audience, brushing the silver locket on my neck. When everyone nods, I push forward. "Are there any other spirits here? Please reveal yourself."

An eerie silence, not even a shallow sigh, as if everyone ceases breathing. The heaviness of the collective expectation curls like smoke above my head. The frosty air seeps from the open windows in the hallway. I squeeze the locket harder, and with a sharp tug in my chest, a torrent of words spills out of me. "Who's here? Reveal yourself now. Come in, come in, come in."

"What in the Lord's name is happening?" a familiar voice thunders from the door. "Nina, have you lost your mind?" I open my eyes and stare at my twin brother, my breath frozen in my lungs. He stands in the door, clad in a long wool coat and shiny black boots. His hair is slicked back. A scatter of freckles across the bridge of his nose looks exactly like mine. He glares at me over his half-rim glasses splattered with raindrops.

"Amos?" I exhale. "What are you doing here?"

"The right question is, What are *you* doing?" He steps inside the room, water dripping from the lapels of his coat. "Who are these people, Nina?" He sounds angry, almost hostile.

I leap to my feet with such force my chair tumbles over, its clatter reverberating through the room. My hands curl into fists when I take a few steps toward my brother. "You sound upset, and I don't know why.

What have I done?" When he doesn't reply, I shriek, "Damn it, Amos. Answer me."

Someone's hand grabs my upper arm and spins me around. "Nina." Leroy's voice has a sharp edge to it. "You're upsetting our guests. You need to calm down."

"Let me go," I hiss. "I need to talk to my brother."

"Dear Lord," Mrs. Thomas whispers hoarsely from the table. "Amos is here. She's talking to her dead brother."

Chapter 20

A roaring silence descends in the room.

The floor tilts underneath me. The room and people in it fade away. A cold and heavy feeling settles in my chest as I slowly pull away from Leroy's grasp and turn to Amos. "I'm angry with you. And also I'm so incredibly sad. But mostly angry."

"I understand," my brother says softly. "And I am sorry."

"Do you really understand?" A fresh current of fury makes my skin burn, but I direct it not at my brother but into fists clenched by my sides. "It's been so hard for me to understand why you did what you did. Did you consider even for a minute what it would do to your family? To me?" My mouth is dry. My voice is rough with unshed tears. "Our parents blamed me for everything. For your sickness. For your absence. And then for your actions." He stares at his shoes, obviously not able to look me in the eye. "You were dead, and I was alive, and they wished it would be the other way around."

He jerks his head up. "It's not true. You know it's not true," he says slowly, as if he's trying to console me. "I'm sorry, Nina. I know it must've been incredibly hard for you. Especially after Father's accident."

"And how do you know that, Amos? You weren't here. You've been dead for a year now. You know nothing about what I've been through."

"I know enough. You've been trying to reach me, Nina. For a very long time. Your letters. They opened the door. But the locket that I sent you from the clinic pulled me through the veil. I'm here now."

"For how long?" With a sharp inhale, I unclench my fists, and I touch the silver locket, pressing it against my collarbone. "Can you stay?" In the pit of my stomach, a knot forms, and I know he won't stay for long.

"I don't think so," he says.

"I've missed you, Amos. So much." My back aches with tension when I reach out to him, but he shakes his head, and I realize I cannot touch him. And maybe I shouldn't even try. "The letters. I wrote so many."

"I know," he says with a sad smile, blue lips stretching taut. The more time he spends in our world, the more dead he looks. As if the other side is pulling him back. As if he's already fading away. "I've missed you, too, but I couldn't come. Every time you wrote one of your letters, I thought I was going to finally break through, but I didn't know how. Until tonight. Something pulled me like a rope."

A rope. Only now I notice a rope wrapped around his neck. And the unnatural tilt of his head. A bone, white and jagged, is protruding through his pale skin on the side of his broken neck. His eyes, sunk into deep hollows, are tinged with blue and black, and if there is anything left of my twin, I cannot see it.

Memories that I was suppressing for a year now break loose and flood my mind. My father told me it was my fault Amos contracted syphilis in the Cribs. "You knew he was visiting the Cribs. Every night you let him out of your window, and every morning you opened the door for him. And all this time, you said nothing." Maybe Father was right. Maybe I didn't love Amos enough to stop him from going out in the night.

"You did it to your brother. All of it. It's all on you," Mother said during one of her grief-infused fits. Her words imprinted into my heart like a permanent wound that never stopped bleeding. I was too frightened, too ashamed by everything that happened, and didn't have enough courage to point out to our parents that it was Amos who did it to himself.

My brother was sent to upstate New York for treatment, where one winter day he hanged himself. The telegram arrived on a cold Tuesday morning, and we all knew, even before Father opened it, that something terrible had happened. That night, when Mother's screams subsided, when Father locked himself in his study, I went to Amos's room, and I tore through his things, searching for answers that weren't there. The shock, the overwhelming agony, made me almost belligerent as I turned his room upside down, throwing his clothes and books on the floor, stomping on them, ripping them to pieces. I found nothing. Not a hint. Not a note or a single sign of why he would do something so violent and despicable.

His destroyed body was delivered to us ten days later. The funeral was small. My memories of that day are hazy, but I remember Lizzie in a wool coat, her black leather shoes with a Louis heel digging into the wet soil. She held my hand, her eyes downcast, too ashamed to look me in the eye.

According to the Blue Book, Mother started going to every single séance she could find in Omaha, and Father found his solace in gambling. I descended into a tangle of guilt and denial. I started writing to my dead brother, desperate to talk to my twin, even though it was hard to see his name on the page, but soon I was spilling my feelings on the paper; the sheer relief of it was what pulled me to the surface, giving me a way to be whole again.

"Are you lonely?" I whisper, tears burning my skin. "Because I am."

Someone gasps, and a chorus of whispers erupts behind me, odd, buzzing sounds. It must be our guests, but I don't care. All I need is Amos. All that matters is my brother.

He steps closer, his gray oxygen-deprived face molded into a mask, and I catch a whiff of freshly turned earth and rot. "Don't be angry at me. I couldn't go on. It was what I wanted. Treatments were not helping, and my body just turned into a collection of slow, burning agony and deterioration. I was dying. I just sped up the process a bit."

"I could've stopped you from going to the Cribs. It was all preventable."

A gurgle breaks loose from the bottom of his crushed throat as he tries to laugh. "No one could've kept me away from the Cribs." He shakes his head, and a curl falls on his pale forehead. He pushes it away. "Father had an obligation to you. To Mother. He should've taken care of his family, and he failed. You need to forgive yourself, Nina. Nothing was your fault. I chose it all." He finally manages to smile, a broken, distorted smile. "Stop blaming yourself. And listen. We don't have much time." He looks around frantically, and the air gets thicker around him. "Something came through the veil. There was a rip. I don't know how you managed to bring it into your world, but you must send it back." He sighs, removes his glasses, and rubs them between his fingers. "It wants to go back."

"What? I don't understand. What do you mean I brought something over?" My throat constricts. My chest is suddenly heavy, like someone is sitting on it. Is he talking about the ghost-boy? How is it that I brought him through the veil?

"Send it back, Nina." His voice is weakening, fading away, but he still sounds very much like the Amos I remember. "That's all it wants."

"I don't know how." A sob erupts from my tight throat. "Don't go. Stay, please. Just a little longer."

Somewhere far away, I hear Lizzie's thin voice saying something and Leroy's low rumble, but I cannot understand them. All I hear is my brother as he says, "But I must." The words are on the breeze that suddenly fills the room. They are seething through the air as my brother looks around, hearing something only he can hear. His head lolls to one side at a sharp angle, and his glasses start to slide down, but he pushes them up the bridge of his nose. "Give it back."

My knees go soft at his words. "Give what back? What do I have? What does he want?" The boy's name—Oliver Rask—rattles at the back of my throat, creeping into my mouth, lacing my tongue.

The whisper of the breeze gets louder. Amos's face turns translucent. It glows with an odd gray light, and I can see right through him, to his joints and bones deteriorated with syphilis. I reach out to my twin, willing to follow him into the abyss, but someone's strong arms wrap around my waist and pull me back. Amos crosses the room in a few long strides; his bones shift and move of their own accord, his frame dissipating into a thick white mist that seeps from the deepest corner of the room and swirls around him. The fog gets thicker with every step he takes. I stand still and watch my brother step into the rip between the two worlds.

The chill in the air is too sharp, too icy. In howling gusts, the wind roars in my head. The lack of light makes the floors and the wallpaper look almost black. Suddenly the walls seem to move toward me, closing down, suffocating.

The last thing I remember is a wail breaking loose from my chest and then complete, all-encompassing blackness.

I come to my senses in Father's study. I'm lying on the small sofa, the heavy mahogany bookcase looming over me. As I slowly emerge from the oblivion, I try to figure out how long I was unconscious. A minute or longer? It feels much longer because the Dawning, full of whispers and howling winds just moments ago, has gone silent. I turn my head, and the relentless drone of the pulse in my temples intensifies. I slowly inspect the room, but there are no ghosts roosted nearby. No evil spirits smiling at me. No churning fog. I feel no fear, no sadness, just complete exhaustion. As if all my strength was stripped away from me and whatever's left—a half of me—is still suspended between two worlds.

Leroy sits in my father's armchair, his long legs stretched out and crossed at the ankles. His evening jacket is gone, and the sleeves of his black shirt are rolled up to the elbows to reveal his strong forearms. His gaze is fixed on the fire in the hearth that Tilda must've built a few minutes ago. The contented look on his face is surprisingly unsettling.

I clear my dry throat. "Where's everyone?"

"Gone." His shoulders loose, he swirls the amber liquid in his glass. "After you collapsed, I asked our guests to leave." He takes a long sip, watching me over the rim. "I think tonight you have established yourself as a true medium, Nina. You were absolutely sensational."

Groaning like an old woman, I sit up, the room slightly spinning. The walls seem to shift again. "*Sensational* is not the word I'd use." I lift my head and study him in the glow of the candles—tracing his cheekbones, his full lips, and the side of his neck where a thin vein pulses. "You seem extremely pleased with yourself."

He chuckles. "I'm pleased with the outcome. And you should be too. On her way out Mrs. Holland inquired about the next sitting."

I straighten my dress. I move my feet. My body feels full of lead, limbs heavy and numb. "That's all you care about? The business side of it?"

"And you? Don't you care about the business side of it?"

I think of everything my family has lost. Of everything we need. Of the Dawning's leaking roof, its crumbling siding, the mold on its walls. I think of Mother. "I chose it because you said it's a profitable business."

"Profitable indeed." With a wide smile, Leroy waves at a small leather-bound box sitting in the middle of the table. "Your tax bill is paid. See for yourself." He hooks his nail under the top and flips it open.

"My Lord." Forgetting about the headache and the moving walls and my unnatural exhaustion, I get up and walk over to the box to take a closer look. "I've never thought séances pay so well." I touch the bills, my fingers light. "It's so much more than I've ever expected." I felt so powerless in the past year. I failed to bring Mother out of her grief, I failed to find money to pay our bills, and I failed to restore my family. But tonight, for the first time in my life, I feel in control over everything that's unfolding within our walls, and it's the most exhilarating feeling I've ever experienced. A sense that this decision to become a part of Leroy's schemes born out of desperation might in fact have been some kind of fate. Something that was meant to be.

Leroy lifts his glass to his mouth but doesn't drink. There is wistfulness and mischief in his face. "And it's all yours," he says, pushing the box toward me. "My share will come out of our future séances. I have a feeling we'll be very busy." He gets up to his feet and pours whiskey into a new glass. "Here." He passes me the drink, our fingers brushing against one another. "Sit down by the fire, have a drink, and tell me about Amos. I'm curious to know how your brother was able to breach the veil."

I take the drink and lower myself into a seat. "Didn't you hear what he said?" I ask, staring into the dancing flames.

"Some of it, yes, but not all. I spent most of my time with the guests. They were quite agitated by the whole experience."

"Agitated? They're lucky they didn't see what I saw." I think about Amos's broken neck, the thick rope, his hollow, dead eyes. My eyes start to burn, and a few tears spill onto my cheeks. Embarrassed, I frantically wipe them away.

"What did you see?" he asks softly.

"My dead brother, his neck broken, his flesh rotting in front of me." I take a mouthful of the drink. "It was awful." I take another sip, and the drink burns, thick and warm, soothing me a bit. But its aftertaste sours my mouth. There's a pit deep down in me, a hole that cannot be filled. I look at Leroy, at the candlelight glowing in his eyes, the wonder in his face, and, feeling entranced by his attention, his proximity, I tell him about the Cribs and the clinic and my brother's death. I talk about my mother's wrath and my own guilt and the all-consuming, obliterating grief and how life can pivot from one outcome to another in a span of mere seconds.

"You're one of the most talented mediums that ever existed," Leroy says when I'm finally done. "Imagine everything you ever wanted. It's right here, in front of you."

Laughing, I nod at the box. "It is indeed."

Leroy chuckles. "That's not what I meant." He gets to his feet, places his glass on the table, and kneels in front of me. My heart rate spikes. "There's so much more we can do." He takes my hand and gently turns it over—palm up. What is he doing? The question runs through me like fever. He looks down at my palm, his thumb brushing my skin. "Together."

There is a moment of silence, broken only by my thunderous heartbeats. He presses his lips to my burning palm. His touch, the pressure of his mouth, explode through me like fireworks. I gasp, and the sound lingers in the air. My breathing is jagged, uneven. He smiles but doesn't pull away. The floor vanishes beneath me, and I'm in free fall. My body's on fire. My mind blank. His tongue—firm and soft at the same time—trails up my hand, to my wrist.

He pauses, lifts his head, and flames of deep unyielding hunger rage in my veins in the wake of his kiss. "Nina." He says my name gently, letting it carry through the space between us. I study the intensity in him, his ravaged-by-desire face. In this moment, seeing him like this, I can let him do whatever he wants, and I won't feel any shame. Just a core-deep yearning for him. But something stops me. Maybe it's my upbringing, my bloody manners etched deeply in my soul. Or maybe it's a shard of doubt that stirs in my chest.

He goes still under my inspection. As I straighten my spine and pull my hand away from his grasp, he gets to his feet. "You and I are meant to be together." His voice is low. Almost hesitant. "But I'm not asking for anything. Not now. When you're ready, I'd like to offer you a life that is not ordinary."

Leroy Marshall, the famous traveling medium and spirit conjurer, the man who had hypnotized Omaha and who never gets attached to anything or anyone—an experienced man with his own strange view of the world—looks at me with such desire, I feel not just seen and wanted but loved. With the echoes of his touch still fresh on my skin, his words offer me the way out of my lonely, miserable, and isolated existence. As God is my witness, I want it. I want Leroy Marshall and everything he offers.

Again, the flicker of a warning inside my chest stops me from leaping into his arms. Instead, I push myself out of the armchair, feeling off-balance. "I'm utterly exhausted. It's time for me to retire." I press the heel of my hand to my forehead. "One last thing. Amos said something crossed the veil." Leroy looks at me, an eyebrow curved in an unspoken question. "Something that was not meant to cross. I wonder if it's the drowned boy, Oliver Rask, I've been seeing. I think he wants his farm back. My family owns the land."

I brace myself for a look of disbelief, but instead Leroy's eyes are firmly affixed on my face. He drums his long, strong fingers against his glass. "Why do you think the boy wants the farm? It's an odd thing for a ghost to want."

"I don't know. Father refused to give the farm back to Mr. Rask. That night Mr. Rask fell into the creek. He was drunk out of his mind. His son, Ollie, jumped in to save him, and they both drowned." My voice wraps around each word like a vise, making it almost impossible to talk. "The family left. And now, I don't know how, but I think you and I brought Ollie through the veil at your séance. At the Hollands'. And he wants revenge. Most likely, he always wanted to avenge what happened to him, his family. We just opened the door for him to come through."

"Did Amos tell you how to send the boy back?"

"He told me something strange. Amos said the boy wants to go back, but he can't. It's like he's tethered to me." I look over at the fire and watch the play of the flames in the hearth, an odd and violent dance. "I have no idea what I'm supposed to do. How do I give the land back to a ghost?"

Chapter 21

In the days that follow, no matter what I do, the ghosts, including my own brother, refuse to come.

I focus on figuring out why the spirits won't oblige me anymore. I try to summon them using the same words, same tone, every single day, but nothing happens. It must be something else that helped Amos to cross over, though what it is, I don't know. Was it my voice? Was it something I said? I don't have the slightest inkling where to search for that one magical trick that can help me.

During my lessons with Leroy, I catch myself looking back at what happened that night, as if my memories might open a door into the unknown and guide me to answers I'm desperately seeking. But the more I push myself to remember, the faster my memories shrivel and wither.

So for now, I try to practice as much as I can: tapping until my knuckles get raw, craning my neck and rolling my eyes as if I'm going into a trance, talking in a low voice, and my favorite—hissing and hollow sounds. When I practice fake conjuring, Leroy urges me to use a deeper voice and convulse more. Every time I try it, I burst into laughter. He guffaws with me, and for a few minutes, under his amused gaze, it feels like I'm the funniest and most beautiful girl in the world.

Every day we remind Tilda not to throw apples with such force that they split in half and leave dents in the walls. She scoffs and frowns, and her eyes always linger on me with some unpleasant undercurrent that sets my teeth on edge. I want to talk to her, to ask her what has changed between us, but her resentment is thick in the air, and there is this heady, noxious flicker in her eyes, and I delay the conversation and hold my hurt inside like a clenched fist.

Our morning lessons make me feel normal. There are no ghosts, no tragic past pressing on my shoulders, no pockmarked-with-mold walls shifting around me, and no reminders of Mother's madness. I exist in moments filled with Leroy's jokes, instructions, and unspoken promises. At times like this, between lingering glances and peals of laughter, between joint meals and long conversations, I can almost feel what it might be like to share my life with him.

When I'm in his company, my guilt recedes, and my anger loses its hooks and sharp edges, as if he has taken a part of me—the broken part—and tucked it away in his pocket. I finally learn to look confident, even though my palms still sweat and my knees tremble when I tap on the hollowed leg of the chair. In the afternoon, we take our tea in the small parlor. I scan the pages of the Blue Book, and we discuss people mentioned on its pages.

In the evenings, we sort through the letters that are being delivered daily. The rumors about our first séance spread through the town like a wild prairie fire, and now, mail deliveries are full of letters from people we don't know, people who ask us if they can be our night guests. Their stories are sorrowful. I know too well how one fateful moment, or a careless decision, can upend one's life in an instant. A girl walks out of her seamstress shop, looking down at a package in her hands, and gets trampled by a horse. A man leaves his home one morning and is hit in the head by a bullet meant for someone else. The letters that unsettle me the most are the ones from grieving parents looking for their missing children.

As the night of our second séance approaches, I get more and more convinced that the ghosts won't come, someone will see through our ruse, and the Wilson family name will be ruined forever. But Leroy's electrifying energy keeps me going. Keeps me practicing.

In the dining room, the shadows from the candlelight play over the pale, intense faces of our night guests. My gaze slides around the table, always seeking him out first. The beautiful planes of Leroy's face soothe me and ignite me at the same time. Tonight, he's wearing a brown silk shirt, but his favorite silk necktie is missing. It's odd because he thinks that particular necktie is his lucky charm. His hair is slicked neatly back from his forehead. He nods slightly, urging me to go on, and following his direction, I close my eyes and start chanting.

"May your hearts be full of light. May the spirits come and reveal themselves to us." I listen to the gaping silence of the room. Wondering if anything will be different tonight. But the house is quiet—no creaks or groans or unexpected drafts. Even Tilda doesn't move upstairs, patiently waiting for our signal. I open my eyes and repeat my chant again. "Whoever is out there, reveal yourself." I fall silent. I must have paused far longer than needed, because Leroy gives me a questioning look. "Spirits of the otherworld, we welcome you home. Come in freely," I continue, pausing between words, as if waiting for a sign or a sound, but all I hear are the ragged breaths of our guests. "Is anyone here? Please reveal yourself." A loud knock from across the table signals me to tell our guests that we finally have a visitor.

We plan to start with a young bank manager who wants to know if he is going to inherit his father's estate or if it'll go to his older brother, who disappeared years ago. But according to the Blue Book, his brother is doing quite well in Chicago and plans to come back to Omaha to claim his father's estate. I'm going to conjure the dead father's spirit to announce the return of the prodigal son. "The veil is opening. Someone's getting ready to step through it. Whoever you are, welcome. Please come in, come in, come in." I wait, but, of course, there is no response. Instead, James, who sits three seats down from me, raps his knuckles under the table.

A few guests gasp. An older man to my right spills his drink on the table and starts wiping it down frantically with the sleeve of his jacket. I hold a finger to my lips to silence everyone.

"Don't be frightened," I tell a nonexistent spirit.

The woman next to me, who lost her fourteen-year-old daughter to influenza, stirs. Her lips smack as if she is about to utter a question but is not sure if she is allowed. I nod at her encouragingly. Perhaps the banker can wait a little longer. A few days ago, she sent me money, paying double what we charge for the entry, ensuring her place at the table. Her bright-blue eyes are wide as saucers, her lips wet with spittle when she leans forward and puts a small doll in a white embroidered dress on the table in front of me.

"My daughter's name was Ethel. Can you ask if it's Ethel who wants to come through?" She pushes the doll into my hands. "It was her favorite doll." She pats my hand, and the sadness for her loss curls around my heart like a vine. Her fingers brush over the doll's face, as if touching it gives her a thread of hope that her daughter will return from the dead. "I beg you. Call for Ethel." The vine around my heart tightens. If I only knew how.

I take the doll and turn it over in my hands. The doll is made of porcelain. Her eyes are black, almost predatory, but her face is cool under my fingers, a gentle whisper of a soul lost too early. I think about a fourteen-year-old girl I never knew and wonder if she liked to read poetry or ride horses. If she smelled of pines and fresh grass. If her mother used to braid her hair and plant gentle kisses on her cheek before bed. And if there was a mischievous glint in the girl's eyes when she smiled.

Holding my breath, I squeeze the doll.

James scoffs and flexes his arm, the tendons of his forearm tense. His gaze flicks to something over my shoulder, and his expression turns smug and self-satisfied. "Someone's moving behind you. Must be the spirit of the girl." Even in the gloom of the room, I can see the sharpness in his eyes.

Anger slowly stirs in my chest. My first instinct is to demand that he leave, but the rational part of me knows we need James to continue with our ruse. The guests follow his gaze, but their focus returns to me instantaneously as I tap with my heel on the leg of the chair. I close my eyes and say, "Ethel, I summon thee. Your mother is here and wants to talk to you. You're welcome here. Step freely through the veil. Come to me. Come to me, Ethel." *Please come.* My words like a prayer reach out to the veil, to the night, and out to the spirit world.

When I open my eyes, a slow breeze brushes over my face. The dark clothes of our guests stand out against the twinkling light of the candles. Their heads are tilted forward. Some sit with their eyes closed, as if frightened of what they might see. Some are studying me with intense curiosity. Leroy's face is calm, but his gaze presses heavily against my skin. Just like me, he must be sensing the shift in the air.

Cold sweat beads at the nape of my neck as a shadow shifts to my left, in the blackest corner of the room. And there she is, crouching quietly in her white nightdress. She has light-brown hair and the same piercing blue eyes as her mother. She's tugging on something with her right hand, something I cannot see. The girl stirs, pulls herself up, her eyes narrowing on me. Her face is gaunt, with sunken cheekbones. The hues of her white nightgown are broken up with brown spots around her ribs and thighs. The fabric looks clammy, as if it's wet. The insides of her arms are covered in wounds gushing with blood. Crimson liquid flows down her arms and drips to the floor. A porcelain doll hangs loosely in her hands. The girl tilts her head and grins, inching closer. Two front teeth are chipped. The chill, marrow-deep, slinks around me, and the hair stands up on my arms.

"Ethel?" I whisper. "Is that you?"

"You're so pretty," the girl says, and my pulse stops, then spikes, and now it is beating in my throat as I stare at the doll, the exact same doll I'm holding in my hand. A low laugh, girlish and pleased, almost kind, but with a pang of darkness, slides down my spine like ice. "Why did you call for me?"

"Ethel," I exhale. "Your mother wants to talk to you."

The mother says something and pulls on my hand, but there is the girl's roaring laughter in my head, and all I hear is the rasp of my own breathing.

"She's such a liar. Always lies. He paid her to come here and make a fool out of you." Ethel points at James, whose eyes are fused to my face. It's all clear now—the overpayment, the woman's eagerness to talk to her daughter, James's pathetic jokes. They were setting me up. "They don't believe you. They think you're a fake." With certain haughtiness, the girl turns and stares at her mother. Her face contorts with hatred. "How dare she ask for me?" Her shoulders jerk violently, as if in some deadly convulsion. "I don't want to talk to her. She's mean. Angry. Always so angry." Tears bloom in the girl's blue eyes, and her voice shakes; she's nearly sobbing. "She used to slap me around. Then she chased all my friends away. And when I tried to escape her, she found me, brought me back home, and whipped me with a belt. Like I was some animal." The girl rolls up her nightgown and shows me festering, bleeding welts on her skinny thighs. "She tells everyone I died of influenza. But it was a blood infection."

The mother leans forward. Her sour breath on my face turns my stomach. "What's happening? Are you seeing anything? Anything at all?"

The air around me is humming with hatred and pain. I hear a trill of dissonant voices from somewhere far away. It must be either the people around the table or the spirits on the other side of the veil. Leroy says something; his voice is trying to break through the noise in my head, but I cannot understand a word.

The mother clings to my hand. "Is Ethel talking to you?" She squeezes my fingers, pulls on the doll, her nails scratching my skin. My thoughts are a jumble. Words are disconnected, but I slowly piece them together.

The ghost of the girl spits at her mother. "I'm finally free of her. Tell her I hope she rots in hell." The girl turns away, stepping into the otherworld, but halts midstep. She looks at me over her shoulder, and there's so much sadness in her, so much pain, I choke on my own sob. "Don't call for me anymore. I won't be coming back."

The hatred that roots me to my seat as I stare at the mother is so overwhelming I can barely breathe. I know now what it feels like to face a monster who's real and not conjured by the underworld. "She's gone," I hiss through my teeth and pull myself away from the woman.

Her entire focus is on her hands, which are clasped around the doll. She seems deep in thought, but I'm intensely aware of her need for answers. What am I supposed to do? Do I tell her I know what she did to her own child, or do I confront her and James and throw them out of the house?

The mother lifts her head and smiles at me briefly with her puckered mouth, but the smile never reaches her eyes. "What did she say? What did my girl say to you?"

"What indeed, Miss Wilson? For you look like you've seen a ghost," James says, and his rough laughter roars through the silent room. How did I let this drifter, with fists like bricks and eyes as icy as the Missouri River, from God only knows where come into the Dawning and occupy a seat at my table? How did he find his way to Leroy in the first place? I lock my gaze on James, ignoring the insolence in his eyes, the burning resentment, and under my stare, something steadies in him. Settles.

The hum of people around me draws my attention to Leroy, who gives me a short, flinty look and turns to James. "Mr. Moore." His voice is low, yet it carries a hint of threat and commands attention. "Do I need to remind you why we are here?" The room goes silent. Leaning back in his chair, smooth and collected, Leroy smiles with the authority of a man in charge. "If you cannot handle yourself appropriately, I'll have to ask you to leave. The spirits must be respected." Everyone watches him in subdued silence. Most men nod in agreement. If Leroy is aware—and I'm certain he's fully aware—of the power he exudes over the room, he does not reveal it. Of course he won't. After all, he is a showman, a magician, a spirit conjurer.

But my breath catches at his last statement. The spirits must be respected? I raise a brow at Leroy. What about me, the medium, the vessel?

James puts his hands on the table. His knuckles are scarred from a recent brawl. "I apologize if I was rude." With a deep sigh, he sprawls in his chair, as if he just came back from a hard day in the field.

The mother grabs my hand again. "Tell me. I beg you. Tell me what happened." I see the years of pain and anger and fear on the woman's face. There is more fear than pain. There is more loneliness than anger. Nausea heaves through me as I make my choice.

"It was Ethel, but she didn't tell me anything, just asked me to not bother her again," I say.

The mother looks fragile for a short moment, her shoulders sagging. "You're a fraud," she says, her voice shaking, and I withdraw into the chair, away from her hateful gaze. "Ethel wouldn't be silent. That girl never knew how to keep her mouth shut." She leaps to her feet. The chair overturns behind her and falls to the ground with a loud thud. "This woman is no medium. She doesn't talk to spirits. She's lying to all of you," she shrieks and points a finger with a long, sharp nail at my face. "Give us our money back, you lying whore."

Every single welt on the girl's body is etched into my bones. My eyes sting with tears, not because of the deep sadness I feel for the girl, but because I'm angry and growing more furious by the second. Rage reaches out to my heart and sets it on fire.

I slowly get to my feet and stand in front of the woman.

"Well now—" Leroy pulls himself up, but I cut him off.

"Your daughter Ethel didn't die of influenza," I say sharply, punctuating every syllable, every word. "She had a blood infection. You beat her with a belt when she tried to run away from you, from your cruelty. Her wounds got infected." I step forward, and the mother flinches. "She's finally free of you. And she wishes you to rot in hell." The woman whimpers incoherently as she's backing away from me. Her eyes are wide; her lips are trembling. "You killed her. And if you don't leave my house, I'll send an army of ghosts after you. You'll live the rest of your life in misery, haunted by the dead."

Behind me, by the table, there are loud, incoherent murmurs, a mix of confusion and excitement. The voices are getting louder, almost bursting into a roar when the woman turns and flees the room. Someone screams, "Murderer!" Someone suggests sending for the police. Someone laughs, and I recognize James's voice, saying, "An army of ghosts? That's new. What does she mean?" Leroy is trying to say something, his voice loud, almost piercing, but no one is listening.

The room quiets as soon as I face the guests. "Shall we continue?"

"James hired the woman to expose us," I tell Leroy as soon as the guests leave, and we settle in the study. "He's dangerous. You need to do something. We cannot continue like this." Leroy doesn't say anything for a long time. All he does is look at the fire snapping in the hearth. My patience is wearing thin, and I push forward, adding, "For the love of God, Leroy. We need to get rid of him. He'll expose us, and we'll lose everything we've worked so hard for. We cannot afford it. I cannot afford it."

I'm puzzled by Leroy's hesitation. He's had many faces, performed multiple roles over the course of our time together—a spirit conjurer turned a trickster turned a mystery turned a business partner—but in that moment I see his perfectly constructed mask of poise slipping. I see him for what he is. A man lacking confidence in his own mediumship and needing a crutch in the face of a drifter like James. And we're just barely gaining our footing. The snobs who wrinkled their noses at me just a few weeks ago are seeking my company now. I may not be invited to fall galas yet, but I know that my social currency is gaining strength. Soon the invitations will come.

"Sadly, I think you're right," Leroy finally says and adds as an afterthought, "The time has come for James to leave."

I narrow my eyes at him. "Sadly?" Anger flows through my bloodstream. "You do realize he's trying to ruin us. And I'm wondering why."

"Jealousy, I reckon. We've been successful before, but not like this." He smiles at me. "You're extraordinary. Tonight was especially good. But I'm sad it came to this. James and I have been together for a long time. There was a time I considered him a friend."

As I lean deeper into the armchair, the Dawning moves around me, a slight lowering of the ceiling, a barely noticeable shift in the wooden planks under my feet. "What are you going to do about James?"

"I'll talk to him. I'll make sure he isn't part of our séances any longer."

"Apologies if I'm interrupting, but I heard my name mentioned." James barks a laugh, his stocky frame filling the doorway. I flinch back from the sound of his voice. How much has he heard? "I saw light in the windows and decided to come back." He walks into the room, heels clicking jarringly in the quiet. His shoes are caked with crusts of mud from the courtyard. "I came to collect my wages. Why delay until tomorrow if I can do it tonight, right?" His gaze slides from Leroy to me and back to Leroy, who nods at James with a sharp annoyance.

"Since you're already here, why delay indeed?" Leroy starts walking around the desk, but I spring to my feet and take hold of his sleeve, pulling him to a stop.

"Remind me: What are we paying him for?" I say, motioning in James's direction. My voice is as smooth as our polished silverware, but inside I'm seething. James shouldn't be here. Not at this hour. Not ever. "He didn't do anything for us tonight. We don't owe him a penny."

"Is she joking?" James turns to Leroy, who towers over my father's desk, his arms folded across his chest. "She better be joking."

There's ringing in my ears. The vein at the bottom of my neck beats against my skin as if trying to burst. "You want to expose us. You hired that awful woman to accuse me of fraud."

James shrugs and points his chin at me. "I wanted to expose you. Not Leroy."

"Why?"

He looks at me, and there's so much hatred in his eyes, I don't need his response. I want this man, this grifter, out of my house. I open the box, pick up a few bills, and reach out to James. "Here." I hand him his wages. "You don't deserve anything, but you can leave now. You won't be coming back. Your services are not needed."

He ignores my words and counts the bills exaggeratedly slowly, licking the tips of his fingers. Finally, he shoves the dollars into his jacket pocket. "Is that it, then?" He addresses Leroy, a glint of anger in his pale-gray eyes. "Just like that?"

"You broke my trust," Leroy says. "It's unforgivable."

James stalks to the whiskey decanter and pours himself a full glass. "So you choose her? This stupid rag over me?" He finishes the whiskey and pours some more, his eyes never leaving Leroy's face. "The spirit conjurer?" He chuckles and turns to me. "What new tricks did he show you to make all these fools believe you talk to the dead?"

"You'll be the last to find out." Leroy's words cut through the air like a whip, fast and sharp. "I'm losing my patience, James. Leave."

James empties his glass, wipes his mouth with the sleeve of his topcoat. "Fine. I'll go." He slowly sets the glass on the desk but doesn't put the decanter down. He gives that short bark of a laugh I hate. "I don't care about your gatherings." He pushes the words out of his mouth slowly. The disdain on his face morphs into fury. "But I care about my wages."

"I suggest you go somewhere else, then." Leroy's voice is surprisingly leveled, no sign of nerves. As if James doesn't pose danger. As if he's not trying to harm us.

James's face twists in a grimace as he spits on the floor. The spittle misses me by a few inches and lands by my right foot. I step aside. "Give me the Blue Book, and I'll never bother you again. This town is big enough for all of us. Imagine a new headline. A grieving father now talks to the spirits." He laughs at his own joke.

Leroy gives me a warning look and steps toward James. "You're drunk, James. We'll talk later. Perhaps tomorrow when you sleep the whiskey off."

James doesn't move, just stares boldly back at Leroy. "You're giving the book to *her*. But I can pay you. I saved up enough."

"The book's not for sale," Leroy says, shifting his weight from one foot to the other. A floorboard creaks underneath his weight—a loud snap, amplified by the silence.

"Why her, Leroy?" James waves his hand around the room. "She ain't that special. She might be good at rolling her eyes and knocking with her heels, but she doesn't deserve the book. What has she done? How long have you known her? She ain't one of us." He inspects me with an oily smile that turns my stomach. "Wasn't she supposed to move away? Like her lunatic mother? This house's full of wraiths. It ain't for the living." He laughs, but his eyes remain cold.

James's words carry the same sentiment as Tilda's. A bitter pang of suspicion expands inside my mind, but what exactly they're trying to do and why escapes me. Driving me away from the house because it's full of ghosts might've worked on someone younger and sillier. It's not going to work on me.

Thud.

I flinch, but Leroy and James don't seem to hear it. Another thud from within the walls, like something heavy being moved and pushed.

"Oh I see." James spits incredulously, oblivious to all the noises within the walls. "It's not just the house she opened for you but her legs too. And whatever you found between her thighs must've blinded you."

Leroy lunges forward and punches James in his nose. A crunch, a wet, sickly sound like a cockroach crushed underfoot. James's head jerks back, and he staggers, hands flailing, mouth agape, blood bubbling around his lips. He gasps through his teeth like an animal, choking on his own fluids. I shudder when I see blood. So much blood. My body goes cold, and I want to scream, to plead them to stop, but all I do is stare. Leroy lifts his fist again while his other hand reaches out to grab

James by the lapels of his jacket, but James spins out of his grasp and smashes the decanter into Leroy's head. The heavy glass connects with the side of his face, near the corner of his eye. Leroy stumbles, holding his hand to the gushing wound. He takes an unsteady step backward and trips over his own feet. He falls on his back, his body rigid, his hands grasping at air. In an instant, James is on top of him.

I finally scream what I think is both their names, but the sound transforms into an incomprehensible howl. I leap onto James's back and try to grab his hands, yank him off Leroy, stop the madness. James twists and pushes me away with one hand. The other is holding a jagged shard of glass. The decanter must've broken. There's blood everywhere—on his face, his hands, around Leroy's head. I fall on my back and hit the floor so hard, the air leaves my lungs in a whoosh. I scramble to my feet, sliding and almost falling again, the floor slick with blood.

"Leroy," Tilda's voice howls as she rushes into the room. She shouts something else. So much noise. So many words. I'm standing, mesmerized by the violence. I cannot believe this is happening to Leroy, to me.

James lifts his head. Murder clouds his face, his thin lips stretching out in a primal scowl. Tilda wrenches a log out of a small mound by the hearth and launches herself at James. Bits of something white, maybe paint, drop from the ceiling and dust the floor like snowflakes. The pipes moan loudly in the walls. The wallpaper ripples. The floor tilts.

Tilda smashes the log into James's forehead, and he crumples to the floor.

October 28, 1903

My darling Amos,

Despite our unexplainable rift, I'm so grateful for Tilda. There was a fight in the house, but all is well now. Sometimes a good hit on the head is all that is needed. James is gone, and we will never have to see him again. He was conscious—a bit disoriented but cognizant—when he stumbled out the front door and disappeared into the night. For his sake I hope he found his way back to town.

I helped Tilda to boil a pot of water and gather some clean towels so that she could clean Leroy's head wound. Kneeling next to him, she cleaned his lips and his face and his cuts. She did it so slowly. So gently. And yet he still winced and jerked and even growled like a wild animal. I watched them for a while, but I was not happy about her touching him in such an intimate, personal way. So I retreated to my room before she was finished. I could not sleep, and I tossed and turned all night.

This morning I spent hours going through our father's paperwork, trying to find information that would help me figure out how I can give the farm back to the Rask family. I searched and searched for what seemed like hours and could not find anything, and then, when I almost gave up, one of the drawers that was always locked—the bottom drawer—suddenly fell to the ground. And what I found there was a documented decade of shady deals.

Our father bought parcels and parcels of land from the government (who bought it from the Omaha Tribe for twenty-two cents per acre—imagine that) and then he turned around and sold it to the railway companies for thousands of dollars per acre. At some point he even formed a land speculation company to ensure his grip on reservation land titles. I found an old map of the Union Pacific Railroad in the drawer all marked up in Father's handwriting. The parcels of land were mostly riverfront lots, but one of the central inland parcels belonged to Mr. Rask.

After six months of working on the piece of land, Mr. Rask paid $1.25 an acre and got his land title instead of farming it for five years as the law prescribed. He borrowed from Father against his land to buy animals, equipment, wheat, and that's how he got into his financial troubles. Because Father was not an honest man, whatever interest he collected exceeded Mr. Rask's resources by far.

Father—as all rich people in our rotten town—did not think twice about the homeless or hungry or poor.

Do you think the boy came through the veil to avenge his family? I wish I could help, but I have no idea how to find his family. They left in a hurry, and no one seems to know where they went to. Can you help me, Amos? Can you send me a sign from the other side?

I do not know how you slipped through the cracks between our worlds, but I keep touching the locket and hoping you will find your way back to me. You told me once the locket pulled you through the veil like a rope.

OH MY GOODNESS, Amos! I think I know what I must do.

With all my love,

Your sister Nina

Chapter 22

I place my silver locket on my father's desk. "I know how to summon spirits. I know what works. I finally, finally figured it all out." I pour myself two fingers of whiskey and turn to Leroy. His lower lip is swollen slightly, and there is a purple bruise on his chin. I wonder how James looks. Hopefully, much worse. "This silver locket. Ethel's doll. It all makes sense to me. I know why the spirits refuse to come." I sink down into the armchair, cross my ankles, and smile, delighted with the discovery. "And it's much simpler than I thought."

"Your silver locket? I don't understand," Leroy says as he puts a log into the hearth. "The locket and the doll. Are these things connected?"

I laugh. "Connected to me in a way. In a very exciting way."

"Is it a riddle, Miss Wilson?" His grin always makes my heart skip a beat. Something smolders in his gaze as he kneels beside me. "I'm not good at riddles. Have I told you that?" He reaches his hand toward me and runs his cool fingers down my cheek. "None of what you're saying makes any sense to me." The fire snaps in the hearth, and the words die on my lips. Firelight makes his face paler than usual, sharpening his features, making him even more handsome. Neither of us says anything. There is only his breath and the thrum of my own heartbeat.

The space grows hot and airless, and to distract myself from Leroy, I take a few sips of whiskey. "The mother brought the doll to the séance to summon her daughter's spirit. And it worked. It finally worked. The spirit of her daughter came. You saw it with your own eyes. You heard what the girl said. The doll was the vessel. And the girl was able to hear me, and she responded."

Leroy chuckles. "Like all dreaded things do eventually."

"But do you understand now?" I point at the locket. "I should've figured it all out sooner. All this time it was right in front of my nose."

Leroy gets to his feet and looms over me, studying the locket. "Are you saying this locket helped you summon Amos? I thought the locket was yours."

"When Amos was sent away, I gave him my locket. A week before his death, he sent it back to me. I didn't know it then, but it was his way of saying goodbye. Maybe even asking for forgiveness." My voice is cracking, my eyes are burning, and I take a deep breath to settle my racing pulse. The gut-wrenching, familiar grief stirs sharply in my chest. I remember feeling the coldness of silver in my hand. I remember the shock. Tilda delivered the mail, and I sat staring at the bright whiteness of the envelope, wondering why my twin sent the locket back to me without writing a single word.

"The locket." There's an urgency to Leroy's voice. "You think the locket brought Amos to you? Is that how it works?" He finally understands.

"Yes, exactly that." I look down at my glass, carefully running my fingers around its cool edges. "I burned my brother's belongings after his death. His clothes, his books, his things. They were living, breathing memories. It was just too much. Mother was livid when I did it. She must've hated me then even more. I had nothing of Amos left except for that locket."

Neither of us says anything for a few moments as we listen to snaps and pops coming from the fireplace. I get to my feet and set my glass on the desk. "How does it work with you?" I ask Leroy. "Why do the spirits respond to you?"

"I don't know. I've never given it much thought," he says slowly. "Must be my charming personality," he adds with a small smile. He's watching me keenly, and something pokes at my heart like a small shard of glass, but I ignore it.

"The letters I write to my brother," I say. "They helped him. That's what he said. But the locket pulled him through the veil."

"The locket. The porcelain doll." Leroy slowly rubs the back of his neck. "Something real. Something tangible." His face is half shadowed when he turns to look at the fire.

"I suspect that's the only way for me to commune with the dead." I'm surprised he doesn't ask me about the origin of my powers, and I don't share my theory. I used to think I was going mad and it was my grief that cracked open my soul and triggered something so powerful, I became a vessel, existing between the world of the living and the world of the dead. But now, I suspect that it was Ollie Rask who breached the veil, sensed my connection to the Dawning, and granted me my childhood wish. Because I'm the only one who can heal his wounds and bring justice to his family.

"Fascinating," Leroy says. "Let's make sure to include that request in the invitations."

Spiritualism proves to be a tiring exercise for body and mind but also a remarkably profitable one. All my family bills, including my father's gambling debts, are paid in full. I even allowed myself to splurge on a new velvet dress in a pattern of black and gold, a bright-red wool coat, and new red leather shoes with a Louis heel to match the coat.

Mother's departure still haunts me. But the crashing guilt that used to spring in my chest in the deep hours of the night has lost its bite. It is still there, tucked away inside me, but I don't feel the same raw disquiet. When I close my eyes, I still see her pale face and long, disheveled hair, and my chest still seizes with sadness, but the load that has been pressing on my heart for eternity has lifted slightly.

As the days turn into weeks, I feel more and more at ease around our guests and the dead who come with them. I stop noticing how my skin tingles with nerves every time a spirit brushes by. Or how cold sweat licks the back of my neck right before I meet hollow, dead eyes and pose a question.

After séances, Leroy and I retreat to the study. He folds his tall frame into my father's armchair and watches me count the bills, a smile playing on the corners of his mouth every time I get excited about how much money we made. We are becoming something I cannot define. Allies? Friends? None of it fits. None of it explains how I feel about him. There's an electric current buzzing in the air every time we're alone. I'm sure he senses it, too, because sometimes I catch his eyes on me, full of unspoken hunger, and it takes everything in me not to respond to it. But with every passing day, with every brush of his fingers against my wrist, with his every joke and every smile, my defenses are getting weaker.

Tonight is no different. I'm perched on the edge of the chair across from him, a glass of whiskey in my hand. "We made so much in such a short period of time." I take a swallow of my drink. "I'm thinking to redecorate the Dawning for the holidays." Mother used to start her Christmas shopping early. Her engraved invitations to our Christmas gala were sent out a month in advance. The house featured bright-red velvet ribbons on the mantelpieces and up our long and curving staircase. Our Christmas tree was always considered the tallest, lushest tree in Omaha, boasting the most extravagant decorations.

His smile is big enough for the two of us. "We don't want to invite strangers into the house, do we?"

"We invite strangers into the house twice a week," I note. "What's the difference?"

"A séance is a controlled environment. Having workers inside the house at any given hour might be inconvenient."

I grin. "Are you afraid they'll discover all your tricks, Mr. Marshall?"

He doesn't smile in response. He doesn't come up with a witty retort. Instead, he studies my face, as if looking for something that isn't there, and doesn't say anything for a long minute.

"I want the Dawning to shine brightly for Christmas," I say. "Maybe we can have our own holiday gala here. Dance, drink." I chuckle. "Be merry."

"Be merry?" His lips twitch.

"I'm tired of being alone, sequestered in the house. Is that wrong of me to want to have a party?"

"You're not alone," he says gently.

I remember then how alone I was before he entered the house. How one small moment, one impulsive invitation, changed my life, and how strange it is that a thoughtless promise has somehow morphed into this: séances, ghosts, a black box full of money in the middle of the desk.

"You ever think about stopping?" He raises a brow at me.

"Stopping?" I meet his gaze and see muscles in his jaw straining. It never crossed my mind to stop doing séances. Not yet. I like helping people find answers they seek. And it gives me power and status, and it pays so well. Sipping my drink, I lean back against the armchair. "There are days and especially nights when I grow tired of all the sadness and sorrow. Of all the tragedy. In moments like that, I want to pause. Take a break, maybe. But I've never thought about stopping." I take a deep breath and look down at my glass. "Before the séances, I thought about leaving Omaha. Now?" I look at Leroy, and suddenly my cheeks heat up. "I'm not so certain."

He pushes himself from the chair, walks over to me, and takes my hand. Then he gently yet insistently pulls me to my feet and into him. He's so close, I see golden flecks in his eyes. There's sadness, the same thing I often see in his face when he's haunted by his thoughts. And there's a familiar need, a longing I see so often too. The one that makes my knees go soft.

"Why don't we take a break and go somewhere else for the holidays? The Dawning will be here when you come back. And so will the spirits." His breath brushes over my lips, his fingers warm and firm as they trail my upper lip, pausing by its dip. "Let's go to Chicago."

I raise a hand to his cheek, and he covers it with his. "A holiday together?" I whisper. His skin is warm, so warm, the heat radiates off him in waves. "It sounds lovely."

He takes me by the chin, his eyes heavy with need. My hands lace around his shoulders, and with a gentle pull, he draws me closer, and his lips are finally on mine, hungry and rough. I press hard against his chest and open up to him, also starving. His tongue tangles desperately with mine, and everything around me fades away. His hands on me, his muscles tightening under my grip, his breath brushing against my skin, and my fingers running through his hair.

He tastes of whiskey, spiced and sweet and blistering. His lips grow greedier; his tongue is more insistent. He withdraws slightly as his hand pushes into my hair and pulls my head back, exposing my throat. Then his mouth is on my skin, and I moan, digging my fingers into his shoulders.

"Nina." His voice is thick as he lifts his head for an instant, and I slide my hand into his hair, pulling him back to me.

Hearing him say my name, making it sound like the most beautiful name in the world, opens something in me—something fiery and all-consuming. My hips move, my head tilts back as his tongue grazes along the edge of my throat, dipping lower to my collarbone. He pulls the dress off my shoulders; the fabric rips, exposing my skin. Heat rising in my chest, I find his lips, catching them between my teeth, and he growls something incoherent. His grip on me becomes almost painful; his hands are everywhere, taking me in—every nerve, every breath, every moan. His kiss is wild and heedless. The fire of his touch consumes me, awakens something feral in me, and I give myself to it. His mouth against my skin, healing my wounds, melting away my guilt and shame and grief.

The door slams behind us, and we both startle at the harshness of the sound.

"Didn't mean to intrude," Tilda says from the door, mouth set in a thin line. She stands still, a tall, lean figure in a pale-blue blouse to match the blue of her eyes. Her arms are crossed against her chest as she makes no effort to hide an unpleasant scowl on her face. Her sharp eyes travel along my exposed shoulders down to my chest. I frantically pull on the ripped sleeves of my dress. She watches me trying to cover myself up, and an unsettling expression flickers across her face as she says, "I'm about to retire for the night. You need anything else from me?" Her hand touches her neck and brushes lightly against it, as if trying to draw my attention to something.

"No," I murmur, tugging on the thin lace, ripping it further. "You can go."

Leroy shoves his hands into his pockets, but right before he does it, I see his hands curl into fists. "You shouldn't be here," he says, his voice low, even dangerous.

"Don't I know it," Tilda says, and her lips quiver for half a second as she continues to brush her fingers across her throat.

Leroy goes completely still, his jaw going slack, as if he's talking to a ghost. The spiced scent of his shaving soap wafts through the air, bringing to mind another spiced scent that seems to be attached to Tilda. The earthy and spiced scent of witch hazel. Leroy's aftershave. The realization tugs on some invisible string in my swelling-with-dread chest, and I'm terrified to pull on it. Because I know there will be no going back from whatever I uncover.

"We won't be needing anything." His usually confident voice trails off. "For God's sake, Tilda. Leave." The way he looks at Tilda, the harsh surprise in his eyes, reminds me of the moment when he studied me at the Hollands' the first time we met—the way his eyes narrowed, the way he faltered, as if he'd seen something unexpected. Something alarming.

"Tilda, wait," I say.

The air seems to have gone from the study the moment I see it. A familiar black silk necktie is fastened around Tilda's long neck. I can't catch a breath when I make out yellow letters embroidered in the corner: LWM. He wore it the first time we met at the Hollands'. He calls it his lucky charm. I haven't seen him wearing it for a while now, but I never questioned what happened to his favorite necktie.

"A gift," Tilda says, answering my unspoken question.

"Nina—" Leroy starts, his face reddening, but I put my hand up, quieting him.

The silence falls, deafening, the air taut with so much strain, the room is about to explode.

I should have realized it sooner. Seen it sooner. All women in the Dawning eventually end up under Leroy's spell. He snaked his way into our house, charmed his way into Mother's heart. I blindly followed in her footsteps. Of course, Tilda is no different and couldn't resist his looks either. I'm certain now it was her footsteps I heard at night while lying in bed dreaming about the man who deceived us all. How many nights has Tilda spent in Leroy's room?

My stomach churns. I'm about to be ill. I cannot bear to look at him. At Tilda. And that damned necktie. A high-pitched sound—a shocking, embarrassing screech—pierces the air as I lurch at Tilda, wrap my fingers around the necktie, and rip it off her neck. She clutches at her throat, her mouth wide open in a scream I don't bother to listen to. I run out of the room before anyone can stop me, and when I get to the staircase, I sense the shift in the air. My head is swimming. I feel dizzy, and when I look up the stairs, I cannot see the end of the staircase; its ascent is steep and endless. With a deep sigh, I squeeze the necktie in my left hand, brace my right hand on the railing, and start climbing.

A damp, moldy smell surrounds me. The ceiling presses lower, but the staircase widens so much I cannot see the walls anymore. My muscles burn with every step I take. The wind wails in my ears, and I begin to shake, violent shudders, bone deep. I trip and fall forward, my hands and knees slamming hard into the floor. Sharp vises burst through the carpet and crawl through the stairs like tentacles, tightening around my ankles, digging into my skin. I yelp, scramble to my feet, weak kneed and whimpering, and try to wrench away my ankles, but the vises cut through my stockings, slice my skin, and burrow into my veins. "Please stop," I moan through the agonizing, blinding pain. "Stop it. Please." As if obeying, the tentacles recede for a few seconds, only to attack my feet with even more force.

Angry, angry, the house whispers.

I force myself to stop moving. Stop fighting against the house. I must redirect my anger into something else, but what? I decide to fight pain with pain. Squeezing my eyes shut, I bite down on the inside of my cheek with such force, blood floods my mouth. I do it again and again, until my head is clear, until tears spill in rivulets down my cheeks, until my anger is fading away.

A few long inhales later, everything is quiet. The carpet underneath my feet is worn, but it looks normal. The banister is smooth and polished, as it was this morning. I can see the walls and the top of the stairs. There are no cuts on my skin. No blood on the floor, just in my mouth. The Dawning has gone back to normal. Sweat beads between my brows, and with a sigh of relief, I wipe it off with the back of my hand.

When I finally reach my room, my legs turn into cotton, my muscles shaky. The world around me is spinning so badly, I barely make it to the bowl by my vanity, where I purge myself of everything that is connected to Leroy. After I wash my face and rinse my mouth, I stand in front of the window. The night is quiet, covering the world outside in a deep-black veil. The trees are only shadows swaying in the familiar white mist.

The boy outside is watching me. A look of unmistakable delight crosses his face as he spreads his arms and slowly ascends to my window. He floats behind the glass, studying me with an amusement I cannot quite fathom. As if he thinks I've done something unexpected. Whatever that might be. His mouth twists into an approving grin, and for a moment, I feel a small bit of pride, knowing that I was able to surprise the ghost. That I am the reason he is amused. I put my palm on the glass, and he does the same. The heavy mist seeps between his fingers but never breaks through the window. I lean my forehead against the glass and close my eyes. When I open them, the boy is gone.

Chapter 23

I sit on the edge of the bed for a long time. What am I supposed to do now? I rub my temples, my fingers digging into the skin.

A loud knock at the door jolts me.

"Nina," Leroy's voice says from the hallway.

I push myself away from the bed and shuffle to the door. I grip the doorjamb as he says, "Nina, please, let me explain." I stare at my hand, my knuckles devoid of color. I set my shoulders, gather whatever shreds of dignity I still have left, and wrench the door open.

His pale face is illuminated by the twinkling candlelight. How many times have I imagined him coming to my room at night? How many times have I fantasized about him closing the door shut and stepping into my embrace?

He leans on the doorframe, watching me. He's holding a candle in one hand; the other is in his pocket. "Nina—" he starts with a sheepish grin, but I put my hand up, and he falls silent. Fury blossoms, bright and ravenous, at my own foolishness. At his betrayal. At my own willingness to be blind.

"There is nothing you can say that would change my mind." I try my best to keep my expression neutral and my words clipped with coolness. His smile gradually disappears as if being wiped away by a cleaning cloth. Just the traces of it touch the corners of his lips when he looks at me more closely, not fully trusting my words.

"You don't know what I'm about to say."

"I'm not interested in anything you have to say. I want you and Tilda out of the Dawning by sunrise."

Uncertainty flickers across his face, but he disguises it with a forced sigh. "Nina, please, let me explain."

"No."

He rubs the back of his neck. "You're not being fair."

"Fair?" My voice breaks because everything inside me is on fire. I'm not just seething; I'm raging. The man who mesmerized me the first time I laid my eyes on him, who moved my heart with his charm, now stands in the hallway reduced to a cheater. "What an odd word you chose considering the circumstances." He takes a half step toward me, and I breathe the scent of him, the familiar tang of shaving soap and whiskey. "Don't come any closer," I say sharply.

He hesitates, squaring his shoulders, but doesn't take another step.

Behind him, the wallpaper starts to simmer, small bubbles spreading in rapid succession. At first, I think it must be shadows from Leroy's candle dancing on the wall and mocking my imagination, but then something groans in the walls. And I know. The Dawning is waking up. The sound moves through the house, closer now—and a second later farther away.

Leroy, oblivious to it all, massages his forehead. "I must explain."

"I'd rather you don't explain yourself to me." I throw the words at him like blades. He shuts his eyes for a few seconds. When he looks at me, there is a question on his face, and I shake my head. "There's nothing here for you. Not anymore."

"Don't." He sounds hollow, depleted. "Don't do it. Don't destroy our partnership. Everything we've built together."

I burst into laughter, a bitter and thorny sound. "Is that what it is?" I ask between croaks of laughter. "A partnership?" Rage, black and agonizing, that has been straining against my rib cage since I saw that necktie wrapped around Tilda's neck engulfs me. Its heat ripples through my veins. I rub my forehead, as if trying to erase every thought that still connects me to him. I hate him with everything I've got. For his open deceit and betrayal, for his inability to admit the truth—and, most of all, I hate myself for allowing him to use me as a pawn. "I'm done being a fool." His face pales, but he doesn't respond. His nose starts to bleed. At first, it's a thin trickle, and then a great gush of blood spills down the front of his face. I watch the blood make its way to his chin and then his shirtfront. "You're bleeding."

He wipes at his face, smearing the blood. He takes a step back, his face confused. "Where did it come from?"

"Your nose."

He swipes at his nose and studies his fingers marked with blood. He staggers backward.

"You need to leave," I say.

He pinches his nose and tips his head back. "I'm not leaving unless you give me a chance to explain. Tilda's an old friend. I've known her for a long time." His eyes narrow as he looks at me. "We've been working together. James, Tilda, and I."

"The three of you?" I remember reading the recommendation in the Blue Book about how to approach Mother. "My Lord. She's the one who told you about Father's accident. About our nightly walks to the cemetery. My letters to Amos." I watch his face for some kind of response—guilt, shame—but there's nothing there. "All that tapping. The knocking in the night. It wasn't you, was it? It was her. You lied to me to protect her." Bile rises in my throat.

"It's part of the business."

I squeeze the edges of the doorframe—the polished wood prickly and uneven under my grip—and watch my knuckles turn white. "But why? Why do you need to dig up the most personal, most shameful things about people? You talk to the spirits. Isn't it enough?"

"He doesn't talk to no spirits." Tilda's voice floats through the air. "He doesn't see no ghosts. It's all tricks." Tilda appears by Leroy's side dressed in a brown smock, her feet stuffed into short leather boots with a fancy heel. Our séances benefited everyone, but blinded by my affections, I missed how much Tilda's dressing has changed. A woman who introduced me to pawnbrokers, who folded bedsheets in the morning and served coffee in the afternoon, who washed dishes and threw apples at the walls pretending to be someone she wasn't is looking at me like I'm nothing and she's a queen.

Leroy looks at Tilda, who's clutching a small valise in her hands, prepared to leave, and then at me, and something shadowy clouds his eyes.

I think I knew it all along. But I was afraid to admit it. Because once you admit you're a fool, you must act on it. Do something to correct your mistakes. To right all the wrongs. "Is this true?" My voice is flat. "You don't talk to the spirits? All of it was a foolish, pathetic ruse?"

"I've been doing it for so long, I don't know who I am anymore. I had so many experiences, I don't know what I believe."

"Stop lying. It's not needed anymore," Tilda says. Her gaze slashes me to my core. "It was so simple. You and your lunatic mother alone in this house. No daddy to pay the bills. No brother to protect you. Such a perfect con. We thought we scare you away with our ghost stories and you'll abandon the house. Your mother signs the deed to Leroy. He pays the tax bill, and the Dawning becomes ours. We were so close. Your mother was an easy mark, but you . . ." She takes a few steps toward me. "You turned out to be something else entirely."

Some places are not meant for the living. It all makes sense now.

"Mother was supposed to sign the deed?"

"Well, she got so crazy so fast, we couldn't talk to her about anything but your father." She shrugs and looks at Leroy, who can't seem to look me in the face. His focus is on his shoes. His mouth is twisted into a frown. "All of it was his idea. A desolate location. No neighbors. Two vulnerable women. A perfect place for séances."

"What changed?" My voice is hoarse and wretched.

He finally looks at me.

"You're the best thing that ever happened to me in my life," he says with a deep sadness in his voice. "And yes, in the beginning, I had this idea of driving you away. You were so lost. So gullible."

My hands twitch. I want to hit him. I want to shout and push him down the stairs and wipe Leroy Marshall from the face of the earth. But through sheer power of will, I force myself to remain still.

"I didn't know you at all. In that unpredictable and exciting way that I got to know you later. As soon as I suspected you had abilities, I wanted to see if I could expand my business. Make it something real. Something that cannot be exposed. And having you by my side, your beauty alone was a great attraction, a selling ticket. Your acting talent kept everyone mesmerized. But then, with time, everything changed. At least for me." He rubs his forehead. "I fell in love."

"Stop it, please. You're getting so dramatic, Leroy," Tilda drawls. "Enough of this horseshit. You never loved her."

I look at Tilda. Really look at her, and as I meet her eyes, I know with an awful, devastating clarity that she's lying. The most valuable lesson of spiritualism is learning how to spot a lie. And by now, I know her face as well as mine. The sly twist of her lips when she tells our guests the windows are closed and there is no breeze. The sharp tilt of her head when she whispers stories about ghosts. I know how wariness darkens the blue in her eyes when she gets a response she doesn't expect. I recognize the quick pulse at the bottom of her throat when she knows she's winning. My body trembles, but not with nerves. With rage. Deep, black, all-consuming rage.

I turn to Leroy, who must be expecting that his declaration of love will fix everything between us. "I was one of your *experiences*," I snarl. "One of your tricks that turned out to be a real deal. Get out. Leave Omaha. I'm sure people will come after you when they find out you used their grief to cheat them out of their money." My voice rises, as I'm trying to talk over the mounting growls deep in the walls. "If you stay, I swear I'll expose all your tapping, knocking, and apple-throwing tricks." Fury scorches my chest and flows through me in waves. Something clangs against the pipes, and this time Leroy hears it, because he jolts and looks around, trying to determine the source of the sound. "And take her with you." I point a finger at Tilda.

Large beads of thick, black mold slide to the floor like drops of rain and sink into the carpet. A foul odor invades my nostrils—something earthy and rotten, as if a casket was left open in the sun. An odd humming noise replaces the groans. The Dawning is chanting.

"Nina, look at me," Leroy says, and I tear my gaze away from the mold. "You're wrong about me. I help people. My ways might be unconventional. But together we can do a lot of good."

I don't answer, and he waits for a while. The longer I remain silent, the more uncomfortable he gets. His nose starts to bleed again. Large beads of blood bloom on his upper lip. Leroy shakes his head, the bloody streaks glinting crimson in the candlelight. "It must be the whiskey. Alcohol sometimes has that effect on me." As he talks, his lips split, and for a second he looks distraught.

"You're not listening. Leave now." I repeat my words slowly, trying to make him understand. Whatever is happening with the house, it's getting worse. The air starts to vibrate, and Leroy must sense it, too, because when I meet his eyes, he sees the threat, the terror. The darkness. His face pales, and he steps away from me, as if I am the source of his fear.

"My God, you're bleeding." Tilda's fingers brush at Leroy's lips, wiping away the blood, and he slumps as if the weight of her touch pushes him into the ground. "We must go. There's nothing for us here." She turns to me with slow, deliberate insolence. "Let her rot in this house. There'll be others."

The walls close in, and a roar erupts out of my chest, full of wrath and agony. It's not just the hurt of her betrayal but also the suggestion in her tone that she's better than I am, smarter in a way I'll never be. The implication there is always someone else out there. Another experience. Another trick. And maybe even a better one.

I leap forward and push Tilda with a force I never thought I possessed, and her back slams into the brown paneling. The chanting inside the walls begins again, low and threatening. The voices are humming under my skin, in my blood, all around me. I want to cover my ears, but I don't dare to move.

A wail pierces the air. Tilda's head is turned to the ceiling; her eyes are wide as she's staring into the space above her. The wallpaper, alive with mold, separates from the wall and brushes over Tilda's hair. Then it violently presses itself against her tall figure. She thrashes, tries to break free, but the wallpaper slopes tightly around her hips, her waist and her chest, and finally her throat. Under its pressure, Tilda's face warps and changes. Her eyes gape wider, the eyeballs slowly rolling out of their sockets. Her jaw twists and turns and rips itself. The sound of her bones cracking is the most awful sound I've ever heard. Her mouth twists into an unnatural, inhuman scowl, but no sound comes out.

A second later, the house pulls Tilda inside the wall.

Chapter 24

"What just happened?" Leroy's voice thunders in the silence. He presses his quivering hand to his forehead. A thick layer of sweat covers his ashy skin. Blood crusts in the corners of his mouth. "Where did she go?" He looks old in this moment—inky hollows underneath his eyes are as deep as ditches in Omaha streets. His face is withered and haggard, as if everything that happened drained him of what little life he has left.

"The Dawning swallowed your lover." A half sob, half deranged laugh breaks through me. "Now you believe me when I say you need to leave?" I lean on the door, feeling utterly exhausted. And somehow much, much older too.

He's gone within seconds, bolting for the front door, and I am left alone. A part of me is still waiting for something to happen—the screams, the chanting to resume, or Leroy's footsteps rushing back, the strong grip of his arms as he carries me away from the house.

I press my eyes shut, waiting, but nothing happens.

Instead, the air clears, the sounds recede, and everything looks normal again.

I turn around and go back to my room.

Chapter 25

The days that follow are a blur of suppressed memories and vivid visions of walls growing claws, slicing through my rib cage, carving my broken heart to ribbons. I drink whiskey, but its burn doesn't help me much.

The toughest part is being alone in the house, walking in its empty hallways, touching Mother's crosses on the walls, going into rooms where dust motes swirl in the air. Memories that flood my mind make it hard to breathe. This space reminds me of the days when there were people here. Living, breathing people who laughed and made plans about the future and who filled this place with life. Now, only ghostly madness lurks here.

During the day, I drift through the house, unsteady on my feet, my fingers wrapped around the bottle of whiskey. I question my sanity and my choices. The Dawning watches me and sighs; its pipes moan and groan in response to my whimpers. There are moments when I think I hear Leroy's boots thudding on the floor, knocking off mud, and I run downstairs, certain he has come back. Of course I don't find him. I don't find anyone. As the days creep along, I'm starting to wonder if the Dawning is testing me.

I cannot stop thinking about Leroy. I hate the way thoughts of him overpower me throughout the day. The hope of his return is crippling. And yet it continues to bite and cut me at every step I take. Why doesn't he come back? He said he loves me. Where did he go? The thought of him fills my days. With the night comes despair, and it settles inside me like a bruise, ripe with blackness.

I hate the hold he still has on me.

Every day I feel the Dawning's invisible eyes, like a weight. It presses on my shoulders. On my chest. Mother's wooden crosses rattle, and the wallpaper blossoms with mold every time I run downstairs expecting to find Leroy. This continues for a few days, and when I stop waiting, stop hoping, the noises stop too. The Dawning's attention retreats, the weight lifts, and I can breathe again.

The acceptance of Leroy's betrayal is like a punch to my already broken heart.

I sob all night.

The next morning, when I stumble downstairs, my eyes watery and bloodshot from liquor, the pipes wail loudly in the kitchen. I don't want to go. I don't want to know what the house has prepared for me. But when I hear the sound of rushing water, I turn on my heel, then walk quickly down the hallway. The pipes whine and spew foul-smelling water on the floor. I shiver and gasp and slowly back away from the kitchen.

No more. A whisper in my head. *No more.*

"No more," I agree, my hands rolled into fists, as though I'm preparing to fight my own thoughts. My throat closes up with pain, but I don't let myself cry. Instead, I let my rage at Leroy's betrayal flow through me. Until my heart settles and my eyes stop burning and I'm free of pain, free of my thoughts of him.

In a few hours, the kitchen is back to normal. Not a trace of water remains.

As days go by, the house and I are merging together, turning into one being full of bones and mold and bursting pipes.

Every room, every wall, every space in the house reminds me of Tilda. How she shrugged her shoulders and how she used to look at me with sadness and a bit of wonder. She made me think I had an ally in the house. Someone who understood my broken promises. Someone who thought I was doing everything right, even when I was doing everything wrong. I ache physically when her last moments break through the surface of my hazy mind. When I remember how her jaw broke, the loud snapping of her bones. When I close my eyes, I get flashbacks to the sound of her final screams, to the smell of Leroy's aftershave as he turned to watch her last moments, to the dripping mold like fat tears sliding down the wallpaper.

At night, I lie awake for hours, terrified to shut my eyes because behind my eyelids lives Tilda's warped face. To avoid recalling her quick and ruthless demise, I force myself to stare at the ceiling and think about the past. I don't dare think about the future, because I'm not sure there is one. When I am too tired to think, I go downstairs to my father's study and drink all the whiskey I can find. It helps me to contain my memories, to encapsulate my thoughts. To let them rot inside me.

During the daylight, I allow images of Tilda on the wall to carve my brain and bleed it raw. In the deep of the night, I fill myself with whiskey, and the heaviness recedes. With the alcohol coursing in my bloodstream, my thoughts weigh nothing. I drink myself unconscious every night. Because whatever the whiskey gives me is preferable to anything that is my life.

I open my eyes in the morning; the air is saturated with the stench of whiskey and my own vomit. It must be a late morning, because the daylight is soft and gray. I feel more wretched than yesterday, and yesterday was awful. The hammering in my temples is thunderous. It hurts to move my eyes. My stomach contracts, but nothing rises up my throat. I must've purged myself of everything last night.

There are no sounds in the walls, and I'm grateful for the silence. For the nothingness. My mind is awake, which means the memories are about to break free. But for now, in an alcohol-induced fog, they are shoved into the furthest corners of my psyche and held together by thin, fragile threads.

I slowly get out of bed and drop my nightdress on the floor into a puddle of my own sickness. I wash my face and untangle the knots in my hair. The pipes groan, and the walls shudder. The brush gets stuck, and I pull and tug and twist until my eyes start to burn. When was the last time I brushed my hair? How long has it been since Tilda and Leroy left me?

I contemplate going into the kitchen and rummaging through the empty pantry, but not in search of food. In search of more alcohol. I remember Father mentioning something about extra bottles he kept downstairs. I work my fingers through the long strands. My movements are slow. My limbs are heavy.

It starts to rain outside. I tense and listen and wait, bracing myself for what's to come. The pounding of the rain is usually accompanied by the wailing, a hollow, keening sound from within the walls. She screams mostly at night, and on a rare occasion her shrieks break out during the day. It doesn't last for long, even though the sound travels freely through the house. When I hear her cries, I wonder if she knows what happened to her. If her heart is tapping violently against her ribs as she tries to free herself. Does she crawl inside the walls, looking for a way out? Does her mind remain intact and understand she's now a part of the house, trapped forever within the walls of the place she was so eager to leave? Is she screaming for her lover to come and rescue her? What does she see inside the Dawning? Does the house speak to her in a hoarse whisper like it does to me?

I don't want to know.

Yet my thoughts coil and curve and go back to her. To her attempts to break through the wall and set herself free. Once I saw her face slowly emerging through the wallpaper. The edges of her broken face were softer, less shattered, smoothed out by paper. But the expression was so furious, I screamed. The Dawning hauled her back at once, but I remained rooted to the floor, staring at the space where her face had glared at me just a few seconds earlier. If only I could talk to her, say something to soothe her pain.

Since then, every morning on my way downstairs, I stand in front of the wall that swallowed her and try to find the words, try to make a sound, but I can't. What would I say, anyway? How her betrayal tore my soul to pieces and I'll never be able to trust anyone ever again? How much I want to know why she had wanted to hurt me? Because to do what she did requires intention and desire to inflict pain. What have I done to deserve any of it? I didn't know Leroy was hers. I didn't know he never meant to stay. I want to tell her how angry I was at her for taking away from me what I thought was mine. And how I long to turn back the time and just let her leave the house with him.

In those moments, when the awful stillness of guilt overwhelms me, I press both my hands to the wall, right at the spot where she vanished, and whisper her name.

This morning I don't stop by the wall. Maybe because I feel not angry but exhausted by everything that happened. I go to the kitchen, find another bottle of whiskey, and drag myself back to my room, where I sit on the bed and pour myself a glass, hoping the alcohol will wipe my mind blank. But the more I force myself not to remember, the more I do.

I will carry her with me always, won't I?

The window shutters quake in response.

I scrape my hair into a tight bun and open my wardrobe to find something clean to wear. I put on the dress I wore to that fateful séance at the Hollands'. A sharp poke into my thigh, and I shove my hand into the dress pocket. There's something inside, something small, wooden, with sharp edges. I pull it out, and in the dim light of my room, I make out a small wooden figurine of a soldier. His face is stretched in a silent scream. His neck is bent at an unnatural, terrifying angle. I found this figurine at the Hollands' and thought it belonged to Lizzie's younger brother.

The air gets icy, acquiring a familiar heavy weight. My spine tenses as I think about the face of the ghost-boy floating behind the window. How he always points a blackened nail at me. How his face stretches and the lips peel back in a mischievous smile, an invitation for play.

How his neck bends backward and to the side at a sharp angle. Just like the wooden soldier in my hand.

Return what's mine.

So that's what Oliver Rask wants. Not his family farm, not the deed to the land, and definitely not revenge. He wants his toy back so he can cross through the veil and return to his father. That's why he granted me my powers. The soldier's small dots for eyes are fixed on me, and I finally know what I must do.

I leave that afternoon.

At the gates, I turn back to look at the Dawning. It stands alone, grand, and ominous. There are still some remnants of wealth left in it as it spreads its wings against the expanse of the prairies and the wide horizon. Both of us are lonely and abandoned by people we thought we loved and trusted and who didn't want us in the end. Both of us bound to each other in some sort of wicked, unexplainable way.

I turn away from the house and walk down the familiar path.

The sky is mottled gray, and the air is sharp with winter cold. In my previous life, before the death and loss and ghosts, this walk used to be a favorite part of my day—nothing above me but the sky; nothing around me but the air and vast prairies. When I think about my life like it used to be, there are moments that come back to me in sharp clarity, moments that cut me deep and stain me like mud. The sound of Amos's laughter as he climbs out of my window into the night on his way to the Cribs. My parents' intimate murmurs in the night. Bobby's figure at the bottom of the stairs waiting for me to come down and greet him, a bouquet of white lilies in his hands. Lizzie handing me a note from one of her secret admirers, her warm breath washing over my face. Tilda's raspy voice as she hums a song under her breath while washing dishes. The smell of freshly baked bread swirling in the air.

The memories now feel like dreams, and I'm not sure those dreams are mine.

The air is fresh, carrying over the prairies in a frigid exhale laced with rain and a hint of early snow. Long dry grass soothingly brushes at my skirt. There is the call of birds in the distance. The coolness of the wind propels me forward despite how tired I feel.

As I get closer to the Rask farm, the breeze dies, giving way to the familiar heaviness that pushes against me like a wall. Every cell, every muscle in me, screams to stop walking, to turn around and go back home. But I don't do any of those things. I keep on walking despite the rank smell that slowly invades my nostrils. Despite the soundless air, where there is no sweeping of grass against my ankles.

A familiar tree line, where the farmhouse is situated, rises to my left. I leave the road and wade through the mud and dead grass swaying in the field that used to be a pasture. From here I can see the house that looks as neglected and washed out as it was a few weeks ago. More windows are shattered, jagged edges of glass sticking out like spiky teeth. I stop in front of the house and stare into the gaping, screaming hole where the front door used to be. I stand in silence, bracing myself for what I must do.

"Hello?" I call out into the blackness, but the house swallows my voice. The quiet is unsettling. The trees don't move. The wind chimes don't clang. "I know you're in the house. I know you can hear me."

A stench of something dead and foul washes over me as he steps out of the shadows, his small frame highlighted by the sunlight. He's wearing a smile that gets wider with every step he takes. His face contorts into a grimace that makes me want to run back to the Dawning, where I know I'll be safe. But instead of running, I square my shoulders and plant my feet a bit wider, taking up more space. The way Leroy used to do it.

The white mist swirls around his feet, gently stroking his legs.

"I know who you are. Your name is Oliver Rask. I know how you died. And I know how you came here, to our world."

Return what's mine.

The mist leaves the boy and slowly creeps toward me. A few seconds later, it pulses around my ankles. My body goes numb. I try not to think about what happens next, the strokes of icy water against me, the awful way he died trying to save his father. I don't think about the house waiting for my return or the woman trapped inside its walls. Instead, I think about the family that used to live on this land and the children who used to play in these fields. And the little boy who loved to play with toy soldiers. "I think . . . I think I know what you want."

He tilts his head expectantly. His eyes inspect me with unabashed curiosity.

"Here," I croak as I extend my hand with the wooden figurine in it. "I didn't know it was yours. I am sorry."

I miss Father. His voice is so soft now. Almost intimate. *Promise you'll burn it.*

"I promise."

The mist rises in ripples, lingering at my feet for a few seconds before snaking back to the boy. My head starts to spin. The daylight dims at the edges. The air tightens around me, and my resolve is beginning to crack. I want to flee, to get as far away from this place as possible. The longer I stay here, the stronger all my emotions get.

Close your eyes.

I do as he asks, and fear overtakes my body, and my heartbeat accelerates. I feel my chest constricting as water rushes and closes over my head. Where has all this water come from? Something inside me is shifting, changing. I can't breathe. Tears burn my eyes from all the sadness inside me. I surrender myself to the coldness that is burning against my skin, flooding my lungs, suffocating me. There is ice in my chest. Mud in my mouth. This must be what the boy felt when he went into the raging creek to save his father. I keep still and quiet, and then all the sensations are gone.

When I open my eyes, the air is warmer than it was. Birds are chirping peacefully from the sky. In the place where Ollie stood—and where there had been nothing but weeds and dry, tangled grass—there are a few red and yellow flowers. Flowers in October. I kneel and touch the ground, and it feels soft and warm.

I get to my feet and go home.

Chapter 26

Coming back was a horrible mistake. But that's the thing about fate: it comes without a warning.

James stands in the doorway to the study, leaning on the wall, his arms crossed over his chest. A pungent stench of sweat swirls around him. His slightly swollen eyes watch me as I approach, resembling a predator waiting for his prey. There are blue-and-purple bruises on his chin and under his eyes, black stains marring his skin and reminding me of the wallpaper mold. There is something primordial about him, something vile in the faded gray of his eyes. I don't know why he came, but I'm starting to suspect he's here to collect whatever he thinks I owe him.

"I let myself in," James says, pushing himself away from the wall. "The front door wasn't locked." He talks to me slowly, as if he wants his words to sink in, take shape, and convey the same threat his eyes have already revealed.

"There's nothing for you here," I say calmly, but my heart is racing against my rib cage like a runaway horse. The Dawning must be sensing my fear, because the ceiling is too high in the grand hall. The wooden planks beneath James's feet are too wide and too long, their edges blackened.

He's blind to all the changes in his surroundings, because he shrugs nonchalantly and says, "I knocked, but no one came to the door."

I swallow, clutching the soldier in my hand as if this little toy is going to save me.

A nasty smirk appears on James's lips. "Is this for me?" He nods at my hand, and my body tenses as if my bones are about to turn into water. "My advice?" His right hand, which was shoved in his coat pocket, is now holding a small pistol. "Don't bring a toy to a gunfight."

I swallow hard and wrap my fingers tighter around the figurine. "Is there going to be a fight?"

"Not if you give me what I want."

"Haven't we paid you enough?"

"You have something that belongs to me."

"I have nothing to give you."

"The book, you stupid cow. You have the book."

The stench of death surrounds James—swamp rot and wood decay—and I know I'm probably going to die here today. "Let's talk in the dining room." I turn my back on him, my knees trembling, my steps uneven, and my feet heavy, as if I have stones chained to my ankles. I have no idea what I'm going to do or how I'm going to protect myself.

I walk inside the dining room, where the curtains are drawn over the windows. They billow as I enter, and I know the house is watching. James follows me, his heavy footsteps not far behind. As we enter, German Opa stares at us sternly from the wall, his figure too big to fit fully within the frame. As if he took a few steps closer to the border of the canvas. As if he's preparing to leap into the dining room.

"What happened to your housemaid?" James asks, his gaze quickly assessing the dirty plates on the dining table and crumbs of toast mixed with dry yolk. I haven't realized how little I have eaten in the past few days. And how dirty everything looks without Tilda's care.

"She left." I walk around the table, positioning myself closer to my grandfather's portrait and farther away from James and his gun. "What do you want, James?"

"I want the book." He points the pistol at my chest. "Give it to me, and I leave."

We both know he's lying.

"I'm afraid there is nothing I can do for you." I bite down on my lower lip so hard I can taste the blood tinging my tongue. "I burned it."

"You what?" His pistol trembles in his hand. "Burned it?"

"It was an awful book full of awful secrets. No one should ever have it."

"And who do you think you are to decide something like this?" He moves forward, taking each step carefully, not letting me out of his sight. "You're lying." He raises the gun to my face. "I know you're lying." As he speaks, his breathing changes. "I can read your face. You always bite down on your lip right before you do your tricks." He exhales in short, rapid breaths, sounding like he's getting agitated. "And you're doing it now."

"Search the house. See for yourself." I pull a chair and sit down, placing the toy soldier on my lap. I am so tired, I don't even know if I care anymore.

"I've searched the house already." His forehead glistening with sweat, he backs away, never lowering his black pistol. "I don't think you burned it. You're daft all right but not that daft."

I cannot allow the book with all my family secrets to get out into the world. I should've burned it, and now I may never get a chance to destroy it. "You're not getting your hands on that book," I say, my breath catching in my throat. *Help me,* I think. *Someone please help me.*

James leaps across the table, and when I jump to my feet to confront him, he slaps me across the face. The first thing that registers is surprise. Then the pain comes, agonizing and joint twisting. My head jerks back, and I stagger, hands thrashing, mouth wide open. I hit the wall so hard, the air leaves my lungs with an odd hiss. *Please help me.*

Ferociousness clouds his face, his thin lips stretching out in a wild scowl. His forearm flexes as he prepares for the next blow. But instead of hitting me, he grabs my arm and jerks it behind my back, his fingers digging into my skin, twisting my wrist. James pushes his knee between my legs, pinning me to the wall, and wraps his hands around my throat in a viselike grip. He bumps my head into the wooden paneling. The world tilts at a sharp angle. "Give me the book, and I'll let you live." His words float to me from far away.

The walls tremble, and for a wild second I expect the wallpaper to come to my rescue. But all I hear is the growl of the pipes reverberating through my body. The floor tilts underneath me. James squeezes harder, and the world stops spinning. I'm going to die. I should have known there was a price. The darkness edges closer and closer, circling me, waiting to be fed. That's what happens when you break promises and inherit all the sins, commit murder, and bring ghosts into this world.

The air turns into liquid and fills my lungs, and it is so heavy and thick, I cannot breathe.

I glance at Opa. The tilt of his head is sharper; the brown of his eyes is lighter than a minute ago.

The glass in the windows rattles.

"James, I'll give you the book," I whisper hoarsely. "Let me go, and I'll give you the book."

He doesn't let me go; instead he savors his victory, pressing his fingers harder against my skin. He laughs, his breath a wash of spoiled meat on my skin. He's too close. Too deadly.

I need to free myself from his grasp because the lack of air is making me dizzy. "Please," I push out the word. "It's in the study. On the third bookshelf." The walls are curling around us, and for a fraction of a second, I wonder if the house is about to swallow us both.

"Show me," he whispers into my ear, his rotten breath trailing around my face.

I nod, and James untangles himself from me. I know I should be afraid when he points his gun, but I'm so, so tired. Living in the world of ghosts made me forget for a while how afraid I should be of living men.

The floorboards moan oppressively.

The ceiling shakes.

Somewhere inside the house, a door slams. Then another.

James startles.

I smile. "It's the draft. The house does it when it's windy outside. You, of all people, should know it."

"Right." He gives a short bark of a laugh and shakes his head. "Just like our séances."

I straighten my spine. "Take him," I whisper. "I beg you." I look up at Opa. His head slowly turns, and he nods.

"Who are you talking to?" James asks, quickly looking over his shoulder. His jaw tenses, but when he doesn't see anyone else in the room, he rolls his shoulders back. "No wonder everyone left you." He chuckles. "You've gone mad. Like your lunatic mother."

I smile, step aside, and smooth the wrinkles out of my crumpled dress.

The house wails. A rush of warmth floats from the ceiling, moves from the walls, from the floors, climbing up my legs and my torso, chasing away the ice, and settling in my bloodstream.

My grandfather's arms leap out of the portrait, getting longer and longer until they finally latch on to James like serpents, bending and twisting around his stocky frame. James opens his mouth, and a wet, phlegmy grunt bursts from deep inside him, an ungodly sound that makes my ligaments strain with such force, I might snap in half. James twitches violently in Opa's embrace. His lips contort and twist, and he is mouthing something I cannot understand. With a quick and violent move, Opa drags James inside his canvas.

It takes me a long time to start the fire in the hearth. But when I'm finally done, I take the wooden figurine and fling it into the flames. The soldier's mouth gets wider and wider in a silent scream as the fire devours him. Something heavy inside my chest lifts, breaking our bond.

When there's nothing left of the soldier but ashes, I go to Father's study and pull the Blue Book off the middle shelf. Sometimes the best hiding places are right in front of you, in plain sight. I'm about to toss it into the hearth as well, but I hesitate. The secrets on its pages run dark and deep. The history of this town is written in blood and shame.

Destroying the book would be an act of kindness to people who don't merit it. Nobody in this damned town did anything to help us. None of them deserve my kindness. If needed, I can wield this book as a sword and use it against those who betrayed us. My own bloody legacy is documented there. I know how the words on the pages taste, how the weight of the secrets feels in my chest. I know the shape of my shame.

My fingers run along the cracked leather spine, looking for reasons to burn the book.

I find none.

November 25, 1903

My darling Amos,

I hope that wherever you live now, you know and see everything. Or, at least, you are listening quietly.

I could have gathered my things and left the Dawning after everything that happened here. I will not lie, I have considered it, but only for a moment. Where would I go? What would I do? And most importantly, why would I abandon our family estate, the only true and real thing that is left of us? When I found my answers, I made my choice.

You always hoped for the best for me. And now, I'm creating a life of my own. It does not get better than that. The feeling of newfound authority over my own life and my own decisions is exhilarating.

My new life of course comes with certain responsibilities. There are so many empty rooms in the house. Why waste all this space when it can be put to good use?

I went to the Cribs and found Peach, Bobby's girl. I offered food and shelter. I told Peach I can haul her and other girls out of the Cribs, out of their miserable existence in Omaha's underworld, and they can build a new life with me in the Dawning. They will be free to leave the house when they wish or anytime they are ready to be on their own. And of course, of course, they can stay as long as they need to.

The girls were terrified of my offer. The Dawning has a dark reputation, and I am a big part of it. In town, people talk about us. There are rumors that something awful happened to Tilda. No one knows exactly what, but the local gossipers whisper in parlors that she had never left the Dawning. James's wife filed a police report about his disappearance, and I was questioned about his whereabouts.

Peach was the only one who believed that despite the desolation, despite the ghosts and the séance business, she would be much safer in the haunted house than in the Cribs. And so she came to stay with me. It takes time to build trust. It takes even longer to start feeling safe. Especially when there are a lot of strange stories circulating in town. But everything ends sooner or later. When all the stories were told, and the gossip got old, the bad spell finally ended.

Three more girls moved in, and a couple days later two more came. Now the Dawning is full of giggles, loud voices, and life. I think the house enjoys it all because not once have I heard its pipes growl. The mold is gone, and no one ever complains about the endless stairs.

In the mornings, after breakfast, I give the girls lessons in math and grammar, and I admire their way of yearning for knowledge, for the betterment of their lives. I wanted to hire a new cook, but Peach would not allow me. Some of the girls love to cook. Some of them love to work in the garden.

When the night comes, when the girls fall asleep, I do my rounds around the house. The only sounds are my own footsteps and the creaking of the floorboards. When I get tired of the silence, I whisper to those trapped within the walls. I ask them if they remember what it feels like to be out in the fresh air, inhaling its sharpness and feeling the breeze on the skin.

They never answer me.

I hired a private detective to track down the Rasks. And I am happy to report that he located the family in Colorado. I gave Jonathan Rask, the oldest son, the deed to his father's farm. The debt is paid, and my heart is finally full.

My days acquired a simple rhythm that I enjoy. My life has a nice routine. Dinners are around nine and séances are held at midnight. Always at midnight. By three o'clock in the morning when my guests leave, I situate myself in the study, where I tie Leroy's silk necktie around my neck.

The first time I called him, I was not even sure he was among the dead, but I thought why not. Why not call his name and see what happens. When he appeared, his face was turned away from me, as if he did not want to look at me. I could see only half of his profile, and I wondered if he was angry with me. If he could not bring himself to look at me. But then he slowly turned, and I gasped in horror. Half of his face was gone. Obliterated by a bullet. Of course he was not angry with me. He just did not want me to see his mangled face. To see what James did to him right before he came to the Dawning to get the book.

Leroy always looks uneasy when he is around me. I understand why. It is hard to be back in the place that almost killed you. It is hard to be with me. And I call for him every night. Together we watch the stars in the sky and listen to those trapped inside the walls.

Punishment comes in many forms, Amos. I offer no apology for my decisions.

I do not know why Mother chose you over me. Why she loved you more. Perhaps because you were born first, and I followed fifteen minutes later. Perhaps she had enough love only for her firstborn. It does not matter anymore. Dr. Fuller tells me she mostly lives in her dreams, talking to no one, seeing no one. I have not visited her since I sent her away, and she never asks for me. Sometimes I wonder if she ever thinks of the house she left. Does she remember she has a daughter? Dr. Fuller sends me an occasional report, and according to him, she spends most of her days sitting in her chair in the garden where she likes to feed squirrels. Dr. Fuller heard her calling one of the squirrels Amos in that cheery and sweet voice reserved just for you, my dear brother.

This is my last letter. I do not want to bother you anymore. I am not even sure this letter will ever reach you, but I need to write it. I never got a chance at a proper sisterly farewell. You were gone so suddenly and all that you left behind was this gaping, yawning hole.

I remember the day we got the news like it happened yesterday. We read the telegram a few times because we were certain there was some grievous error, and it was not you but someone else who died. I woke up the next day thinking you were not dead, and it was just an awful dream. It lasted only for a few seconds, and then the reality hit me so hard, my heart almost stopped.

The realization of your death was like being plunged into frigid water—your heart stops, your lungs spasm, and you cannot catch a breath, and then everything accelerates around you. You wish you were dead, but you are acutely alive and feel every pang of pain, every agonizing contraction of your soul, and there is nothing you can do but just scream and cry and hope for it to end.

It never ends, Amos. It dulls around the edges eventually, but it is always there—the agony, the longing, your name whispered at odd times and in random places.

You have to learn to live with it.

I think I finally did.

I must go now. The dinner is ready, and the girls are waiting.

With all my love,

Your sister Nina

Acknowledgments

The journey of writing *The Night Guests* wasn't easy. It was filled with self-doubt, questions, and hesitation. It was wild and unpredictable. To this day, I'm not sure how I got here. Thankfully, I wasn't alone on this journey. I'm eternally grateful to work with people who support and encourage me along the rocky road of publishing.

To my incredible agent, Melissa Danaczko, who works tirelessly and champions my work like it's the best in the world and who possesses a supernatural power (no pun intended!) to guide me to the story I was sure I couldn't deliver. I'm so fortunate to have you!

To my wonderful and exceptionally talented editor, Nancy Holmes, who fell in love with my book and saw right into the heart of the story. I'm incredibly lucky to be able to work with you. To Clete Smith, whose keen editorial insight, enthusiasm, and impeccable humor brightened my days. To Joanne O'Neill, who designed the most hauntingly beautiful, heart-stopping cover. To the phenomenal people at Lake Union Publishing and APub who worked tirelessly to bring this book to life and into the world.

To my insanely talented writing friends who suffer through my messy drafts.

To Jenna Aker, thank you for always being there for me, reading everything I write over and over again, wading with me through my awfully muddy first drafts, and responding to my random texts at random hours. No words can express my deep gratitude for your friendship.

To Erin Litteken, for your unbelievable patience (truly!) and brilliant insight into my stories. Your wisdom and your talent inspire me every day. Your undying and unwavering belief in me is all I need to continue writing.

To Amanda McCrina, a creative, unstoppable force and my infinite source of inspiration. Thank you for reading every word I write, for our conversations, and for your friendship.

To David Neuner, for reading my early drafts, providing your insightful feedback, and staying with me through all the ups and downs of publishing. Thank you for always making me laugh through all of it.

To Paulette Kennedy, for the unlimited wise advice and enormous kindness.

To Gabriella Saab and Olesya Salnikova Gilmore, for letting me share this journey with you.

Finally, to my husband, Bryan, who witnessed all the madness and remained sane. I don't know how you do it. You're my rock in the endless sea of chaos.

Book Club Questions

1. When Nina first realizes she's seeing things that may or may not be real, she fears she's losing her mind like her mother. Did Nina's wavering mental health make you sympathize with or distrust her, and why? How did you interpret this in the context of what we know about mental health today?
2. Belonging and ostracism are two central themes throughout the novel. How did your feelings toward Nina and her mother evolve as the mother becomes increasingly distant, especially when she chooses Leroy over her own daughter?
3. Leroy is a master manipulator. In what ways does his behavior mirror examples of manipulation in today's society, whether in your social circles or in politics?
4. Nina's use of her powers plays a key role in the story. Did you find her return to society using these powers to be gratifying, expected, or surprising?
5. When Nina reads the Blue Book, she uncovers some of Omaha's darkest secrets and uses them to her advantage. What does this say about Nina's questionable moral choices and her willingness to cross certain lines? How much do you think her decisions are shaped by free will versus Leroy's influence?
6. As the house begins to change, did you interpret the changes as a reflection of Nina's emotions and thoughts or as simply the deterioration of an unkept estate seen through Nina's

perspective? How did you interpret the symbolism of rage confined within the walls?

7. Corruption within Omaha's society is another major theme of the novel, and both Nina's family and the Rasks are victims of it. How does this darkness feed into the novel's ending, and how did you feel about the way things turned out?

About the Author

Photo © 2021 Laimis Urbonas Photography

Marina Scott was born and raised behind the Iron Curtain in Vilnius, Lithuania. She graduated from a local university with a master's degree in library science, but a short stint in a Soviet library changed her mind about being a librarian in the USSR. After immigrating to the United States in 2000, she attended Weber State University in Ogden, Utah, where she earned her master's degree in accounting. Scott now resides with her family in Salt Lake City. She loves visiting haunted houses and old cemeteries and enjoys all things Gothic. You can connect with the author on Instagram at @marina_v_scott or her website at www.marinascott.com.